Praise for *Lost,*

"A perfect romance—charmi... ...y, and a rescue dog that steals ...
—Jennifer Probst, *New York Times* bestselling ... of
The Secret Love Letters of Olivia Moretti

"Like the proverbial dog with a bone, I devoured this book in almost one go. It's the adorable tale of a movie star dog at the heart of a rescue doggie custody battle . . . which is actually a love match rescue. Pure delight!"
—Julia London, *New York Times* bestselling author of
It Started with a Dog

"The most charming love triangle of the season. It's a good thing one of them has dog sense. I especially loved the inside peek at movie-making with the cutest canine ever. Spencer will steal your heart."
—Shelley Noble, *New York Times* bestselling author of
Imagine Summer

"Victoria Schade continues to dazzle with *Lost, Found, and Forever*. Fetch this adorable book for lighthearted romance and one of *the* best doggos, Spencer."
—Tif Marcelo, *USA Today* bestselling author of
In a Book Club Far Away

"For everyone who has loved a dog—or a human—this warm and fetching story is an absolute delight. With a charming and intimate small-town setting alongside Hollywood glamour, a winning romance, and one precocious pup, all wrapped up in a bighearted tale of a woman's journey toward passion and purpose, *Lost, Found, and Forever* is a real treat."
—Phoebe Fox, author of *The Way We Weren't*

Praise for *Who Rescued Who*

"Move over Marley and Enzo—there's a new dog in town! Chock-full of heart and humor, anyone who has ever been redeemed by the love of a dog will treasure this uplifting, big-hearted novel. A treat from start to finish!"

—Lori Nelson Spielman, *New York Times* bestselling author of *The Star-Crossed Sisters of Tuscany*

"Victoria Schade is that author who could write anything and I'd read it. *Who Rescued Who* is the perfect feel-good book with charismatic characters, swoony romance, family secrets, and snuggly puppies. Grab your furry friend and start reading now."

—Amy E. Reichert, author of *The Kindred Spirits Supper Club*

"Pet lovers will rejoice over this too-cute 'tail' about Elizabeth Barnes, who travels to her late father's family homestead in the English countryside." —*Woman's World*

"A delightful romp through the English countryside . . . resplendent with sheep, dogs, cats, and lovely people. Beyond her irresistible story, Schade writes with beautiful descriptions. Readers will laugh, cry, and love this charmer." —*Booklist* (starred review)

"You don't have to be a dog person to love this heartfelt book, but you will be by the time you finish it. Victoria Schade has written a timely, heartwarming story for everyone who longs to break free of the rose-colored filter of our Instagram age and rediscover the messy perfection of life, love, and the people—and pets—who shape us."

—Lyssa Kay Adams, author of *Isn't It Bromantic?*

TITLES BY VICTORIA SCHADE

Life on the Leash
Who Rescued Who
Lost, Found, and Forever
Dog Friendly

dog friendly

VICTORIA SCHADE

JOVE
NEW YORK

A JOVE BOOK
Published by Berkley
An imprint of Penguin Random House LLC
penguinrandomhouse.com

Library of Congress Cataloging-in-Publication Data

Names: Schade, Victoria, author.
Title: Dog friendly / Victoria Schade.
Description: First Edition. | New York: Jove, 2022.
Identifiers: LCCN 2021059771 (print) | LCCN 2021059772 (ebook) |
ISBN 9780593437391 (trade paperback) | ISBN 9780593437407 (ebook)
Classification: LCC PS3619.C31265 D64 2022 (print) | LCC PS3619.C31265 (ebook) |
DDC 813/.6—dc23
LC record available at https://lccn.loc.gov/2021059771
LC ebook record available at https://lccn.loc.gov/2021059772

First Edition: June 2022

Printed in the United States of America
1   3   5   7   9   10   8   6   4   2

Title page photo by Mary Swift / Shutterstock.com

For my parents, who introduced our family
to the Grey Lady over twenty years ago.

dog friendly

chapter one

"Ticks have legs, nipples don't. Those are definitely Tucker's nipples."

It wasn't the first time Dr. Morgan Pearce had needed to help a client understand the distinction between a parasite and a body part. She was sitting cross-legged on the floor of her favorite exam room petting a shaggy senior shepherd mix, who didn't seem to mind being on his back on the cold tile while they stared at his stomach. The woman on her knees across from Morgan, a new client named Carol, blinked back at her in silence for a few seconds.

Uh-oh. I know what's coming.

"But . . . Tucker is a *boy* dog," Carol said slowly. "Right?"

Morgan struggled to maintain her poker face.

"Yup, he's a boy. Male dogs have nipples too, just like male humans," she answered, hiding her smile. The last thing she wanted to do was make her client feel bad about trying to care for her new dog.

"So, you're telling me all of those little black things are *not* ticks?"

Morgan shook her head. "Nipples. I promise you."

Carol ran her hand down the dog's lower stomach wearing a dubious expression. She'd called the Bristol Animal Clinic in a panic, convinced that the rescue dog she'd just adopted was infested with bugs.

"Okay, but what about all the fleas? Look, right here. He's *crawling* with them." Her voice went up a worried octave as she pointed to the dotted pink skin by his rear leg.

Morgan leaned closer to examine Tucker even though she'd identified the issue the second he'd flipped over. "I have more good news for you. Those are freckles."

"But . . . how can you tell?" Carol asked, frustration evident in her voice as she shoved her glasses on top of her head and leaned closer to study the dog's belly.

"Fleas never stay still." Morgan gently pushed on a freckle and Tucker's tail slapped the ground. "See? It didn't move. Plus, Tucker would be really itchy if all of these freckles were actually fleas. Have you noticed him scratching?"

Carol sat back and looked at Morgan with her bottom lip trembling.

"Hey, are you okay?" Morgan asked gently, searching the woman's face.

The floodgates opened.

"I don't know what I'm doing!" Carol wailed as tears rolled down her cheeks. "I'm screwing everything up. I've wanted a dog my whole life, but my husband wouldn't let me have one. The first thing I did when we separated was run out and adopt this guy, but I think I might have made a mistake."

"Oh no," Morgan said in a soft voice. "Of course you're overwhelmed, adopting a dog for the first time is a big responsibility. It's scary! Did you get him from a rescue or a shelter?"

"Rescue," Carol managed through her tears.

"Okay, then I bet they'll have a couple of options to help you. They might have a trainer on staff who will give you advice, or if it's all too much and you feel like this isn't going to work out, I bet they'll take him back and find him another great home."

"No!" Carol yelped, leaning forward and putting both hands on her dog protectively, as if she thought Morgan herself was going to take Tucker away. "I love him already. So much."

Carol dropped her head and sobbed harder as Morgan scooted closer to her.

"Listen, I think you're doing a *great* job," she said as she rubbed Carol's back. "You thought something was wrong and you brought him in as quickly as you could. That shows how much you care."

Carol hiccupped, tucking her white hair behind her ears. "I do care. Because he's the best boy." She sniffled and ran her hand down Tucker's belly, causing the dog to slap his tail against the tile again.

"I agree, he's a sweet guy." Morgan said. They both stared at the dog, who seemed content just to laze on the ground with his belly exposed. Of all the dogs Carol could've adopted as a first-time pet parent, it was clear she'd lucked into a perfect match. "Should we do a quick exam, while you're here? Get his weight and stuff? That way you'll walk out of here knowing he's healthy."

She nodded again. "Yeah, that would be good."

Fifteen minutes later Carol and Tucker headed to the front

desk to check out, loaded up with pamphlets, dog food samples, and a heaping dose of hope.

If only they were all that easy.

Morgan could handle the tough stuff—she actually *liked* the complicated cases—so it wasn't that she could only tolerate freckly seniors and their nervous moms. But after starting her day with an emergency that left her feeling like a wrung-out dishrag, the easy tick-nipple appointment was a much-needed home run. Morgan grabbed her tablet as she headed out of the exam room and noticed two small spots of dried blood on the screen. She used her fingernail to quickly scrape them off, then squeezed her eyes shut, willing the stress tentacles to loosen their grip around the base of her skull.

No time to think about it. Just stop. On to the next one.

"Sorry, the screen froze again," Morgan said, flashing an apologetic smile at new-puppy clients Jared and Allison Lerner. Their white-and-tan mixed-breed pup was latched on to the bottom of her jeans and was tugging away, making adorable little growling noises.

Morgan had already managed to accidentally piss the guy off by being five minutes late to their appointment, and the technical difficulties weren't helping. Moving from paper records to tablets was one of the many changes implemented when the former practice owner, Dr. Simmons, sold his business to a huge veterinary consolidator. The upgrade to paperless records had seemed like a good idea when it was rolled out, but the confusing and glitchy system was yet another headache that Morgan and her colleagues didn't have time for.

The device didn't show any signs of life, so Morgan squatted down on the chipped tile floor, placed the useless tablet down next to her, then reached out to pet the pup, wearing a genuine smile. She felt her whole body relax when the puppy turned crescent-shaped with glee and wiggled into her palm. She wished she could inject the furry oxytocin hit into her veins like a junkie.

Thank God for puppies.

"Bailey is absolutely adorable."

"Yeah." Jared laughed. "Good thing because she's a pain in the ass."

"Stop," Allison said softly as she swatted him on the shoulder.

Morgan ignored the comment and started quickly cataloging the little dog's health and temperament as she petted her, running her fingertips along the pup's body from her ears to paws and taking note of how she reacted to the handling. She had about two minutes for the get-to-know-you pleasantries if she wanted to make up for lost time, especially since she had to worry about her productivity goals. Morgan looked down at the happily squirming puppy. "We're going to have a good time, okay?"

The *whoosh* of the tablet booting up on the ground next to her startled Bailey, and the puppy dashed under a chair.

"I guess someone is a little nervous," Morgan said, glancing at the couple. She sat down on the ground, crossed her legs, and peered at the puppy. "Hey, Bailey? We'll take it nice and slow, my little friend."

Bailey came out with her head held low but her rear end wiggling, and Morgan breathed a sigh of relief. She loved an easy patient that was all about wags and kisses and would be reluctant to leave her when the exam was over. And when it came to the other side of the table, she needed pet parents who were eager to take her advice on the importance of socializing their nervous puppy in order to prevent a lifetime of fear responses and stressful exams.

"Let's get your weight, little one," Morgan said as she reached over to pick Bailey up.

The puppy immediately threw her head back and started biting Morgan's hand with needle-sharp teeth.

"Uh-oh." Jared laughed. "Looks like she hates the mean vet lady already! Get 'er, Bailey, before she grabs the thermometer!"

Morgan plastered a less-genuine smile on her face as she expertly maneuvered to avoid punctures on her already bruised hands. "No, this is totally normal. Nipping and play biting are common at this age. I have a great little booklet that describes the puppy stages you'll go through with Bailey; I'll make sure you get one before you leave."

"Does that cost extra?" Allison asked, her eyes darting around the exam room as if searching for price tags.

"Nope, it's part of our new puppy packet. All of our clients get them." Morgan zeroed out the exam scale, then placed Bailey on it. "Her weight looks good."

"Hey, Morgan, got a question for you," Jared boomed, crossing one leg over the other in a way that seemed to take up half the space in the small room.

Seriously?

"Morgan"?

She took a second to compose herself before turning away from Bailey to face Jared.

"Of course, I'm happy to answer all of your questions. But

you can call me Dr. Pearce." She forced herself to smile widely, hoping it would blunt her words. She didn't want to piss off new clients, but she wasn't about to let him ignore her hard-earned title. She always endured the "sweeties" and "honeys" from senior citizens without comment, but she wouldn't stand for the insecure man-spreaders flexing on her by using her first name. There was a reason why she was staring down $150,000 in student debt, and it was spelled *DVM*.

"Oh, excuse me, *Dr. Pearce*," Jared replied in a tone that made it clear he wasn't used to being corrected. "Anyway. About housebreaking . . . I caught Bailey pissing in our family room and I gave her a good smack. Was I also supposed to shove her nose in it? Because I remember my parents used to do that with our dog."

Deep breath. Count to five. Pleasant expression. Try not to murder him.

Morgan massaged the puppy's shoulders in an attempt to vent some of her frustration.

"I'm glad you asked me about that. Actually, it's outdated advice. Hitting your puppy does nothing to help potty-train her, but what it *will* do is make her afraid of you. Bailey doesn't know where she's supposed to potty at this age, so it's up to you to help her learn. Believe it or not, accidents in the house are people problems, not puppy problems."

"Told you," Allison said under her breath, looking down at her hands.

"Huh. So, no smacks?"

Morgan shook her head vigorously. "No smacks, ever, for any reason."

Jared frowned. "Everybody's a snowflake these days, I guess."

He leaned over in front of his puppy on the exam table. "Want to talk about your *feelings*, Bailey? Will that keep you from shitting in the house?"

Allison laughed nervously. "Jared, stop."

"I know some excellent puppy trainers I can refer you to," Morgan said, looking at Allison. "They can help you with potty-training." She glanced at Jared. "Manners too."

"Sure, whatever," he replied, settling back in his chair. "As long as it's not too expensive."

Morgan slipped her stethoscope from around her neck and placed the ends in her ears, grateful for the few seconds of quiet to come as she listened to Bailey's heart. The puppy licked her hand as she positioned it on her chest, as if to offer her a little love and support.

"I heard what happened this morning," Adrienne the office manager said as she gathered her Tupperware from the break room table. "So sorry, hon."

Morgan flinched. She'd managed to not think about the early-morning triage all day. "Yeah, me too."

You did your best. Stop replaying it.

"Have you seen the email from corporate?" Adrienne seemed to shrink as she asked the question, her shoulders hunching up toward her cap of gray hair.

It was lunch break, or what was formerly known as lunch break but had become more of a lunch *pause* if they were lucky since Smithfield Inc. had bought out the practice. When Dr. Simmons still owned it, they used to lock the doors for an hour so the staff could catch their breath and refuel before the afternoon rush began. But Smithfield was all about maximizing every last second throughout the day and had immediately done away with the locked-door lunches, allowing for just twenty-five minutes of shotgunned sandwiches and mad dashes to the bathroom. Plus, there were the drop-off patients to attend to. People could leave their furry best friends in the hospital's care in the morning and then pick them up after work, which meant more patients forced into already over-crowded schedules in between regular appointments. Morgan usually found herself diagnosing and treating instead of eating, which was the reason why her stomach was growling as she got ready to examine a rabbit with overgrown teeth. Sometimes it made so much noise that it scared her patients.

"Not yet. Is it bad?"

Adrienne squinted behind her glasses, like she was trying to see something in the distance. "Sort of? It's about our ACTs and PPDs . . ."

"Again? Seriously?" Morgan stomped her rubber-soled clog in frustration. "I guess my email didn't matter."

Of all the changes that had been instituted since the take-over, the push to increase their average client transactions and patients per day had been the toughest for Morgan to stomach. How could she give her clients and patients her undivided at-tention when she felt like she was a slave to a stopwatch and a cash register? She'd written a heartfelt plea to the overlords at Smithfield, asking them to think about the quality of care in-stead of their bottom line, but never heard back.

"*Yeah.*" Adrienne drew the word out slowly. "They included a doctor-by-doctor practice scorecard in it. Dr. DeWitt is con-cerned."

Morgan felt an uneasy ripple pass through her. She'd never been last place in anything, but she had a feeling she knew exactly what the report would show. "Let me guess. I was at the bottom."

Adrienne tipped her head and shrugged, giving her the same sympathetic smile she used when handing over big surgical bills to clients.

Morgan whipped her phone out of her back pocket to check for the email, only to find the screen filled with alerts and texts.

"Whoa, hold on. Did something happen in the real world?" she asked Adrienne as she unlocked her phone. Morgan scanned through the messages quickly, trying to make sense of the flood of communication. The texts from her friends were vague, but they all mentioned Dr. Sophia Williams, the shining star of her graduating class.

All of the coded, triggering words were there. No one *said it* said it, but they didn't have to. Her heart thudded and she looked around the room in a panic. Morgan realized that she was holding her breath, and when she finally exhaled she was rewarded with a wave of nausea.

I'm in shock. I can't believe it, a text from her lab partner at Cornell read, with a link attached.

She didn't want to click on the article. There was no space in her head to process what she knew she was about to read.

Morgan opened it anyway, and the second the headline flooded her screen she wished she hadn't.

chapter two

Morgan's hand drifted to the warm body curled up behind her before she even opened her eyes. She'd slept with the windows wide open in her bedroom to let the early-summer air into her little cottage. The pressure of her dog George's body behind her knees was just the right amount of snuggle for the season. She adjusted her legs around him and gave him a little squeeze, hoping he'd lift his head up to rest it on top of her calf and make his little contented noises. Morgan reached back to give him a scratch and when she made contact, she realized that it was a pillow pressed up against her.

The reality washed over her as she came to, so suddenly that it took her breath away.

George.

Gone.

She curled into a tight ball and willed the tears away, just like she always did.

After six months, it felt like the wound from losing her thirteen-year-old Rottie–pit bull mix was finally starting to scab over, but for some reason the death of a classmate that she didn't even know personally seemed to have ripped the scab right off again. Instead of surrendering to the tidal wave of grief inside her, Morgan tried her usual technique of quickly reasoning through what she was feeling before locking the thoughts away for good. Simple sentences worked best.

You've made peace with losing George now. You're okay.

And Sophia...

Try as she might, there was no way to distill the news about her former classmate into a simple sentence she could file away, because Sophia Williams, DVM, had killed herself.

The news existed in two distinct parts of Morgan's brain. The "it makes absolutely no sense" section and the parallel "it's statistically probable" section. The fact that veterinarians were 3.5 times more likely to die by suicide than the general population was an open secret in her profession. Everyone knew what compassion fatigue was, but no one would cop to having it.

When she'd stumbled on an online quiz titled "Are You Suffering from Compassion Fatigue?" she'd answered a few questions about whether she was impacted by her patients' suffering and if she had feelings of hopelessness before she realized that she was taking it at the end of a long, tough day. Who *wouldn't* feel hopeless after diagnosing an adorable new puppy with parvo?

She was nothing like Sophia Williams. She was fine.

Maybe Sophia had that weary-to-the-bone exhaustion that made her feel like she had no other choice? It was probably part of the reason why the condition had the word *fatigue* in it. But it was a shadow syndrome in her profession, because there was no way a bunch of overachieving perfectionists felt comfortable admitting to feelings of anxiety or depression.

Stoicism for the win.

Morgan rubbed her swollen eyes, then stared at the sky-blue ceiling she'd painted back when she could still take on fun projects. The old Morgan tried on new hobbies every few months. Terrarium planting, scrapbooking, photography, needle felting, baking bread...she used to want to do all the things. The current Morgan could barely fix her hair.

The birds outside her window were already putting her to shame, up before the sun finding mates and building nests. Her dad had taught her to identify the songs when she was a girl, and she could hear the unmistakable scolding of robins, the screechy meowing of catbirds, and the white-throated sparrows singing the first few notes of "Here Comes the Bride."

It was her day off, and as usual she had more things on her to-do list than she could accomplish in a month. Everything from the essentials, like attacking a towering mound of laundry, to the never-gonna-happens, like the decoupage project she'd started the year before. Then there were her little herb garden pots that were filled with weeds instead of seedlings. Maybe she could at least clean them out? Without George staring up at her with his sad eyes begging to spend half the day on a hike, she had no excuse not to accomplish *something*.

Morgan rolled over to grab her phone. The alarm set to wake her at nine was more of a pipe dream than a reality. She couldn't remember the last time she'd slept a full night or woken up because of an alarm. The fact that she'd dozed off and on until seven felt like a miracle. She clicked it off and stared at her lock screen photo, an old image from a clinic Christmas party long before Dr. Simmons sold it. Morgan was in a sparkly black dress and surrounded by her drunk and happy colleagues. She enlarged the photo and stared at the smiley, more stable version of herself. She'd done her hair that night, and the long chestnut waves still looked smooth even though the photo had been taken toward the end of a night of sweaty dancing. Her green eyes were in squinty half moons, probably because she was laughing at something fellow doctor Vidya Nachnani had said as she draped her arm over Morgan's shoulder. She'd always been self-conscious about her smile, since even braces couldn't tame the minuscule gap between her two front teeth. In this photo, her natural smile beamed through, looking as pretty as people said it was.

She dropped the phone to her chest and shut her eyes.

Okay. Let's start with getting out of bed.

The more she scolded herself to get the hell up and achieve something, the heavier she felt. She'd never been a time-waster. Back when she'd been a newbie veterinarian, Morgan had felt like she'd practically invented bullet journaling, proudly checking off her colorful to-do list like it was a measure of her worth. She was the queen of getting shit done. But lately? Nothing seemed important enough to begin or, if it was a task in progress, to finish.

A text message buzzed in, making her jump.

Good morning sweetheart! Are you awake yet? it read, followed by three sunshine emojis and a bluebird.

Her mom, Jean, aka her number one cheerleader.

Barely, Morgan texted back, sans emojis.

Calling you now!

Trapped.

Morgan had no choice but to pick up when her mom's special ringtone sounded off. The morning calls on her day off were a ritual that she didn't have the heart to skip even though she wasn't in the mood for a dose of Jean's motivational-speaker-level positivity.

"Hi, Mom." She amped up the lilt in her voice. Morgan knew that if she didn't manage to sound upbeat, she'd be in for some armchair psychology, and she didn't want to be lovingly picked apart or told how easy it was to just to pull yourself up by your bootstraps.

"You okay? You sound stuffy."

Damn it, Jean, I said two words.

"I'm still in bed, I haven't cleared out my sinuses yet."

"Oh, okay. Blow your nose and gargle with salt water if you're still feeling phlegmy, that should help. And let me know if it's shaping up to be a cold, because I have some lovely new teas I can send you. It's not a cold, is it?"

"Nope, I'm fine. All good," she lied. The achy body and tickle in the back of her throat felt like the beginning of *something*, but she didn't want to worry her mother or trigger more care packages. Morgan already had stacks of boxes filled with herbs and potions from her massage therapist mom.

"So, I'm guessing you've talked to your brother?" Jean sing-songed.

The answer was obviously no, but her mom liked to pretend her two children were still close. Morgan couldn't remember the last time she'd directly communicated with Mack. She knew he still crept on her Instagram stories and she occasionally got curious enough to dip into his, but that was the extent of their contact. And she was totally fine to leave it at that. After all, there was only so much "shred happens" and "deadlift gains" shirtless content she could handle.

A million years ago they'd been as tight as twins. He'd looked up to her and she'd doted on him, but everything fell apart the summer he turned twelve and went to sleepaway camp. Sweet, chubby Mack had attracted the attention of bullies who'd teased him relentlessly. The bullying followed him once he went back to school the following year, and when she'd told their parents how bad things were Mack had lashed out at *her*, redirecting his anger to the last person who deserved it.

Things eased up once their parents and Mack's teachers got involved, but the damage was done, and Mack was cemented as the weird kid who ate lunch alone. When their parents had offered him the chance to go to a private high school farther away, he'd jumped at it. The bullying stopped and Mack managed to find a small group of friends that were as into sci-fi and D&D as he was. Morgan tried to be there for her brother, but she knew he was envious of how easily she navigated high school. Everything she did only seemed to make him angrier at her. Eventually, she stopped trying.

"No, what's up with Mack? Is he okay?"

"He's *more* than okay, sweetie!" Morgan could hear the smile in her mom's voice. "Oh, Morgie. I wish you'd just call him. Would you do that for me? So you can get the news right from him?"

Morgan took a deep breath and rubbed her temples with her free hand.

Why do I always have to be the peacemaker? Why can't he reach out if he has something to say?

"We'll see. I've got a busy day ahead of me," she lied. "Besides, he never picks up."

"I know, it's a terrible habit." Her mother paused and Morgan could almost hear the calculations going on in her head. Jean had never been good at keeping secrets. "Okay, fine, fine, I'll spill it, but pretend you don't know when he tells you. Mack and Elle got engaged last night!"

Morgan sat straight up in bed, her tension headache momentarily forgotten.

"Wait, *what*?"

"I know!" she trilled. "Your father and I are so excited. We're going to have our first wedding!"

"But, Mom . . . I mean . . ." Morgan searched for a way to shorthand her confusion. "They've only been dating for, like, four or five months. It's way too soon, isn't it?"

"Honey, you've lost track of time again. Mack's been with Elle for almost a year."

Really?

Elle had been at the family Christmas gathering, but that didn't mean that it was *serious* serious. Mack cycled through women like he cycled through diets, so Morgan didn't even bother to learn the names of the pretty faces who showed up in his feed. She assumed that Elle was yet another shiny blonde that looked perfect next to her brother, but she had to admit that the woman had more sass than she expected. When Morgan and her mother started clearing away the dishes after lunch, Elle had joined them, then razzed Mack for not helping out until he was shamed into grabbing a few plates. But as much as she liked how Elle didn't seem to take any of Mack's shit, Morgan knew better than to invest time getting to know a woman who was sure to be punted eventually.

"Want me to send you the photo of the ring? It's stunning."

"That's okay, I'm sure it'll be plastered all over his social media."

Knowing Mack, he probably bought a rock the size of a paperweight.

"You sure you're okay, honey? You don't sound good."

There was no point unloading on her mother. Of course, good old Jean would say all the stuff she thought would help, about the necessity of sleep, "me time," and eating right. Over the years, Morgan had learned that the only way she could cope with the running tally of traumas she faced every day was to keep them to herself, push them out of her head, or pretend that they didn't happen. When she'd first started working, she'd spent hours on the phone with her mom talking through the mistakes she'd made or crying together about the pets she couldn't help. Eventually she'd figured out that bottling it up was better for both of them. It wasn't fair to subject her mom to the gruesome stuff she faced on a daily basis, and the truth was, she knew her mom didn't want to hear about it.

Morgan swallowed the lump in her throat. "Yeah, doing fine. Just trying to figure out my day."

First up? My morning nap.

Morgan fell back against her pillow and pulled the sheet that was in need of a wash up to her chin.

"Okay." Her mom paused. "I thought maybe you were feeling strange about the Sam stuff. There's a lot of wedding news flying around and it's probably a little overwhelming."

Morgan's heart sank at the mention of her ex-boyfriend's name and "wedding" in the same sentence.

"What Sam stuff?" she asked, even though she already felt the answer in her bones.

Her mom was in a book club with Sam's aunt, and between the trickle-down from their gossipy get-togethers and Facebook posts, her mom wound up knowing more about her ex than was healthy.

"Oh, sweetie, I thought you'd heard by now and didn't want to talk about it." She paused. "Sam got engaged a few weeks ago."

The news sliced through her like a razor blade. It didn't matter that she had been the one to end things with Sam two years prior.

Oh, Sam. I hope she deserves you.

On paper, Sam Watson was perfect. Tall, Paul Rudd–cute, quick to laugh, easygoing, and totally devoted to Morgan, he seemed destined to be her forever. At least that was what *he* thought. And while Morgan loved everything about him, it finally dawned on her that she wasn't in love with *him*. A person who loved as purely as Sam deserved wholehearted, crazy-passionate love in return. It had taken Morgan months to realize that she needed to set him free, and there were times when she still questioned if she'd done the right thing. Now, her heart toggled between jealousy for the girl lucky enough to love him the right way, and happiness for a man who deserved it.

"Wow, good for him," she managed. "That's great. Sam and Kelly, getting married."

Morgan pulled the sheet all the way over her head even though she was sweating a little.

"Morgie, you don't sound like you. I'm worried. Can I come visit for a weekend? I'll do some relaxing cranial sacral work. I'll cook lasagna for you and take care of your laundry. It'll be lovely. Let me do this for you, sweetheart."

By the worried tone in her mom's voice, Morgan knew the

offer was verging on an intervention. Even though her parents were only three hours away in Connecticut, she hadn't seen them in months. She wasn't ready to get the loving motherly beatdown about how tired she looked, or how much weight she'd lost. It was easier to keep her at arm's length.

"No, that's okay, Mom. Things are too crazy right now. We'll do it soon, I promise."

Jean let out a long sigh in response, like she didn't want to give up but knew she had no choice.

"You'd tell me if something was wrong, wouldn't you?"

Morgan sat up a little. "Yup. Of course. But I'm fine." Her voice quivered as she said the words, so she cleared her throat and steeled herself. "Seriously. Don't worry."

"I'll always worry about you," she responded. "I love you. Call your brother, okay?"

"We'll see."

Morgan hung up, shut her eyes, and did her best to think about nothing.

chapter three

I'm just worried about her," Eugene Pak said, shooting a look at his partner, Karl Reynolds, while he cradled their quivering dog in his lap. "I hate to see Bernadette uncomfortable. You know how happy she usually is when you walk in the room. This isn't normal."

The Pak-Reynolds family always added some much-needed sunshine to Morgan's schedule, even when they were dealing with senior dog challenges. They were always quick to set up an appointment when something felt off with Bernadette, their salt-and-pepper miniature Schnauzer, and they followed Morgan's advice to the letter. A consult with them was usually enough to lift her spirits for the rest of the day.

Bernadette shifted in Karl's lap, kicking her back legs against his stomach and groaning every so often. She was one of the smallest Schnauzers Morgan had ever met, weighing in at a whopping twelve pounds. The Pak-Reynoldses kept her silver beard precisely trimmed and her coat cut tight and neat against her body, leaving her leg fur a bit longer so it looked like she was wearing little pants.

"You're right, she's not herself. But you got her in quickly, so try not to stress out," Morgan replied, meeting Eugene's gaze with soft eyes for a moment before scrolling through her tablet. "We'll have her feeling better in no time."

"It's my fault," Karl said with a heavy exhale, running his hand through his coppery hair and making it stand up. He always wore head-to-toe black as if to try to tone down his ginger-ness, but the red swooping hair, full ruddy cheeks, and salt-and-paprika goatee defined the man. "I threw away the uncooked bacon and didn't snap the lid shut on the trash can. She got into it and now . . ." He broke off with a frown and gestured to her.

"Accidents happen," Morgan answered, dropping into her soothing voice. "Don't beat yourself up."

The low, reassuring tone was almost unconscious for her. Not that she didn't feel the appropriate emotion behind it. The fact was, she felt too much of what went on in the exam rooms . . . despair, hopelessness, fear, worry. Didn't matter if it was the person or the animal going through it, by the end of the day she wore their combined darkness like a heavy wool jacket. And since the news about Sophia on Friday, it felt like she couldn't take it off. The accompanying brain fog made it almost impossible to be present for her patients and clients.

"Dr. Pearce, did you hear me? Are you okay?"

She blinked at Eugene. "I'm sorry, what was that?"

"I asked if we need to adjust the time we do her next insulin injection." He swept his eyes up and down Morgan's body, pausing on her clogs, and frowned. "What's going on? Something's not right with you today."

It didn't surprise Morgan that he was calling her out, but she wasn't sure if it was for her melancholy vibe or her rumpled cloth-ing. Eugene Pak was the very definition of dapper, a sweater-vest, bow-tie, spit-shined-shoes kind of man with his own swoop of inky hair to complement Karl's.

The Pak-Reynoldses had been bringing their medically frag-ile senior to see her since she'd started at the practice four years prior, and the line between clients and friends had quickly blurred. Even though they were home decorating celebrities with a social media empire, a bestselling book, and an upcom-ing design partnership with Target, they passed through the clinic like regular citizens. They considered Morgan a miracle worker since she'd diagnosed grumpy Bernadette's diabetes and taught them how to do her three-times-a-day insulin injec-tions in a way that the old lady could tolerate.

"No, I'm fine," she lied. "Just a little distracted today. Sorry."

"Hm, it's more than that," he continued, scanning her face. "Don't hate me for saying this, but you look tired, like you just rolled out of bed."

"Ouch, Eugene," she said as she patted the messy bun on top of her head. He never sugarcoated anything, and she usually loved him for it, but this time he was hitting a little too close to home. "Thanks for the fashion critique, but there's not enough time to talk about my mess. Let's get Bernadette feeling better, okay?"

He nodded, but Morgan got the sense that he wasn't done with her.

Ten minutes later, she was back in the exam room after run-ning some blood work to confirm her pancreatitis diagnosis and coming up with a treatment plan for them.

"Bernadette's going to get some relief pretty quickly, so there's no need to worry," she said as she finished outlining everything. "Any questions for me?"

Eugene and Karl exchanged a look.

"Actually, yes," Karl said, shifting Bernadette in his lap. "But it's a strange request. Can we steal two more minutes with you?"

Morgan silenced the stopwatch ticking in her head and settled back against the counter. "Of course. What's up?"

"We need a little help this summer," Karl said.

"Don't lie, we need a *lot* of help," Eugene interjected. "And we figured you could point us in the right direction."

Karl adjusted Bernadette gently. "Target launches this summer, in late June, and we're going to be doing appearances in stores all over the country for it. But you know that to us, summer always means Nantucket."

They'd invited her to visit them in their second home on Nantucket dozens of times over the years, but getting away for more than an overnight felt impossible.

"As much as we want to bring Bernie with us on tour, we know it's not a good idea. Our old lady needs stability, and someone who can handle her, uh, quirks." Karl gestured around Bernadette's body as if it had a force field. "My mom was going to do it, but she broke her foot so she's out of commission for a few months. That's why we're hoping you can recommend someone to stay with Bernie in Nantucket during the launch. We'll be in and out, but we want someone to set up camp at the house to keep things easy for her. Now, it has to be someone with training, not just any teenage dummy who thinks they know dogs."

Eugene tsked at Karl.

"Honestly? We would love for *you* to do it, but we know that's not possible." Karl paused and stared at Morgan. "It's not . . . possible . . . is it?"

Is it?

For two glorious seconds Morgan envisioned spending the summer stretched out by the Pak-Reynoldses' pool with Bernadette at her side and a cold beer and novel on a table next to her. The vision fizzled when a dog started howling just outside the exam room.

"I wish. But it's just not possible. Let me think about if I know of any vet techs who might be interested."

Eugene frowned. "We were hoping that by some miracle you'd be able to sneak away. No one can handle her the way you do, not even your best tech on staff here! Everyone gets freaked out by her . . . communication style."

"Well, you gotta admit, old Bernie's got some scary pipes," Morgan said, nodding at the lovable curmudgeon on his lap.

"But she's all bluster, she's a total sweetheart outside of the office," Karl said. "You know that. She doesn't even notice her injections now."

"And that's why I'm sure we'll be able to find someone who can handle her," Morgan teased gently.

"We wish it could be you," he said. "Some time away would do you good, young lady."

"Karl, don't pester her." Eugene turned back to Morgan. "Please give it some thought and let us know if you come up with someone you think is worthy. It's short notice, but hopefully a beautiful, mostly empty home on Nantucket plus a nice little paycheck will be enough to find the right fit."

"Yes, would you like to see photos of the pool house? The dog sitter will have *complete* privacy," Karl said, reaching for his phone. "It's charming. Here, look."

Morgan suspected that "charming" was an understatement. A tiny part of her wanted to see it but there was no need to torture herself with the missed opportunity.

"Stop trying to butter her up," Eugene scolded, and pushed Karl's phone away. "She's a busy woman, she doesn't have time to hang out in paradise with the best dog in the world." He paused. "Although honestly? You look like you could use a vacation."

Morgan laughed. "Are you guys negging me? I get it, I look tired, and I need a break. It's just not possible for me right now, though. I'll let you know if I think of anyone. Keep me posted on our girl, okay?"

"Always," Karl answered as he stood up and adjusted Bernadette in his arms. "Thanks for taking such good care of her, you're amazing and we worship you."

Dopamine hit engaged. Thank you, gentlemen.

Morgan escaped through the door that led to the back room, unable to ignore her bladder before her next appointment. She nearly collided with her favorite vet tech, Rebecca, as she speedwalked to the bathroom.

"Hey, DeWitt is looking for you."

"Okay, I just need to—" Morgan pointed down the hall and grimaced. "Do you know what it's about?"

"Nope, but he didn't look happy," she replied, mimicking the man's perma-frown.

The numbers conversation.

But she was prepared. A few extra hours on her laptop the night before meant that she was ready for battle.

chapter four

"Please close the door," Dr. DeWitt said to Morgan as she walked into his cramped office. "Have a seat."

His face was grim, but he wasn't known for smiling. New to the practice since the takeover, Dr. Curtis DeWitt had settled uneasily at the helm as medical director. He was the sort of doctor who had a hard time looking clients in the eye, and he wasn't much better with his colleagues. Coming into a practice to manage a team of people with an established camaraderie, then hiring on new staff as well probably wasn't easy, but he didn't even try to fit in. His 1970s porn star glasses and constant frowny "something smells bad" expression didn't help.

Morgan straightened her back and met his gaze as confidently as she could, considering her hands were starting to tremble. It had been happening recently in high-pressure situations, including during a routine spay surgery. She dug her nails into her palms as she sat down on the edge of the chair opposite him.

It's okay. I'm ready for this.

"Dr. DeWitt, I know my ACTs and PPDs are low, and I'd like

a chance to explain why. I had a feeling that you'd want to talk about them, so I made a spreadsheet comparing my numbers from last year to this year." She pulled her phone from her back pocket. "I can email you my documentation so you can see—"

"Dr. Pearce, your numbers are a concern, but I need to talk to you about something else." He paused and Morgan mentally scrolled through a thousand other potential issues. "Can you tell me what happened with Lillian Stanwick's cat?"

She froze.

Oh shit. Oh shit.

The walls in the small room edged closer to her and Morgan felt the static of numbness scramble along her fingertips.

"Um, Lillian. Right." Morgan flexed her hands under the edge of his desk. "I'm sorry about that. She was really desperate. I couldn't say no." She felt a suffocating mix of anxiety and anger rising inside her at being called out like a naughty schoolgirl. "I didn't use any hospital materials, I swear. And it was on my own time."

"Dr. Pearce, you treated a current patient outside of the hospital. You know that's against Smithfield's code of conduct." He adjusted his glasses and glared at her.

"It was a onetime thing, I swear. I ran into her at the grocery store on a Sunday and she showed me a photo of the abscess on Orson's forehead. She was there buying antiseptic cream hoping it would help. He was in bad shape. It was a fight wound, a puncture that closed, and the infection was pretty advanced. I told her to bring him in the next day when we opened, and she told me she couldn't afford the price of an office visit, let alone what the treatment would cost." Morgan paused, heart pounding in her chest so hard that she swore he could hear it. "Lillian is old, Dr. DeWitt, and she's on a fixed income. It wasn't a big deal, really. I lanced it, flushed it, and gave her some of the left-over antibiotics I had. That's it."

He blinked and his eyes were closed for so long that she thought he was meditating. "It's not just the loss of revenue that concerns me. It's the *tendency.* You let a client take advantage of you once, at least that I know of, so what's keeping you from doing it again? Besides, your plate is full enough taking care of our paying clients."

It was the closest thing to an acknowledgment of her work-load that she'd ever heard from him, and it shocked her into silence for a moment. Did Dr. DeWitt . . . *care* about her?

"She wasn't taking advantage of me, I offered. And you have my word it won't happen again," Morgan answered quickly, her voice shaking. "Trust me, I don't want to get in the habit of treating patients outside the practice." She frowned. "How did you find out about it anyway?"

Dr. DeWitt picked up a flowery greeting card from his desk and brandished it at her like it was a royal flush. "She wrote a thank-you note to say how wonderful you are, and how lucky we are to have you on staff."

She . . . what?

In any other life the sweet gesture of gratitude would be celebrated. In Dr. DeWitt's outstretched hand, the card was a weapon, undisputable proof in writing that she'd screwed up.

The rush of emotions came on so suddenly that Morgan didn't even have time to try to collect herself. She felt her throat constrict and Dr. DeWitt's scowl turned into a blurry haze as she realized that someone had taken the time to put pen to paper to say thank you. With a stamp, even!

She stared at the card in the middle of his desk, wondering if it would be weird for her to grab it since it was essentially a land mine. Morgan had made a small fabric-covered keepsake box back when she still had the bandwidth to be crafty, where she kept the little notes and pet-themed gifts clients had given her. She used to pull it out when she needed a lift, to remind herself that she *was* helping, but lately the good-note-to-bad-day ratio had become lopsided. Plus, she'd practically memorized every line on every card, so there was no need to look at them. Now, though, she'd have new poetry to learn, if she could find a way to steal it from him.

Morgan dropped her gaze to her lap and cleared her throat a few times, waiting until the storm inside her settled before raising her eyes to look at Dr. DeWitt again.

"I apologize. It won't happen again. I promise." She tried to come up with something that would shift her back into his good graces. "I'll, uh, take on some of your paperwork if you want."

"That would be fine." He pursed his lips and nodded. "Good."

She hurried out of the office before he had a chance to bring up her numbers.

You don't know what the hell you're talking about.

Morgan's last client's words echoed in her head. Given her ongoing case of imposter syndrome, she normally would've believed what the woman had screamed at her. But in this scenario Morgan had no doubt that her advice was correct. She'd been trying to talk the woman out of declawing her cat, explaining that the procedure could result in nerve damage and ongoing paw pain, only to be told that Dr. Google said the surgery was fine.

And now that woman is going to find a clinic that'll do it and her poor cat is going to have part of its feet amputated because you couldn't make a convincing enough case against it.

Morgan wiped her nose, then shoved the wadded-up piece of toilet paper in the pocket of her lab coat. The stress tentacles had a choke hold on her throat, but she couldn't keep hiding out in the bathroom. She still had more than half the day ahead of her.

"You okay?"

No one could hide their blotchy cheeks and watery eyes from Dr. Vidya Nachnani. She was so perceptive that Morgan often wondered if she'd be better off as a therapist or profiler.

Morgan sniffled and nodded unconvincingly as she walked toward her friend.

"Yeah, same," Vidya said, frowning as she smoothed her sleek black bun. "A semiferal cat punctured my thumb this morning, and I just had a client tell me that they're going to treat their dog's ear infection with essential oils because they don't believe in antibiotics."

Morgan could only manage a grumble in response.

"Exactly. He was in a lot of pain, but who am I to tell her what to do, right? What do I know?"

They paused in the tiny alcove that did double duty as the on-site pharmacy and gossip hideaway.

"Have you been keeping up with the stuff about Sophia Williams?" Vidya asked her in a quiet voice.

Morgan froze. She'd managed not to think about Sophia since the weekend.

"She was in your class, right?" Vidya continued.

"I didn't know her," Morgan reminded her quickly, hoping to avoid the conversation.

"Everyone keeps saying there was no way to tell that she was in trouble because she was always so happy." Vidya frowned and shook her head. "Denial is a hell of a drug." She pulled out her phone and scrolled to a Facebook post that featured a close-up of Sophia's smiling face. "They're doing an online vigil for her and everyone is posting memories. I thought maybe you'd want to see it."

She handed Morgan her phone as Adrienne pulled Vidya aside to discuss a scheduling issue for later that day. Morgan scrolled through the comments and photos, piecing together the life Sophia had led since college. Standing by the outdoor sign at her first job. Volunteering at spay-and-neuter clinics. Attending a nationwide veterinary conference. Morgan clicked through the photos quickly as a dull pain started to throb in her chest.

It was a life that looked . . . familiar.

She scrolled through the photos faster and faster, wishing that Vidya would grab her phone back because she couldn't stop herself. She kept going until she found the photo she knew would be there, the grainy, out-of-focus image of a tiny girl holding something soft and furry in her hands, a triumphant smile on her face.

Deep breath. In and out.

She felt her mouth go dry.

Morgan put Vidya's phone on the counter and backed away silently until she was pinned against the wall as if held in place by hundreds of invisible arrows. Her forehead went clammy. Her breath came in short, shallow bursts and her vision clouded. Even in her distress she started self-diagnosing.

Dyspnea. Tunnel vision. Diaphoresis. Vertigo.

Her rubbery legs could barely support her as the stress tentacles tightened around her throat and cut off her air supply.

Is this what it feels like? The moment when hurt wins and there's nothing you can do about it?

All the pain she'd been burying ripped through her like buckshot. Morgan reached out to try to find something to steady herself but wound up gripping air.

"Hey, you okay?" Vidya asked from far away, her voice echoing down a long, dark corridor. "Morgan?"

The lights dimmed until all she could see was blackness.

chapter five

Morgan closed her eyes and tilted her face up to the sun. A wave of goose bumps scattered along her arms as a gust of wind swirled her hair into a tornado. The temperature was regularly hitting the low eighties back in Princeton, but over twenty miles out in the Atlantic Ocean, she found herself wishing for a sweatshirt.

She'd followed Eugene's advice to make her way to the top deck before the ferry left the dock, so she'd have a prime spot as it eased out of Hyannis Harbor, past the gray-shingled houses and into the open water. The ferry was the first hint that she had no clue what she was getting into. Based on the photos on the Steamship Authority website, Morgan realized that she wasn't going to be boarding a cruise line, but she wasn't expecting the hulking white school bus on water parked at the dock. Wasn't Nantucket supposed to be fancy?

"The slow ferry is the perfect way to reset and start the process of leaving everything behind," Eugene had told her as they finalized their plans. "The high-speed ferry gets you there in an hour, but we force all first-timers to take the slow one. Those two hours on the water feel like a giant reset. You'll love it."

The traffic-snarled six-hour drive to the port in Hyannis had made her late, stressed out, and questioning if a reset was even possible. Then there was the struggle to find long-term parking once she arrived. She ended up leaving her car in the back corner of a sketchy yard turned parking lot owned by a man who looked like a pirate but talked like a Kennedy.

Everything you're doing feels like a mistake.

When she'd finally come to after falling on her ass next to the medicated shampoos and dewormer, the first face that greeted her was Dr. DeWitt, as unsmiling as ever. But as everything swam into focus Morgan realized that it wasn't displeasure on his face, it was concern. When she tried to hop up, embarrassed that her colleagues were gathered around her, he forced her to stay put until the color came back to her cheeks. When he brought her into his office the next day, it wasn't to scold her. "Something's got to give, Dr. Pearce," he said with a compassionate expression that was completely unlike the one he usually wore. "We're worried about you."

Between Dr. DeWitt, Vidya, and her parents' stressed-out meetings and calls, it felt like she was in an intervention. At first even she admitted that she needed a break. But now, standing on a boat surrounded by happy vacationers, the two months away to care for Bernadette felt like a gift she didn't deserve. Morgan tried to absorb some of the carefree vibes from the people around her, but her mind kept wandering back to work.

Is it a mistake? Does taking time away make me look weak? Am I weak?

The more she thought about it, the clearer the answer became. Yes, she was. Her colleagues were equally burned-out and battle-weary and *they* weren't running away for the summer. They sucked it up and rolled with the highs and lows every day.

She had no reason to be sad, or depressed, or overwhelmed, or whatever she was. Morgan had wanted to be a veterinarian since she was a little girl, so she was literally living her childhood dream every day. She could remember the exact moment the idea had taken root inside her. When Morgan was about eight, a bird crashed into the picture window in their family room. She fought her way through the prickly shrub in front of it to find the broken brown form lying on the ground. She picked up the bird gently, placing its wings against its body in a way that looked more natural, and tucked it in her shirt. She sneaked it into the house and past her parents to find a spot to care for it, settling on her silky pajama top nestled in her princess jewelry box. Morgan placed the unmoving bird inside the folds of pink fabric, scanning its tiny body to see if it was breathing.

She imagined the bird waking up and careening around the house in a panic, so she took it outside, climbed on top of the picnic table, and sat in the sunshine with the jewelry box in her lap, waiting for a miracle. It was uncharacteristic for her to be still, and after a few minutes her father joined her.

"Sparrow flew into the window, huh?" he asked, peering into the box, then at Morgan's face. She nodded as tears welled in her eyes. He grasped her shoulder gently. "Aw, Morgie, it happens. And you did a nice thing for him. We can give him a proper funeral, I have a shoebox we can use."

"He's not dead, Daddy!" she shouted. "Watch!"

"Okay, okay," he replied. "Let's give it a few minutes and see what happens."

He sat next to her on top of the picnic table, and they waited in silence, Morgan with her eyes glued to the bird and her father watching her. Morgan reached into the box to run her fingertip down the bird's body.

"Morgie, you probably shouldn't touch him . . ."

He stopped talking abruptly when the bird's wing moved. Morgan gasped. The bird shifted from side to side, eyes still closed.

"Daddy!" she shrieked.

"Shh, don't scare him," he answered gently.

They watched as the bird opened his eyes, then stood on wobbly legs. He looked around at the satiny bed, then glanced up at Morgan and her father with an unbothered posture. He hopped up to the edge of the jewelry box and paused, bowing his tiny head in Morgan's direction, then took off for the trees.

"You saved his life, Morgie!" her father exclaimed. "You've got the magic touch, young lady."

Morgan had swelled with pride and felt something else she couldn't identify at that age. As she'd gotten older she realized that it was a magical moment of connection. A feeling of communication and bonding that transcended species. And the secret knowledge that *she* had been the reason why the bird survived.

"Maybe you should be a veterinarian?" her father had suggested as he stood up. "You've obviously got a gift."

And with those two sentences, her future was sealed. She had the magic within her that could cure animals and she would dedicate her life to using it.

The healing I can handle. It's everything else that sucks.

The image of young Sophia Williams proudly holding the little animal flitted through her mind.

You need this. You're on this ferry for a reason.

Morgan let go of the rail with one hand and scratched along the neckline of her T-shirt. She felt itchy, like all of the seams of her shirt were fleas jumping along her skin. She gripped the railing again and looked around the ferry feeling panicked.

This is stupid. You're an idiot. You can turn around and go back home once you get there. You've only lost a day.

A dog barked somewhere close by, and Morgan was reminded of the promise she'd made to Eugene and Karl, to care for Bernadette while they were away. She was stuck.

Looking out at the endless blue before her made it even plainer. Between the long drive to Hyannis, the wait to board the ferry, and the two-hour boat ride itself, the trip to Nantucket was a commitment. Getting back home quickly wasn't an option, and half the reason why she was on the boat was the buffer it provided from everything she was leaving behind. There would be no quick trips to the practice just to help out for an hour or two on a busy Saturday.

She was *doing* this, worthy or not.

Morgan clung to the railing as a seasick feeling that had nothing to do with the boat rolled through her. She turned from the horizon abruptly and nearly tripped over a fawn French bulldog dragging a pretty, dark-haired woman with a stranglehold on the leash.

"Violet, be careful!" she scolded the pup, then looked at Morgan. "Sorry about that. She's excited, she knows exactly where we're headed."

"She's adorable. May I?" Morgan asked, gesturing to the dog. She desperately needed some canine TLC to ground her.

"Oh my God, please do." The woman smiled at Morgan like they were already best friends. "She thinks she's the official Nantucket welcoming committee."

Morgan knelt and didn't have to wait long before the Frenchie jumped up on her and demanded a pat. She noticed the dog's angry-looking reddish paws as she massaged her shoulders.

"It looks like she's been—" Morgan stopped talking abruptly, before she could point out that the dog's paw licking was probably due to allergies.

Try as she might, she couldn't turn off her diagnostics. Interspersed with the healthy dogs she encountered out in the world, she noticed luxating patellas, arthritic hips, and tartar-coated teeth. When she'd just gotten out of school she'd always been quick to offer a tip or two. But as the years ground her down, she realized that a word of advice would usually drag her into a full-on consultation. And people in Nantucket would likely ask her why she wasn't practicing, a topic she barely wanted to consider in her own head let alone with strangers. She needed to protect herself, now more than ever.

For the duration of her time on Nantucket, Morgan decided that she was going deep undercover. Most of her colleagues had fake identities when they were socializing, to keep people from either telling them their heartbreaking euthanasia stories or asking for free medical advice. Outside their practices, they were accountants, cashiers, daycare workers, and bank tellers. Solid, dependable jobs that had nothing to do with life-or-death decisions.

"...like she's been enjoying the boat. Or ferry, I mean," Morgan continued hastily, squinting up at the woman. Between the pinkish Nantucket sweatshirt and overstuffed weekend bags on her shoulder it seemed obvious that she was another vacationer. She had the handsome, makeup-free all-American good looks of a middle-aged L.L.Bean model, with a smooth chestnut bob, gold hoops, and a few delicate chains tangled around her neck.

"Oh yes, she loves the ferry in more ways than one," the woman agreed. "The truth is she's looking to pee in as many spots as possible." She lowered her voice. "Violet is a girl who marks, that's why we try to stay outside."

Morgan laughed.

The woman scanned her, like she was also looking for clues about her background, but Morgan's jeans and white Madewell T-shirt didn't offer much to go on. "Are you a first-timer?"

"I am. This is all new to me." Morgan stood up, leaned back against the rail, and hugged her arms to her chest. "I'm guessing you're not?"

She nodded. "Regular. We're here for the whole summer every year. I stay with my son and our nanny, and my husband flies in on the weekends."

Morgan had assumed that anyone wearing Nantucket gear was a vacationer, like the tourists in New York who insisted on wearing their "I ♥ New York" T-shirts during their visit. She checked out the other people around them and noticed even more Nantucket sweatshirts, hats, and tote bags. Now she wasn't sure who was who.

"Okay, since you're a regular then maybe you can tell me what *ack* means?"

The three letters obviously had something to do with Nantucket because they were everywhere. She'd thought about pulling out her phone to look it up, but part of her pact with herself was to stay more in the moment instead of hiding behind a screen.

"A-C-K is the airport code for Nantucket. You'll see it everywhere." The woman pulled her white canvas bag from under her arm and pointed to the orange letters on the side with a grin. "How long are you staying?"

Morgan was about to answer when a little boy with a cap of dark hair came running up to them with a frowning, ponytailed young woman a few steps behind him.

"I'm *hungry*!" He stomped his little foot.

"Nice to meet you, hungry. I'm Mommy." She held out her hand and he swatted it away with a grumble. The young woman shot his mother an apologetic look.

"Stop it!" he pouted. "Give Ginny some money so she can buy me a hot dog."

"Wow, Evan, that's *rude*," she scolded gently. She glanced at Morgan as the boy grabbed and pulled her hand while Violet tried to drag her in the opposite direction with the other. "Sorry, duty calls. I hope you enjoy your stay. Don't forget your penny when you leave!"

Morgan tilted her head, confused. "Huh?"

"It's a tradition," she said over her shoulder. She used her elbow to point at a squat white lighthouse that was coming into view on the horizon. "Throw a penny in the water by the Brant Point Lighthouse and it guarantees your return trip!"

You're an idiot.

Morgan had changed into shorts and biked into the center

of town on one of Eugene and Karl's red bikes to find something to eat. She realized as she hopped off that she forgot a bike lock and weighed the risks of leaving it leaning against one of the many benches along the sidewalk. How likely was bike theft on an island where even the smallest homes cost a million dollars?

When the cab had dropped her off at the Pak-Reynolds residence, she'd felt her guilt about being away quadruple. She was setting up camp in a slice of preppy paradise and she didn't deserve it. The huge gray-shingled house was set back from the road and had a tall, dense hedge all around it, which gave the property enough privacy that she could run naked through the golf-course grass if the mood ever struck her.

Once inside, Morgan was greeted by a luminous oil painting of Bernadette in the foyer that looked like it belonged in a museum. She moved closer to admire it and realized that she followed the artist on Instagram, a woman named Bess who lived a charmed life in England.

Morgan continued into the open-plan house and took in the wide-plank whitewashed floors, massive windows everywhere, and calming shades of light gray and white punctuated with pops of blue. The beach-house-meets-meditation-retreat vibes made the place feel like a high-end hotel, but not stuffy. It was like Karl and Eugene: perfectly put together but still comfortable. She felt instantly at home.

Her stomach growled as she threaded the bike through the shoppers on Main Street and kicked herself for not doing restaurant recon before she left the house. She'd hoped to find a spot to force herself to enjoy a lazy lunch alone at a corner table, a little toe dip into a slowed-down life, but she knew she wouldn't be able to relax if the bike wasn't locked up.

Morgan downshifted to a crawl behind a trio of senior citizens holding open maps and fought the urge to squeeze through them. She was still coming to terms with the fact that for the first time in too long, there was nowhere she had to be. Hurrying was her way of life, and the absence of some sort of deadline made her feel like she was standing at the edge of a cliff. *Something* was going to blow up. That was just the way life worked.

The leisurely pace forced her to window-shop as she surrendered and let the crowd carry her down the sidewalk. Town had a tidy, manicured quality, perfectly suited for a charming vacation photo backdrop no matter which way the camera pointed. Cute T-shirt shops in historic-looking buildings were sandwiched between art galleries featuring six-foot-long paintings of the ocean, and jewelers displaying oversized watches sat next to clothing stores with pale cashmere sweaters stacked in the window. Whether you wanted to drop thirty grand on an original work of art or thirty dollars on a T-shirt, it seemed like Nantucket had you covered.

Everything around her felt . . . unhurried. Like the question of the day was whether to stop for an ice cream appetizer or hold out on dessert after filling up on seafood paella. Sure, there were women with white bobs, creased canvas shorts, and purses that looked like repurposed baskets striding down the sidewalk like they were on a mission, but the majority of the people around her seemed happy to bumble along.

She wound up at the bottom of Main Street where people with suitcases were gathered in a brick courtyard looking grumpy. Morgan couldn't blame them. There was nothing worse than facing the end of vacation while everyone around you was still in the middle of theirs. She walked her bike past them and couldn't help but feel a little smug.

But you're not on vacation. You're here to work.

The uncomfortable tickle ran along her spine again. The feeling that she didn't deserve time away. She'd felt the same creeping sensation when she'd kicked off her flip-flops and stepped into the shallow end of the pool to test the water. It was bathtub warm, but the decadence of even *considering* a swim at two o'clock on a sunny Friday was enough to make her jump back out. Learning to relax was going to take all of her focus.

Morgan spotted someone with a wheeled food cart a little farther down the brick sidewalk, just before where the long dock dotted with sailboats and yachts started. She couldn't figure out what type of food the person might be selling beneath the navy-and-white-striped umbrella. Cupcakes? Ice cream? Whatever it was, she needed it.

As she got closer she could make out the blocky orange lettering on the umbrella.

Peachy. Huh?

Not much of a hint.

She got in line behind a few other people and strained to hear what the tall white-blond guy facing away from her was saying as he reached into the refrigerated cart.

Speaking of peachy.

He leaned over and Morgan was treated to a front-row view of his reddish boat shorts straining across his butt. His legs had the tanned well-defined look of someone who spent a lot of time outdoors doing sweaty sporty things. She let her eyes drift up his body, taking in his faded T-shirt with a faint shark logo on the back, and was studying his messy hair when he turned suddenly, looked past the next person in line, and locked on to her.

He met her eyes and grinned like she was an old friend, gracing her with a perfect, gleaming white smile that was so genuine she turned to look behind her to see if it was meant for someone else. He was still staring at her when she turned back to him.

"Hey there," he said, keeping his blue eyes locked on hers. "You thirsty?"

Oh shit.

chapter six

I am, actually," Morgan answered without looking away from him even though it took all of her strength to keep from fidgeting. His gaze was unwavering and . . . curious. Like he was trying to place her.

He looked like the hot slacker guys at school who used to skateboard or play soccer in the quad by the library. Morgan remembered watching them out the window while she crammed for an organic chem or stats test, wondering how they could be so carefree. But it wasn't like art and philosophy were stressful majors. They had time to enjoy life.

The guy looked like he was trying to camouflage his all-American-quarterback-Ralph-Lauren-model good looks beneath a layer of scruff and relaxed clothing. But the sharp angle of his jawline was magnified by the golden stubble, and every time he pushed his hair to the side it seemed like the sun threw highlighter on his cheekbones. He was hands-down the most naturally beautiful man Morgan had ever seen in real life. He belonged on a billboard in Times Square, not hawking food in board shorts.

"Sorry, my ferry is leaving in a second," a pretty blond woman said as she dragged her body-bag-sized duffel in front of Morgan with an apologetic frown. She turned to the guy. "Hiii, Nathan. Can I get three bottles of Great Fruit?"

Morgan looked over her shoulder and realized that a smaller ferry than the one she'd taken had materialized at the dock a few feet away.

"Hey, Becca, no prob. You coming back soon?" he asked as he reached into the cooler and put his ass on display again.

"Yup, you know I can't stay away from you." She poked his side with a manicured pink nail, then tossed her head back, laughing like she'd actually said something funny.

He chuckled back good-naturedly and handed her three glass bottles with a green striped print on them. "Should I bill you?"

"Always. C'mere, you," she said, clutching the bottles against her with one arm as she drew him into an awkward hug with the other.

The line for the ferry started moving and the stragglers milling around made a beeline for it.

"Whoops, that's me. Bye, love!" The woman drag-hauled the duffel away while cradling the bottles.

"Sorry about that," the guy said to Morgan, jutting his chin at the retreating woman. "She cut in front of you."

"It's fine." Morgan shrugged with feigned nonchalance, trying to ignore the fact that he was staring at her in a way that made her feel both studied and appreciated. "She's got places to go. I've got all the time in the world."

Admitting it out loud made a twitchy feeling bloom in her chest.

"Well, *all right!*" he replied with a nod, the ever-present smile widening. "You're my kind of people. Is this your first time trying Peachy?" He gestured to the cart behind him.

"Yeah," she nodded. "Is it just . . . soda? Or flavored water?"

He threw his head back and laughed so joyfully that it made Morgan want to laugh too.

"Not even close! Do you have a sec? Can I tell you about it?"

She kicked her foot up on one of the bike pedals and leaned on the handlebars. "Like I said, my schedule is wide open."

And I'll keep saying it until it stops feeling weird.

"Excellent! I'm Nathan Keating, founder of Peachy."

He thrust out his hand and she reached for it warily, like she was afraid it might scorch her. His inexplicable friendliness sent her hackles up like she was a nervous cat confronting a vacuum.

"I'm Morgan Pearce."

"Nice to meet you, Morgan." He pumped her hand up and down. "Glad you stopped to talk. So, Peachy is a cold-pressed, effervescent, functional beverage," he continued in a practiced cadence. "We have three flavors, and each one is fortified with a special mineral blend to deliver a different benefit. Our flagship flavor is Peachy Clean, which has an immunity boost in its DNA. Want a sample?"

Her stomach rumbled for real food, but she wasn't ready to walk away from him to continue her foraging. It was like Nathan had her paralyzed in his high beams. "Sure, okay."

"Once you try it you'll be hooked, I promise." He reached into the cart and pulled out a black-lidded plastic shot glass filled with a murky-looking liquid and handed it to her. "Resist the urge to throw it back. You gotta sip it to enjoy it."

Morgan felt him scrutinizing her as she peeled the lid off and took an awkward slurp. Her tongue came alive as soon as the liquid touched it, like she was drinking Pop Rocks candy. She felt her sinuses constrict as a mixture of peach and ginger overwhelmed her mouth. For a moment she had a nostalgic flavor throwback to her grandmother's homemade peach jam.

Which I hated.

"It's different," Morgan said diplomatically. "I wasn't expecting the . . . carbonation."

"Effervescence," he corrected gently. "You like?"

"Mm," Morgan answered vaguely with a nod and a fake grin, holding the cup like it was a hair-of-the-dog shot of Jäger.

"You gotta finish it," he coaxed. "The first sip is training, the second sip is mastery. I promise you."

Morgan caught herself frowning as she tilted the remaining liquid into her mouth. She expected the same bubbly jolt but instead was met with a clean hit of peach flavor. Her eyes went wide. It was like something out of Harry Potter.

"Wow, what *is* that? Magic?"

He grinned. "Sort of."

"It's actually amazing. I'll take a bottle, please." Morgan closed her eyes and took a deep breath of the sea air. "I feel like I just used a neti pot or something."

"That's what I like to hear," Nathan said as he reached into the cart and pulled out an orange-striped bottle. "It's $8.95, please."

Is it made of peaches imported from France? What the actual hell?

Morgan tried to keep her face neutral as she dug into her back pocket and handed him her credit card.

"How long are you here?" he asked as he ran her card.

"Two months."

A band between her shoulders tensed up.

Steady. It's fine. You're okay.

"Fantastic," he exclaimed, beaming at her again. "First time, or are you a regular?"

"First time. I just got here today, actually." Her stomach growled loud enough for everyone on the dock to hear. "I need to find something to eat, but I'm sort of stuck with this bike since I didn't bring a lock. How safe is it to just leave it somewhere? Because it's not mine and I'd hate for it to get stolen on my first day."

"I feel that," he said, pointing to the front of his cart, which Morgan realized was attached to a bike. "No worries, I'll watch it for you. The best pizza on the island is right over there." He gestured near where the ferry had docked. "My friend owns it."

"Oh, you don't have to do that," Morgan protested. "You're working."

"I can multitask, don't you worry," he chuckled. "Let's make it a trade: you bring me back a slice of black truffle and goat cheese, and I'll keep your bike safe." He reached into his pocket and thrust a rumpled twenty-dollar bill at her.

Morgan sized him up again. He was almost *too* friendly, like an overeager youth pastor. But it wasn't enough to stop her.

"Deal," Morgan said, taking the bill from him.

Ten minutes later, she walked back holding a plate with a slice in each hand, only to see Nathan surrounded by a crowd holding sample shots. She placed the plate on the corner of the cart, and he winked at her and mouthed *thank you* as he explained the benefits of turmeric to the gathered people. Morgan stood off to the side until she started to feel weird and stalkery.

So much for that.

But it wasn't like she had the headspace to even think about a summer fling. She hadn't been with anyone since Sam and it felt like her sex drive had gone into stasis. Sure, she noticed the attractive single men who came into the practice, but it was more like art appreciation, not horniness.

Morgan put the bottle of magic juice in the bike basket and balanced the paper plate on the handlebars as she walked down to where the dock began. She found an empty bench facing the water and settled in to devour the pizza, wishing she'd gotten two slices as she polished it off. The Peachy drink did its magical thing in her mouth, and the more she sipped the more she could justify the cost.

So now what?

Eugene, Karl, and Bernadette weren't due to arrive until later in the day, which meant that Morgan was completely untethered. She tried to lean into it, staring out to where the sea touched the sky, and willed herself to feel okay about being away. To soak up the beauty of where she was and appreciate the gift she'd been given, exactly when she needed it.

For about three minutes it actually worked, until a text buzzed in. She glanced at her phone and saw her brother's typical greeting.

Yo.

She refrained from taking the bait and waited for him to say more. She glanced at their text history and realized they hadn't connected in months.

The next message came a few seconds later. Can you talk?

Mom must've pestered him to the breaking point if he's reach-ing out first.

Hey, yes I can.

Her phone rang the second after she pushed send.

"Hi, Mack." She kept her voice neutral.

"Hey, Morgie, been a while, huh?"

We're cool with nicknames again?

The cynical side of her thought that he was using the nick-name to tug on her heartstrings, hoping for a big reaction to his announcement, but a small part of her felt strangely moved that he'd called her that. They'd been M&M for years, Mackie and Morgie.

"Yup, it has. What's new with you?" Morgan asked, giving him the floor.

Mom said to act surprised . . .

He snorted. "Mom told me she told you about the engage-ment, you don't have to pretend."

She sighed in relief, happy she didn't have to muster up the energy to put on an act. "It's awesome news, congrats. I wanted to reach out, but I was waiting for you to formally tell me."

"Well, now it's official." He was breathing hard, and Morgan figured he was probably on the treadmill. "But this call isn't just about me. Mom let me know about your . . . uh, what happened. I wanted to reach out, but I wasn't sure if you wanted to talk about it. You doing okay?"

Morgan closed her eyes and exhaled slowly. The combina-tion of Mack bringing it up and the fact that none of her family was willing to put a name to what she'd been through embarrassed her. She wondered if Mack thought she was weak too.

"Yeah, I'm feeling better every day." *That's a lie.* "Thanks for asking."

The line went silent except for the sound of his labored breathing. It was still an effort to find common ground, but at least he was trying.

"So, Nantucket, huh? Nice gig. Sounds like a fun summer. The real estate there is *insane.*"

Mack was a partner in a high-end boutique real estate company in New York and rarely turned off the property valuation portion of his brain.

"It's not a vacation, I'm caring for a diabetic dog while I'm here." She paused and looked around at the boats and ocean and blue sky. "But yeah, it's pretty nice so far."

The pinprick of tears came out of nowhere. Maybe it was the fact that Mack had reached out to her, or her uncertainty about what the hell she was doing in paradise when she didn't deserve it, but suddenly all she wanted to do was cry. A couple carrying shopping bags walked past her and down the dock to the boats, so she sniffled and sat up straighter.

"Hey, speaking of time away, Elle and I were talking about some summer trips and Nantucket was actually on the list before we even knew you were going to be there . . ."

She grabbed on to his tentative olive branch. Maybe it was time to try again now that she was going to have a sister-in-law?

"Oh, Mack, you should definitely come!" Morgan fiddled with the Peachy lid. "I'd love to see both of you.

Maybe we can act like grown-ups now?

"Cool, cool, cool." He met her enthusiasm with his usual detached air. "I know you just got there, but do you have any suggestions for inns? Obviously, cost doesn't matter."

Morgan ignored his humblebrag as the words came out of her mouth before she could stop them.

"No, stay with me at Eugene and Karl's. They said I could have guests, and the house is big enough to sleep a million people. I've got their whole summer schedule locked in so we can pick a weekend when they're off island."

It felt fussy to say "off island," but it was how Eugene referred to their time away.

"Okay, great. I'll let Elle know it's an option," Mack said. "She might want to stay somewhere else, I'll leave it up to her."

Way to blame your fiancée for your baggage, Mack.

"Okay, sure. Whatever," Morgan said, hoping she didn't sound as conflicted as she felt. He was trying to make a connection with her, and she appreciated the effort, but deep down she wondered if they were just too different now.

"Anyway, time for me to dip," he continued. "Good talk."

The line went quiet except for his breathing again and Morgan realized that as the oldest, it was up to her to try to reassure him that it wouldn't be weird for them to hang out after ignoring each other for so long.

"I'm really happy for you. And I hope we can make a visit happen. It'll be fun." She decided to put herself out there. "The truth is, I miss you, Mackie."

His panting softened and all she could hear was the rhythmic pounding of his feet on the treadmill.

"Same."

In just one word, Mack had told her everything she needed

to hear. They were both going to try. Morgan smiled despite the tickle in her nose. "I'm looking forward to getting to know Elle better."

"She's amazing, you're going to love her," he gushed. "I'm so lucky."

They hung up and Morgan slugged back the remainder of the peach concoction, wondering if maybe it *was* magical, because all of a sudden her life was starting to feel pretty darn sparkly.

chapter seven

The next morning Eugene and Karl stood in the garage looking like they were getting ready to send their only child off to college. Both men had morphed from their typical monochromatic shades of black outfits to clothing that was country-club ready, from Karl's pink linen shirt to Eugene's khaki shorts covered in embroidered red whales.

"Are you sure you can handle the extra weight?" Eugene asked Morgan, his fingers steepled under his chin. "Bernadette can be wiggly in the basket, and the cobblestones close to town make riding tough."

Morgan was used to overprotective pet parents, but the Pak-Reynoldses were next-level worriers. Even with their shared history at the practice, the thought of sending Bernadette into town on the bike with Morgan to check out the farmer's market had them pacing.

"Are you forgetting that my patients range from kitten to Great Dane? I'm strong," Morgan answered, flexing her arm. "I won't let anything happen to her, I promise."

Her answer seemed to placate them, so Karl grabbed a sturdy-looking basket complete with roll bar from the shelf.

"Here's the deal, Morgan," he said as he secured it on her bike in the open space next to a red Jeep. "I'm not sure if you've noticed, but Bernie doesn't like to walk in public. When you get to town you'll have to carry her everywhere."

"Wait . . . really?" She frowned. "Is it a pain thing? Do I need to do an exam? Or is it behavioral?"

Eugene and Karl exchanged a look.

"Neither. It's a diva thing," Karl answered, looking a little sheepish.

Uh-oh. Proceed with caution.

Bernadette was standing beside them turning in excited circles, acting happier and spryer than Morgan had ever seen her. The little dog was never at her best when she visited the office, and Morgan rarely saw her when she was at their house in Princeton because the party hubbub kept her away. The change in behavior made her feel like she was meeting Bernadette for the first time.

"Does she ask to get picked up? Like, does she climb up your leg or something?"

Karl leaned over the handlebars and tightened a screw on the basket. "Nope, I just pick her up and she settles in."

In all the times she'd seen them in the office she'd never made the connection that Bernadette was rarely on the floor. Morgan felt herself slipping into diagnostic mode. "What do you think would happen if she had the chance to walk around in town? Would she be aggressive?"

"Huh." Eugene looked down at the dog as she did another

happy spin for him. "I don't *think* so. She's only crotchety when people do grooming and vet stuff. I mean, I wouldn't call her outgoing . . . She's more like a cat, really. You know that."

"I do," Morgan nodded. "But if it's okay with you, maybe I'll let her try to be a dog for a bit? Sniff around, that sort of thing."

"Oh." Karl's brow creased and he stopped working on the basket to stare at Bernadette. "I don't know . . ."

"Let me try today, it might be good for her," Morgan said. "Put some pep back in her step."

Bernadette dipped into a play bow, then barked at them, and the men looked at their dog as if they didn't recognize her.

"We need to stop being ridiculous," Eugene finally said. "Of course you know what you're doing. Fine, let her walk if you think that's best."

"I'll text you photos and videos. It'll be adorable," Morgan said, reverting to her "you can trust me" voice.

"Speaking of adorable," Karl said. "Our friend Sydney volunteers with the rescue here, Beacon of Hope. They always have a booth at the farmer's market, you should stop and say hi. They do an incredible fund-raiser every summer, and I bet they'd love to have someone like you on the team."

Morgan winced, realizing that they still needed to have the uncomfortable discussion about wanting to be incognito for the summer. Karl and Eugene were her clients, and she didn't want them to think that she hated her job, but it was important for them to know that she needed distance from it while she was there. When they'd had the conversation about her coming to Nantucket to watch Bernadette, she'd been vague about why she needed time away from the practice. But she'd caught the knowing glance that passed between Eugene and Karl as she danced around exactly what she'd been through. They got it.

But how do I explain this part without sounding like an asshole?

"I forgot to tell you that I want to be, uh, *undercover* while I'm here. I know it sounds weird, but I don't want anyone to know what I do for a living." She paused to see how they'd react and was relieved that neither one looked scandalized. "The second people find out I'm a veterinarian, they start asking me to diagnose their animals. I guess I just want to be a regular civilian for a bit. Does that make sense?"

"Of course," Karl replied with a nod, his kind eyes locked on hers. "We totally understand. It's not the same thing at all, not even close, but people ask us for free design advice too when all we want to do is enjoy a cocktail. Don't worry, your secret's safe with us."

"Ooh, you need a backstory, just in case someone asks," Eugene said, looking way more invested in her subterfuge than necessary. "Cryptocurrency millionaire? Trophy wife? Foot model? Because I could help you come up with something *really* juicy."

"Yes, there's a reason why he's the creative director of our company," Karl said drolly, shooting a roguish smile at his partner.

Morgan smiled. "I don't need to lie, I'm just going to tell the current truth: I'm a dog sitter."

Fifteen minutes later, Morgan and Bernadette had successfully navigated their way into town and locked the bike to a signpost at the top of Main Street. She watched Bernadette before taking her out of the basket, looking for signs that the dog was nervous or overwhelmed by the early-morning activity. Bernadette was fixated on everyone passing by, but her little paws dancing in place and her relaxed expression were enough to convince Morgan that her instincts had been correct.

"Okay, my friend," Morgan said as she took her out. "We've got this."

She started off down the sidewalk holding the blue-striped leash so there was slack in it, watching Bernadette to make sure she seemed okay. The little dog sniffed along beside Morgan, pausing to pee every few steps and not seeming to mind the crowds of people passing by. Her stubby tail wagged the whole time.

"They were wrong about you, old lady!" Morgan said to Bernadette, who kept walking like she was on a scent.

"Hey, Morgan Pearce!"

The shout startled her. She stopped in her tracks, frowning as she looked around the crowded sidewalk.

"Over here!" A bike bell sounded off.

Morgan turned to face the cobblestone street and froze when she realized it was Nathan the soda guy, pedaling his bike cart down toward the dock where she'd met him the day before. He slowed down as he smiled and waved, not seeming to realize that he was holding up a parade of cars behind him.

Holy shit, he's perfect. Even riding that dorky bike cart.

She waved awkwardly. "Hey there!"

"You should come visit me later! Same spot," he bellowed so that the few people who hadn't been watching now turned to stare.

It was like they were old friends and he wanted to catch up

with her, until she realized that it was probably part of his sales pitch. Make everyone feel like a buddy, then get them to open their wallets for juice that costs as much as a glass of champagne.

He'd slowed down to almost a stop waiting for her to answer. Morgan couldn't believe the cars lined up behind him weren't honking.

"Okay, I'll try!" she offered, hoping he'd move along and everyone would stop watching them.

"Cool!" He stood up on the pedals and leaned forward, his calves straining at the effort to move the heavy cart on the bumpy street. He threw another glance at her as he gained momentum. "I like your dog."

"Oh, she's not mine . . ."

"Huh?" He slowed down again.

Morgan realized that she was now part of the reason for a major downtown backup. The Volvos and Land Rovers were stopped all the way to the imposing brick building at the top of the street. "Nothing! Bye!"

He waved at her again and finally pedaled off.

He's like that with everyone, just stop.

Morgan found her way to the closed-off side street crowded with farmer's market merchants but still relatively free of other shoppers. She kept an eye on Bernadette as they headed in, watching to make sure her posture didn't change. The little dog's maiden voyage in town on four paws had to be as positive as possible. Morgan snapped a quick photo of Bernadette standing at the entrance to the market near a flower merchant and sent it to Eugene and Karl.

"We'll do a quick walk-through, Miss B," Morgan said to her. "Then maybe we'll stroll down to the docks."

Duh, of course you're going down there. To see him.

They kept to the middle of the street and Morgan peered at the goods for sale from a distance. She made a mental note to check out the handmade jewelry and natural soaps and lotions with cute mermaid logos another time, since her first priority was focusing on Bernadette. The dog was too busy sniffing and exploring to let her ponder which Nantucket bracelet to buy.

"Hey, I know you!" a voice called out from behind her.

What is it with this island?

Morgan turned and saw the woman from the ferry standing at a table with a Beacon of Hope banner slung across the front of it and piles of brochures on top.

"Oh, hi there!" Morgan exclaimed, a little nervous that she was about to officially start her career charade with someone from the dog rescue.

"Cute pup! What's the name?"

She realized that she had no choice but to walk over and engage.

"This is Bernadette, I'm her, uh, caretaker. Her dog sitter. And I'm Morgan." She held out her hand and glanced down as Bernadette squatted and left her calling card next to the table leg.

"Of course, I didn't recognize her without Karl carrying her! I'm Sydney Coleman," she answered as she shook Morgan's hand. She'd paired her slim-fit white "Beacon of Hope" T-shirt with a delicate strand of pearls and black leggings.

"They mentioned you, nice to meet you," Morgan said. "Looks like a great organization."

"Yup, I've volunteered here for ages. We've got a big benefit coming up at the end of next month with a fashion show. I'm selling raffle tickets, you should check out the prizes."

Baskets of dog treats and toys, I'm sure. I'm good, thanks.

"We've got a weekend stay in Bermuda up for grabs, that's the top prize," Sydney continued. "But we've also got a $2,000 cosmetic aesthetician package and a private yoga retreat for four people in Rexford, New York, available too."

Her jaw dropped as she realized that a Nantucket fund-raiser was something entirely foreign to her.

"Tickets are fifty for one chance, ninety-five for two."

Morgan choked and tried to cover it up with a huge smile.

"Wow, that sounds great, but I don't have my wallet with me," she lied. "I'll swing back."

"How long are you visiting? Because we're always looking for volunteers, and it looks like you're in the business," Sydney said, nodding to Bernadette. She handed Morgan a brochure. "We need everything from dog holders at adoption events to people who can foster. And we need a ton of support during the big fund-raiser. It's a blast, I'm one of the chairs."

"Uh-huh," Morgan said, focusing on Bernadette as she stuffed her nose in a duffel bag under the table. "I'm here for two months."

"Oh, fantastic! If you're here that long, you could foster . . ." She trailed off and handed Morgan a sheet with color photos of dogs and cats. "Eugene and Karl fostered a puppy with us a few years back; they're due for another one, if you ask me."

Morgan scanned the sheet. The biggest photo in the center of the page was of a gorgeous blond dog named Hudson who was posed with a smile and an irresistible head tilt.

He looked like a Disney character brought to life, complete with a starry-eyed expression and a filtered halo of sunlight around his head. At first glance she thought he was pure yellow

Lab, but the dark muzzle and oversized ears suggested that there was something houndy mixed in his DNA.

"Wow, this guy Hudson is adorable. How is he not adopted?"

Sydney frowned. "Poor Hud. He's a great dog, but he's got some challenges we need to work through. He has to go to a special foster or adopter, someone who understands how to deal with grumblies. He's got some stranger danger and he's not a hundred percent dog friendly when he's on leash."

Don't say anything. Don't open your mouth. Don't do it.

Morgan nodded. "My old dog was leash reactive. His rehab went really well. The training is pretty straightforward, you just need to stick with it."

"Oh, you have experience with reactive dogs?" Sydney's eyebrows flew up.

Morgan blinked at her and realized that she'd bragged herself into a corner. "Um. A little?"

A lot. I have an absolute shit-ton of experience.

While she'd never call herself a *trainer* trainer, Morgan had hired a few to help with George and had gone on to do enough research on her own to basically qualify as one. She loved the behavioral stuff, and her meticulous note-taking and eye for analysis made her good at it. Under her care, George had eventually grown into a confident, happy, well-mannered dog.

"Then you've got more experience than the average foster parent." Sydney reached under the table and pulled out a stack of papers. "Forgive me for being forward, but here's a volunteer form, and more information about Hudson from his intake eval. Even if you can just give us a few weeks, it would be a *huge* help. Think about it. Eugene and Karl would be okay with it, I bet."

The thought of taking on a needy foster dog when she was supposed to be recharging made her want to pick up Bernadette and run away. She barely had enough juice to get herself through the day. But it wasn't like she wanted to explain why she couldn't foster him on a sunny Saturday morning with a stranger, so she opted to put the blame on Bernie.

"If he's reactive, I bet he needs to be an only dog . . ." She pointed at Bernadette, who was now half-inside the bag beneath the card table. "Plus, the size and age differences between them would make it tricky."

"He's usually only grumpy on leash, or if a dog gets too pushy with him off leash. He played with my Violet and was great," Sydney said. "If you wanted to give it a try we'd do a bunch of meets with Bernadette to make one hundred percent sure they're okay together. You could even do an overnight trial! No pressure, but he needs someone like you."

Morgan glanced at Hudson's photo again and felt an almost physical tug on her heart. She was the world's biggest sucker when it came to the hard-luck cases. Coupled with her inability to say no, she knew she was teetering on the edge of making a stupid snap decision.

"Where is he now?"

Sydney hid a smile. "He's with one of our fosters, but things are getting dicey with her resident cat. And he's been regressing on leash. We'd love to place him with someone that can help get him ready for adoption. He's a wonderful dog, really. He just needs some polishing up." She gave Morgan a hopeful look.

Morgan intended to keep secrets during her time in Nantucket, but it was time to reveal one of them: she'd been preaching the foster gospel for years and had never actually done it herself. She used to blame it on George, who would've had a tough time sharing his home with another dog. But by the time he was gone, she barely had enough headspace for her own needs let alone another creature's.

"Honestly, I'm not sure I'd be a good fit," Morgan said, shuffling a few steps away. "I've never fostered before."

"Oh, it's *easy*! And you clearly have dog sense beyond your own dog, otherwise Karl and Eugene wouldn't let you anywhere near Bernadette. We can support you every step of the way."

The pull to help was almost impossible for her to resist.

No. You're here for a recharge. Save yourself so you can save others.

"Okay, maybe. We'll see."

Idiot. Just say no.

Morgan made a kissy noise and Bernadette finally came out from under the table.

"Fantastic!" Sydney's eyes were shining with hope. "Can't wait to hear from you. I *knew* I met you for a reason."

chapter eight

"Hey, there you are!"

Morgan felt her stomach dip when Nathan's gaze locked on to her and he waved.

The ferry had just left so the sidewalk was relatively empty, which meant that Morgan was about to be the sole beneficiary of Nathan's attention. His blond hair was as blinding as ever even in the shadow of the cart's umbrella. He seemed dressed up for the weekend tourists in a loose, wrinkled white button-down, navy shorts, and flip-flops, with a thin braided leather rope around one ankle.

Morgan looked down at her faded black-and-white-striped tank top, jean shorts, and dirty Keds, and wondered if she needed to step up her game.

"Who's this?" he asked as she walked closer, squatting and waiting for Bernadette to approach in a way that suggested that he had dog sense too. There was nothing worse than a guy who insisted "all dogs love me" only to watch him force himself on a disinterested dog.

"Her name is Bernadette, she's not mine. I'm her, uh, dog walker for the summer."

"Lucky pup!" Nathan said as he reached for the dog.

Points deducted. You need to let her come to you.

"She can be a little standoffish with new people," Morgan cautioned, pausing a few feet away from him. "I'd let her check you out before you try to touch—"

But it was too late. Nathan duck-walked to Bernadette and the little dog closed the distance between them with a wagging hind end. She turned in circles against his leg like a cat as he patted her.

I guess no one's immune to him.

"Aw, Bernadette, you're sweet." Nathan looked up at Morgan. "How old is she?"

Morgan felt a jolt rush through her. Men like Nathan weren't supposed to be walking around in the wild like regular mortals; they belonged on catwalks or judging people from beachside cafés in Capri with fellow supermodels. It was hard to have a conversation with him because her brain couldn't process anything other than the fact that physically, he was as close to perfect as a human could be.

He acts like he doesn't know it, but he has *to know it.*

"Eleven," she managed to squeak out.

"You don't look a day over ten. Right, cutie?" He rubbed Bernadette's ear and she closed her eyes in ecstasy. "My dog's only a year old and he's nuts."

"What kind?" Morgan couldn't stop speaking in fragments.

"A pittie named Archer. Best dog in the world." He looked down at Bernadette. "No offense."

"Aw." Morgan felt like her tongue wasn't working. She couldn't come up with a thing to say.

"You thirsty? Want to sample something else?" Nathan stood and walked over to the cart. "I'm trialing a new drink for the summer, Watermelon Mint. It just came in this morning and I need to get feedback."

"Sure, but I'm probably not the best tester," she replied, finally snapping out of her trance. "I'm not a fan of mint."

"Don't worry, it's not the *flavor* of mint, it's the benefits. It soothes and relaxes."

God knows I could use some of that.

He handed her a shot glass filled with a pinkish liquid. "Take a sip, then say the first word that comes to mind. Don't think too much, just go with what your gut tells you."

Morgan could feel his expectant gaze on her as she tilted the drink into her mouth and waited for the zing. She was under a lot of pressure, throwing back a shot of mystery liquid and trying to catalog her reaction all while being watched by the dock god. This time instead of a shock, her tongue felt only the slightest tingle as the familiar taste of watermelon filled her mouth.

Nathan watched her with a hopeful expression on his face. "First word, please. Be honest."

"Front porch," Morgan said before she could figure out why.

He laughed and it made her want to get him to do it again. "That's weird and I like it. Can you explain?"

She drained the rest of the drink. "I feel like I'm sitting on a front porch eating a cold slice of watermelon. It's *really* good."

"Yes!" Nathan punched the air and bobbed his head. "That's exactly the vibe I was going for. Best description I've heard so far. I hope everyone agrees with you because I'm totally stoked for this flavor."

Bernadette nosed her way around the cart, pulling Morgan a few steps closer to Nathan.

"Do you have any employees helping out or is it just you?" she asked, hoping for more details about his life.

"I'm a one-man operation for now. I wanna stay nimble while I figure stuff out, you know? I've got great distro going with a bunch of restaurants on island, but I'm not ready to scale up quite yet. I'm just treading water this summer, getting a temperature read on my stuff, and then I can go hard once I head home to Philly come fall. What about you? You a full-time dog sitter?"

Morgan cringed and wished she'd given more thought to her cover story. Eugene probably would've created an entire dossier for her if she'd asked.

"I am, but I scaled back this summer so my only client is Bernie," she replied, hating the lie. As much as she needed distance, it pained her to be dishonest. Especially when he was looking at her like that. "She's special-needs, so I'm taking care of her while her people travel. Eugene Pak and Karl Reynolds? Do you know them?"

He shook his head. "Nope, only been here a month. My college friend's grandmother has a house here, but she passed away so they're letting me hang out for the summer to do test runs on Peachy flavors. It's been great." He smirked. "Surfing's hit or miss, though."

Makes total sense that he's a surfer.

Morgan glanced down and noticed that Bernadette had her eyes half-closed and was panting in the shade of Nathan's umbrella. She'd left the bowl and water she'd packed in the bike basket at the top of Main Street.

"Shit, she's thirsty. You wouldn't happen to have—"

He was already halfway in the cart before she had a chance to finish. "The Peachy cart serves all," he said as he presented a glass jug filled with water and a bowl. "I keep this stashed for me and all the dogs I meet." He winked at her as he filled it, then placed it on the ground by Bernadette, who lapped it up. "And now on to your beverage needs. Want another Peachy?"

"Please. I'll take the new one."

It didn't matter that his drinks cost as much as an entire sandwich back home, she already craved it like a junkie. The fact that the dealer was hot made it the perfect gateway drug. He handed her the bottle.

"We can set up billing if you want," he said, a hopeful expression on his face.

Exactly. You're just another customer to him. Don't fall for it.

"Sure, that works," Morgan answered, trying to keep the disappointment from her voice as she handed him her credit card.

A trio of teenage girls walked to the cart shoulder to shoulder, clutching their phones to their chests and giggling behind their hands.

"Is this, like, *beer* or something?" one of them asked, causing them to burst out laughing.

"Hi, ladies," Nathan said good naturedly. "No, Peachy isn't beer, it's a cold-pressed, effervescent, functional beverage. We have three flavors, plus one that I'm trying out. Want a sample?"

The girls clamored around him and he reached over their heads to hand Morgan's card back.

"All set," he said with another wink that would've been ridiculous coming from anyone else, but from him it was like foreplay.

The chatter from the girls got louder, causing Bernadette to pull away from them. Morgan took it as her cue to leave.

"Thanks," she said, taking a few steps backward, holding the bottle in the air. He was busy helping the girls, so he didn't even realize that she was leaving.

She gulped the drink as she walked away, convinced that it was spiked with something addictive.

"Hey, Morgan," Nathan called to her, causing her to choke on a mouthful as she whipped back around. "A bunch of us are going to—" The girls' chatter drowned out what he said, but it sounded liked *Sisto*. "You should come. We'll be there at seven."

Her heart sped up to triple time.

Maybe I'm not just a customer after all? But who's in the "bunch"?

"Okay, great. Maybe I will." She had no idea what Sisto was, but she figured Eugene or Karl could fill her in. "Thanks again for the hydration for two."

She threaded through the people on the sidewalk, trying to keep from getting too excited about the invitation. For all she knew, Nathan could have a girlfriend. Hell, the meetup could be a customer appreciation thing. How stupid would she feel if she went and discovered a bunch of other hopeful, dumb women with heart eyes for the drink dude.

Morgan checked her phone and realized that Bernadette was due for her next injection within the hour. "I think that's enough excitement for today, ma'am. We need to head home," she said as they started back to the bike. "But you did great."

Bernadette wagged her tail and smile-panted like she knew it.

Town had gotten busier since they'd arrived, so instead of walking directly up Main Street, Morgan veered off to a quieter side street. It was just as quaint as the main thoroughfare, dotted with cute shops and restaurants.

And you've got two months to explore it all.

Morgan waited for the waves of guilt to flood her. For needing to get away, for being weak, for thinking she deserved time off from the career she loved . . .

Bernadette barked before the stress spiral overtook her, forcing her back into the moment.

"What's wrong, Bern?"

She barked again and Morgan spotted a giant sleeping lump of a dog in the shadows of a tree up the block, who didn't seem at all worried about the twelve pounds of senior attitude heading toward it.

"Let's cross the street, Bernie. Off we go!"

Morgan knew better than to let Bernadette meet a huge dog whose owner wasn't around. There was no one else on the sidewalk, so they were on their own if the dog woke up and decided to charge them. Bernadette barked again and the dog lifted its head slowly, like it was considering if the threat was worth waking up for.

"*Shhh*, Bernadette," Morgan whispered, realizing that there was no easy escape for them if the massive pile of brown fur decided to make the little dog an appetizer.

It seemed that being ignored was too much for Bernadette to take, so she cemented her little paws in place and threw her head back, scream-barking from across the street. As Morgan flicked her eyes between the dogs, she realized that Bernadette was alternating between barking and play bows. Her bluster was more a mix of frustration and silliness, an invitation to have fun, not battle. Morgan felt her shoulders relax. Her years with George had made her extra careful about leash safety, and meeting strange dogs on walks was a huge no-no. But while she felt okay about how Bernadette was acting, she had no clue what the other dog was capable of.

"Don't worry, he's friendly," a young woman in a woven straw hat said as she appeared from behind a tall hedge. "He's wishing he could meet your dog, but he's too lazy to get up."

Yeah, right. Just like all the unleashed "don't worry he's friendly" dogs that used to try to start shit with George. Not buying it.

"This isn't my dog, I'm just the dog sitter," Morgan called back to her, pointing at Bernadette. "I haven't seen how she is around other dogs yet."

"No better tester than Palmer. He's the most laid-back dog ever. He met a dog that bit him in the face, and he shook it right off and walked away. No biggie." The woman scratched her chin with the back side of her dirty glove and Morgan saw that she was clutching a small plant.

She thought of the photo of Hudson the rescue dog folded up in her back pocket. It actually *would* be a good idea to get a read on Bernadette's dog-dog skills. If she was a nightmare, Morgan could write off Hudson without feeling bad about it. Not that she was even considering meeting the foster dog.

But still. It might be good to see how Bernadette is with a bomb-proof dog. Just in case.

"Would it be okay if I did a quick trial run?" Morgan asked. "Do you mind?"

"We'd love it, please do," the woman said, leaning down to pet her dog.

She was outfitted for work, from her ankle boots to her multi-pocket shorts filled with pruning instruments, to her snug, dirt-smudged green T-shirt. She had the compact, muscled look of someone who was physical for a living. Morgan could see a row of studs and hoops along her ear that disappeared beneath a swirl of dark hair peeking from under her woven hat.

Rather than walking in a straight line for the dog, Morgan zigzagged their way over. She led Bernadette to the nearby trees the dog had likely marked, and after breathing the scents in, Bernie added her own pee signature to them. All the while, the dog watched them with his head still glued to the sidewalk. When he didn't move, Morgan let Bernadette wander over and sniff a few feet away from his tail. Bernadette inched forward, so focused on breathing in his vital stats that when the mountain of a dog raised his head she jumped back in shock. He got up slowly into a combination downward dog stretch and play bow, making it clear that he was totally chill. Bernadette crab-walked over to him, wagging her tail at half mast and batting her eyelashes. After some polite communal butt sniffing, they moved on to doing mirrored play bows over and over.

"See? Everybody loves Palmer. There's just something about him," the woman said, smiling at the two dogs as they goofed with each other. It was an approachable smile, the kind that made her eyes crinkle.

"What is he? I definitely see Newfie, and maybe some chocolate Lab, but what else?" Morgan asked.

"I did a DNA test on him and it said he was Newfoundland, Lab, Greater Swiss Mountain Dog, and *Chihuahua*."

Morgan shook her head. "They've always gotta throw in that weird one, right?"

The woman laughed in agreement. "What's her name?"

"Bernadette. She's usually a very reserved eleven-year-old, but I'm seeing a new side of her today." The little dog took off after Palmer and dragged Morgan a few steps, almost causing her to drop her bottle of Watermelon Mint.

"I see you met Nathan," the woman said, pointing at the bottle.

Morgan tried not to perk up at the mention of him. "I have. You know him?"

"A little. I went to his rival high school in Pennsylvania. Everyone seems to love his drinks."

Morgan tried to act natural even though she was dying to do a full inquisition. "What was he like then?"

"Honestly?" she rolled her eyes. "Total player. But I don't want to gossip. People change."

Morgan's heart sank. Her gut instinct was right.

She shrugged it off since it didn't matter anyway. They watched the giant and the pixie working out how to play together.

"These two are having a blast," the woman said. "We should set up a play date so Bernadette can be off leash with him. How long are you here?"

"Two months."

Her voice was strong as she said it.

"We can definitely make it happen, then. Here." She reached into her back pocket as she strode toward Morgan and thrust a business card at her. "I know it's old-school to have a card, but a lot of my clients are seniors. They like paper, so I always have them on me."

Morgan looked down at the card. "Hortensia Gardenscapes?"

"Yeah, I'm Tess Wilkie. *Hortensia* is the Latin name for hydrangea, which is basically a weed on Nantucket. I do window boxes, beds, and general yard upkeep."

"Of course, I love all of the hydrangeas. I'm Morgan Pearce." She reached out her hand and Tess put down the plant and whipped off her glove to shake it.

"Nice to meet you. Text me when you feel like meeting up. We're heading into my busy season, but I need a break now and then."

"I hear you," Morgan said.

If anyone knows about needing a break, it's me.

chapter nine

Cocktails, Miss Morgan! Come to the house if you want one."
Karl's voice echoing through the yard woke Morgan
from her unexpected nap. She sat up abruptly, blinking in the
dim light, and checked her phone.

Did I seriously just sleep for three hours?

Morgan flopped back against the way-too-comfortable
cream-colored couch and stretched like a cat, batting away the
guilt over wasting the rest of the day.

I'm acclimating. Recalibrating. Like it's a different time zone.

Napping was fine on her second day on the island, but there
was no way she was going to spend the summer hibernating
and feeling sorry for herself. Wasted time made her feel useless,
but it was like the Pak-Reynoldses' guest house was designed to
encourage lazing around. The couch and chairs were slip-
covered in soft white canvas and were so deep that her feet
didn't touch the ground when she sat in them. Even though it was
a small living space, with just a sitting area, kitchenette, bedroom, and tiny bathroom, the soaring beamed ceiling and wall of
glass doors looking out onto the yard made it feel expansive.

Morgan knew that she needed to fill her days with enough activities to keep the stress tentacles from regenerating. But there was *plenty* to do on Nantucket. After taking care of Bernadette's needs in the mornings, she'd spend a few hours exploring on her bike. She'd definitely have to visit the whaling museum. Obviously she'd go to the beach now and then. See a movie in the beautiful theater in town. Buy a Nantucket sweatshirt and a bracelet with a map of the island on it. Try the ghost walk. Pick up journaling again. Read bestsellers by the pool. And stock up on Peachy whenever she went to town.

I'm going to do all the things this summer.

Morgan looked down at the rumpled clothes she'd worn into town that morning and decided to follow her hosts' lead and dress like evening cocktails and dinner meant something. She changed into her go-to white cotton halter dress that was versatile enough to take her from beach cover-up to dinner attire depending on shoes and accessories. Her scrunchie was half out of her hair, so she pulled it all the way off and ran her fingers through the mess to tame it, threw on silver hoops, and headed out to meet them.

Bernadette was waiting for her in the yard with wags and kisses. She followed her into the main house.

"She's been dying to see you, but we made her wait so you could rest," Karl said from the kitchen. "She adores you."

"It's mutual," Morgan said, scratching Bernadette gently under the chin until she closed her eyes.

"You look gorgeous," Karl said as he poured brown liquid into a tumbler. He held it up. "Old-fashioned?"

Morgan pulled a face. "The hard stuff doesn't like me. Any other options?"

"Of course. Name it and we have it." He headed for the glass-front refrigerator. "Chard, Pinot, Merlot, champagne . . . ?"

"Chef's choice. Where's Eugene?"

Karl pointed down the hallway to the formal dining room. "On the phone. Hey, check this out." He tilted a wood tray filled with an assortment of meats and cheeses on it. "I put the *cute* in *charcuterie.*"

It was the silliest thing she'd ever heard him say. Nantucket seemed to take the edge off him, and she hoped it would eventually do the same for her. Morgan laughed and grabbed a piece of cheddar as Karl poured her a glass of champagne.

A few minutes later, Eugene wandered back into the kitchen wearing a smile that made him look like he was up to no good.

"I hear Bernadette wasn't the only one who made a friend today." He held his phone up. "That was Sydney Coleman."

"Oh, yeah. I met her on the ferry and saw her in town this morning. She seems nice."

"She's out for a walk, so I invited her to drop in for a drink."

"Oh, fun."

But not really, because she'll want to talk dogs and I'll have to stick to my cover story.

They moved out to the patio and settled into the double-wide lounge chairs. Morgan was still adjusting to the sheer *comfort* of it all: the Pak-Reynoldses' home, the gorgeous weather, the chill Nantucket vibe . . . it was impossible not to relax. The air was cool and the setting sun threw golden-hour light on them, making her want to pull out her phone for a few photos. But it wasn't like she could post them. How could she boast about where she was when she knew her friends were still dealing with stuff like hard-to-find veins on fractious geriatric cats?

"We leave on Monday for the first leg. Do you have everything you need, Morgan?" Karl asked.

"Yes, do you feel confident about being here on your own? We have surveillance cameras everywhere outside, so if you happen to be the first murder victim on the island since 2004, we'll have *tons* of footage for the police."

"Would you stop it?" Karl chastised Eugene. "Obviously, the Jeep is yours if you need it. And the bikes."

"Please don't worry about me," Morgan said as the bubbles from the champagne started to do their thing. "Your girl and I are going to have a great time together."

"Do you want me to drive you to the grocery store before we go?" Eugene asked, his eyebrows knitted together with concern. "It's a little confusing, there's a roundabout that's a literal nightmare since the tourists don't know what the hell they're doing."

"Nope, I'm good, thanks."

"Any questions about where to eat? Or the best beaches?" Eugene asked, sounding like a concierge. "Not that we get to the beaches much, but we know what people like."

Nathan's invitation echoed in Morgan's head.

Where did he say he was going tonight?

"Actually, I do have a question. What's Sisto?"

Karl frowned. "You mean *Cisco*?"

"Yeah, that sounds right."

Morgan took a huge gulp of champagne. She felt twitchy even following up on it, especially given what Tess had said about Nathan.

"Well, it's a couple of things. Cisco is a beach and it's also a brewery bar about ten minutes outside of town. Why?"

Stop. It meant nothing. You're not going to show up and embarrass yourself.

"Someone mentioned it today. I was just curious, no big deal." Morgan shrugged it off.

"Someone who?" Eugene pressed. It was like he had a nose for gossip.

Morgan was about to make something up when the gate door clattered.

"Hi, guys," Sydney trilled. "Can you meet me out front? I brought *someone*!"

Morgan's eyes went wide as she started to put it all together. "What did you do?"

"Nothing!" they exclaimed in unison, feigning shock and doing a crap job of it.

"We've got an open-door policy. If our friend brought a friend, the more the merrier," Eugene replied, sounding like he was trying to defend himself.

Morgan followed them around the side of the house to the front yard, where Sydney Coleman was standing in a pink patterned dress that looked like beachy hotel wallpaper, holding the leash of none other than the handsome yellow rescue dog from the flyer.

"Look who's here!" she said, waving and grinning. "It's Hudson!"

Despite how sweet he'd looked in the photo, there was nothing cute about the dog in real life. He stood frozen next to Sydney with his ears plastered to his head and his body low to the ground, tail tucked, and his eyes fixed on the three of them.

"He's adorable!" Eugene exclaimed as he started walking toward Sydney.

"Wait!" Morgan karate-chopped her arm into his midsection to stop him. "Don't go up to him, he's nervous."

"She's right," Sydney said, glancing down at Hudson. "He's funny with new people at first."

"What's your protocol for this type of situation?" Morgan asked her, watching the dog warily to see how he was tolerating being the center of attention.

"Total avoidance if it's strangers out on the street. Slow intros if we're trying to build a relationship."

Hudson licked his lips, then opened his mouth in a head-shaking yawn so wide, Morgan swore she could see his epiglottis.

"Then why don't we sit?" Eugene asked, motioning to the backyard. "Let's have a drink and chat."

Morgan wanted to tell Sydney to skip the visit and keep walking to avoid stressing the dog out further, but it was clear that she had an ulterior motive that went beyond just a casual drop-in.

Can't hurt to assess him really quickly.

Everyone started moving toward the backyard and Hudson let out a few loud barks.

"Hold on," Morgan said, shifting into her work persona. Straighter posture, direct phrasing, and a slightly bossier tone. "The three of us will go in first and sit down, then you can come in after us. I'll put a chair a few feet away for you. Did you bring treats?"

Sydney shook her head sheepishly.

Oof. Rookie mistake.

"Do you mind if I steal some of your fancy cheese to use?" Morgan asked Karl.

"Please, whatever it takes. I'll even break out the Stilton Gold if it helps."

Morgan speed-walked to the back of the house and set up three of the heavy chairs across the yard, then placed one a few feet in from the fence door. She dragged a side table next to it and placed a napkin filled with cheese on top of it.

"You two can sit down over there," she said to Eugene and Karl, pointing at the far chairs. "Is Bernadette inside?"

"She is, sound asleep," Karl said.

Morgan answered with a terse nod, half-grumpy about the subterfuge and half-excited to try to help the nervous dog.

"Okay, Sydney, you can come in," she yelled. Morgan turned to Eugene and Karl. "I know it's hard, but don't stare at him, okay?"

"We trust you," Karl answered. "Whatever you say."

Sydney came in through the gate, and Hudson looked like a different dog, wagging his tail and sniffing the grass happily.

Sniffing is a good sign. Means he's not completely shut down.

He swung his head to take in the rest of his surroundings, then froze when he spotted the three of them seated on the opposite side of the yard.

"He's a little nervous now. Sydney, can you sit down over there and give him a piece of cheese?"

She nodded and did as she was told. Morgan watched Hudson creep along beside her, shooting nervous glances at them. Sydney gave the dog a small slice of the Gruyère.

"He ate it?" Morgan asked.

"Oh yes. He's looking for more!" Sydney laughed as Hudson nosed along the edge of the table.

Another good sign. He's comfortable enough to eat with us nearby.

Treat-motivated dogs were her favorites. The ones who lapped up spoonfuls of baby food in the exam room made the blood draws and palpations that much easier.

"Does he have a bite history?"

"No." Sydney shook her head vigorously. She frowned. "Well, the truth is he can get mouthy when he plays, but he probably never learned not to nip. It's not painful, he just lets his mouth drift off the toy. His other foster's been working on that with him."

Excellent. He knows enough not to chomp down on skin.

Hudson sat next to Sydney, glancing at her face, then at the cheese table, over and over. He was tall enough to dust his nose across it and grab a slice, but he opted to wait politely.

Manners. That scared boy is minding his manners.

"You have to admit, he's a gorgeous dog," Karl said, adding to the list Morgan was trying not to compile in her head. The last thing she needed while trying to work though her own mess was a project.

"Isn't he?" Sydney said proudly. "And that's part of the issue. Everyone thinks he's this big sweetheart, but sometimes when people try to walk up to him he goes crazy and sounds ferocious. He needs someone to help show him the way."

Everyone went silent and turned to stare at her.

"This is an intervention, isn't it?" Morgan asked. "You're all ganging up on me."

"No, it's not like that," Sydney said quickly. "We would never force you into anything. But Eugene and Karl said you were so gifted with dogs . . ."

Morgan shot Eugene a look and he pursed his lips and shook his head gently to convey that her secret was still safe.

"But what about Bernie?" she asked, grasping at the last acceptable objection to fostering him. "We don't know if they'll get along."

"We'd confirm everything first," Sydney replied. "And we always suggest a separation as foster dogs settle in. They'd have plenty of time to get to know each other slowly and safely."

The distant sounds of kids playing filled the silence as everyone tried not to stare at the beautiful, nervous dog.

Admit it. If there ever was a time to take this on, it's now.

"I can't make miracles happen in just a few weeks," Morgan finally said. "That's a lot of pressure. Behavioral changes don't happen overnight."

"We don't expect a miracle, I promise you," Sydney said gently. "*Anything* you can do to help would be amazing."

Morgan watched the dog watching her from across the yard. His tail thumped the ground once and he shot a hopeful glance up at the cheese table.

George was worse. He'd still be barking and snarling at everyone. Hudson might be tough, but there's hope.

Morgan looked at her hosts. "And you guys would be okay with a foster dog?"

"We talked about it and we would," Eugene nodded. "We think it's a great setup for him here. You staying in the pool house is perfect. If he's not comfortable having us around when we're home, you can keep him totally separate."

She stared at Hudson, who'd lowered himself into a sphinx-down and was glancing between them. The dog was stunning, which would no doubt work against him given his issues. She'd seen it happen at the clinic too often: an adorable dog gets adopted, then starts showing decidedly un-adorable behaviors and gets returned, over and over.

Do you really want a project dog?

Hudson sighed loudly enough that she could hear it from across the yard, then put his head down on top of his paws and looked up at her.

Damn it.

I do.

"I guess at this point it's not up to me. Bernadette makes the call."

chapter ten

"Awesome sniffing, Hud," Morgan said softly as her first-ever foster nosed his way through the morning fog along what had to be the only patch of weeds on the island. Karl had told her that Nantucket was a place where millionaires mowed the lawns of billionaires, and based on the perfect landscaping and home prices, it sounded about right. "Good boy."

They'd spent their first few days together getting to know one another, slowly feeling each other out until they had a shaky foundation of trust. Hudson had moved into the Pak-Reynoldses' pool house the day after a bumpy but ultimately successful introduction to Bernadette, right as Eugene and Karl set out for the first leg of their Target tour. Morgan could tell that the two dogs would eventually be fine together, but she wanted to keep them apart until she felt one hundred percent comfortable with Hudson. That meant double everything: mealtimes, walks, play times, and snuggles.

The day before Hudson was due to arrive, Morgan had biked into town with Bernadette to pick up something she didn't realize how much she'd missed: a pretty, blank journal. She'd spent way more time than necessary scouting out the perfect one, taking Bernadette in both of the bookshops and every souvenir shop she could find. She settled on a spiral-bound lined book with a navy toile print that featured Nantucket landmarks, the white sign with NANTUCKET written in black lettering, a whale, a sprig of hydrangea, and the perfect squat lighthouse that had greeted her as the ferry pulled in. Even though it was easier to take notes on her phone, something pulled her to journal about Hudson on paper, just like she used to with George when she'd first gotten him.

Her old George notebook had slowly transitioned from keeping track of his training progress to incorporating details about what was going on in her life as well. She'd mention the weather, how her little garden was doing in the summer, and what types of birds were at her feeders in the winter. Sometimes she'd tell the stories of patients that had broken her heart, and the ones that had mended it. She wrote about what she and Sam were up to. Her nights out with friends. The silly things her mom said to her. By the time she hit the last page, the book was less about George and more about her own life, with insights so personal that she hid the thing in between her mattress and box spring. There were still moments when her fingers itched to vent her feelings on the page, but she was afraid of what might happen if she allowed the floodgates to open. It was easier to box up the emotions and move on.

Morgan studied Hudson as they strolled down the narrow street that was crowded with gawk-worthy yards and homes. Despite how tightly wound Hudson had been the first time they met, he was a pretty chill dog. She'd started a list in her journal of all of his positive qualities that at first had been limited to his good looks ... the golden fur, the subtle black shading along his muzzle, the big ears that telegraphed more information about his emotional state than his tail. But each day together brought new insights about the mystery at the end of the leash, like the fact that he didn't pull during walks. He never jumped up on her no matter how excited he got. He always dropped fetched balls at her feet. He didn't guard his food bowl, toys, or his bed. And best of all, he was always DTT.

Down to train.

Hudson *loved* training. It was like he'd been thirsty to prove to someone how clever he was, so no matter what she attempted with him, he happily played along.

A bike bell sounded off behind her and her eyes immediately went to Hudson. The second thing she'd written in her new journal was a list of all of his "triggers"—the things they encountered during walks that tipped him from stable to scary. It included people in all forms, from casual strollers to runners, other dogs on leash or behind fences, and garbage cans. Now she was about to see if she needed to add bikes to the list as well.

"Morgan Pearce! Are you stalking me?"

Her pulse surged. The voice was already familiar.

It's him.

As much as she wanted to turn around to greet Nathan, her first priority was making sure Hudson was okay. The dog's head whipped around the second he heard Nathan's voice and Hudson froze when he saw the bike approaching, a low growl rumbling from deep in his chest. Morgan scanned her surroundings and realized that her best bet was to duck behind a black Range Rover parked half on the street and half on the crooked sidewalk. Working with Hudson behind a barrier would keep the dog calmer than trying to do it just a few feet away from a trigger, like a ridiculously good-looking man on two wheels.

And Hudson isn't the only one triggered by him.

She waved at him over her shoulder and jogged the few steps to the car so that Hudson couldn't see Nathan.

"Hi, sorry. He gets weird around people. He's in training."

Morgan flicked her eyes to the dog and was happy to see him focused on a black pole with a horse head on top of it that was likely covered in pee along the bottom. She tossed him a treat.

Nathan had stopped in the middle of the cobblestone street on his cart-mobile, one foot on the ground and the other on the pedal.

"You've got quite the dog-walking business. But I thought you said Bernadette was your only client?"

He remembered.

Morgan grinned at him while she tried to remind herself that he was just a gifted salesman and nothing more. "Yup, Bernadette is my client, and Hudson here is my new foster dog for the summer. Wanna adopt him?"

The dog alerted at the sound of his name and Morgan tossed another chunk of freeze-dried liver so that he had to chase it down the sidewalk. She hoped she'd filled her pocket with enough treats so that she could chat with Nathan while keeping Hudson happy.

"Maybe I'd adopt him if I could see him," Nathan answered, pretending to peek over the Range Rover. "What's wrong with him? Why are you hiding him?"

She bristled at his insinuation. "Nothing's wrong. He's a great dog, he just needs to learn some people skills."

Foster mom protective instinct initiated? Check.

"Gotcha. Good on you for working with him."

The phrase stopped her. "I've never heard anyone say 'good on you' apart from my Australian friend from college."

"Nice catch." His smile widened. "I've spent a lot of time surfing in Australia. And New Zealand. Kia ora."

What kind of life does he lead?

Her eyebrows shot up. "World traveler. Good for you."

Morgan made a mental note to do some online stalking.

"Not for a long time now, thanks to this." He pointed at the cart. "Hey, why didn't you come to Cisco the other night? I was looking for you the whole time."

Okay, I was wrong. The invitation was real.

"Oh, uh, that was the night I met this guy," she replied, pointing at Hudson.

"Competition," he said, squinting toward where Hudson was sniffing around on the other side of the car. "I don't stand a chance against that dude."

Hold on, what's happening? Why is this perfect creature openly flirting with me?

It wasn't like the guys she'd dated in the past were basic. Sam had been scouted to do catalog modeling at college, and the rest skewed "cutest guy in the bar." But Nathan was on another level.

Morgan felt her face go hot. "So, what did I miss at Cisco?"

"Just a good hang with good people. Hopefully we'll get another chance. Hey, you wanna grab lunch with me today? That is, if you can tear yourself away from that *other* guy."

A Volvo turned the corner and headed down the narrow street way too fast.

"Don't get smushed," Morgan cautioned, pointing at it since Nathan seemed incapable of looking anywhere but at her.

"They can wait two seconds," he replied, standing up on the pedals to get ready to move. "So, lunch? I can lock this bad boy up and we can grab sandwiches at Provisions and sit on the dock. The weather's going to be perfect today."

It was hard to believe, given the veil of morning fog still ghosting through the yards around them.

Tess said he's a player.

But playing can be fun if you know the rules going in. I'm here to relax. Do it.

"Sure. What time?"

The Volvo idled a few feet behind Nathan. Morgan was shocked that the person hadn't beeped yet.

"I'm usually slower from eleven to eleven thirty and any time after one," he answered, glancing over his shoulder at the car. "Why don't you text me when you head down. Let me give you my number."

She nodded, pulled out her phone, and entered it with a shaky hand while gripping Hudson's leash with the other.

"Cool," he said as he leaned back to gather the strength to pedal on the uneven road. "Hey, Hudson, hope we get to meet some day, my dude."

Morgan gave an apologetic wave to the car's driver as it passed by and wondered if the flirting that had just gone down in the middle of India Street was obvious to them too.

"It's nothing, Hud," she said to the dog, who looked up at her expectantly. "He's just being nice."

But I can use a little more nice in my life.

· · ·

A sweat broke out on her forehead as she pedaled in the midday sun to meet Nathan.

She'd kept herself busy up until lunchtime with Hudson's training and notes and Bernadette's walk and play session. As efficient as it would be to bring the dogs together, she knew it was smarter to take her time. It helped that Hudson seemed to appreciate the quiet of the pool house after his brain-teasing training sessions. His former foster family had two kids, a dog, and a cat, and Morgan got the feeling that it had been a little overwhelming for him. It was as if they *both* needed time to decompress.

The swingy black skirt she'd impulsively decided to wear kept flipping up every time the wind blew, so she had to alternate between holding on to the handlebars with one desperate hand and trying not to flash everyone as she navigated the narrow streets. When she finally made it down to Nathan's usual spot near the docks, she was full-on sweating. She walked the bike past the usual crowd of people near the outdoor gazebo bar and the line for the ferry.

"Hey, there you are," Nathan said when he spotted her walking toward him, giving her a newscaster's smile. "Right on time."

Right on time for me is ten minutes early, so, no, I'm not.

Morgan gave him a little wave. "Hi, I'm sweating."

She winced the second the words were out of her mouth.

"Same, it's warm today," he answered as if it was a perfectly normal thing to say. "I'm also starving. What can I get you to drink?" He placed his hand on top of the cart and gave her an expectant look.

"Whatever I haven't tried yet."

Nathan handed her two bright pink-and-green bottles, then moved the cart to an open space near where the charter fishing boats were docked. He locked the cooler and the front wheel, then clapped his hands. "Okay, let's eat."

Morgan fell in step beside him and felt like every woman around them was sizing her up as they passed. She tried to imagine how they looked walking beside each other. Did they make a good pair?

"Provisions. It's right over there," he said, pointing to a small restaurant set back from the outdoor bar. "They've got an unbeatable caprese sandwich."

Ten minutes later they were set up on the same bench she'd sat on the day she arrived, staring out at the water and the puffy clouds dotting the horizon.

"Holy crap, that's a huge yacht," Morgan said, using her sandwich to point down the dock. She squinted. "What's the name of it?"

He gazed at the end of the dock. "The *Her Madgesty*, spelled like the woman's name. I've been on it, actually. It's wild."

"Really?" Her eyes bugged. "How?"

"I've got a very social job," Nathan answered, raising his bottle to her as explanation. "It's easy to get to know people, especially the ones who pass by my cart every day. All the yacht folks and their staff walk by constantly, so I've gotten to know most of the regulars already. The owner, Brooks, likes my stuff." He shrugged sheepishly. "What can I say? Quality bevs open doors."

And it has absolutely nothing to do with the way you look.

She expected to feel too nervous to eat while sitting next to him, his tan thigh just a few inches from her pale one, but there was a force field of calm around Nathan that put her at ease.

Plus, she was starving. The Nantucket air had kick-started her appetite and all she wanted to do was eat anything she could get her hands on.

Morgan's phone buzzed and she automatically grabbed it like there was an emergency bloat surgery on the other end. It would take a while for her reflexes to calm down. "Sorry, bad habit."

"No, feel free. I'm addicted to mine too."

She peeked at it and saw it was a text from Mack, asking if she'd found any inns for him.

"My brother," she said, tucking her phone under her thigh.

She felt a glimmer of hope about what was going on with Mack. Maybe things could go back to a version of the way they used to be, even though they were both different people now.

"Nice," Nathan answered with his mouth full. "Any other siblings?"

"Nope, just us. Mackenzie and Morgan. M&M."

"I'm guessing you're the older sibling?"

She smiled at him. "How can you tell?"

Nathan paused to take her in, his gaze traveling around her face and pausing on her lips for a second longer than necessary, making her wonder if she had pesto on the corner of her mouth. "You just seem . . . I don't know. Organized? Like you've got a to-do list that you actually check off."

Morgan was shocked that he'd picked up on that. "Yeah, I like my lists."

If you only knew how far from together my shit was these days.

"You two close?" He gnawed off another hunk of sandwich in an unaffected way, still studying her.

Even though it had been years, the question still smarted. She took a gulp of her Cuker-melon to buy a few seconds.

"Not anymore. We used to be. He was my best friend for a while." Morgan shrugged and stared out at the calm water. "But stuff happens. We grew apart."

"That sucks," he answered, a frown darkening his sunny face. "Do you miss him?"

Nathan asked it casually, like he had no idea that he was potentially stepping into familial quicksand. She'd expected their lunch to be awkward and peppered with talk of surfing and soft drinks, but Nathan seemed ready to go deep with her.

This feels like therapy. And I sort of like it.

"It's weird," Morgan mused, strangely comfortable having the conversation with him. "If you'd asked me that six months ago, I would've said I don't miss him, but he just got engaged and, I don't know, I feel like it changes stuff."

"Why is that? Do you like his girlfriend? Or, I guess she's his fiancée now."

She shrugged. "I've only met her once, but I did like her. She was . . . unexpected. She kept him in line."

Nathan threw his head back and laughed. The sound made her smile. "Spoken like a true older sister."

"What about you?" Morgan asked. "Any siblings?"

He studied his sandwich and pushed a glob of mozzarella back into the bread, then licked his finger in a slow, lazy way that made Morgan wish she was a dairy product too.

"Nope, just me. I used to pray for a brother when I was a kid."

His expression looked so wistful that she felt a pang of sympathy.

"Well, Mack is probably coming to visit me. I'll let you borrow him."

"Only if he's as cool as you."

Morgan laughed. "Oh, trust me, there's no one cooler than Mackenzie Pearce. Just ask him."

She could see him grinning as he took a long swig. His leg drifted against hers as he tipped his head back, and the heat of his thigh against hers sent a pulse through her body. They ate the last few bites of their sandwiches in silence, watching the boats coming in.

"Well, I should probably get back to my baby," Nathan said, polishing off his drink.

"Hold on, I didn't get a chance to grill you about your life. No fair."

He stood up and gathered his garbage, then used the edge of a napkin to wipe where a tomato had fallen on the bench so no one would sit in it.

"Trust me, this isn't the last you've seen of me. There's plenty of time for grilling," he said as he crumpled his trash into a compact ball.

Her heart did a stuttery two-step as he grinned at her.

Is this really happening?

"I mean, you promised me a brother, so . . ." He cocked his head in a way that made Morgan a little dizzy, like she was on a boat and didn't have her sea legs yet. "We've got more hangouts to come. At least I hope we do."

Morgan felt her face go hot.

What is even happening right now?

"Sure," Morgan said, sounding way more casual than she felt. "That would be fun."

And that's what this summer is all about. Fun. As much as I can get, in as many ways as possible.

chapter eleven

Half an hour. That's it. Forty-five minutes max.

Morgan walked her bike up the driveway crowded with luxury minivans and SUVs and leaned it against the gray-shingled garage.

The night Sydney brought Hudson over she'd mentioned in passing that she was worried about some potential dog safety issues during the fund-raiser. She'd invited Morgan to show up to the next planning meeting, saying that she could use a knowledgeable ally looking out for the dogs. There was no way Morgan could say no.

But I'm here for the dogs, not the drama.

Violet the Frenchie greeted her with a bark through the screen door, and a tall woman with a shiny black bob beckoned Morgan in.

"Hi, welcome. We're just getting started," she said with a friendly smile. "I don't think we've met. And you are?"

"Morgan Pearce, but you might also know me as Hudson's new foster mom." She thrust out her hand.

"Oh, you came!" the woman exclaimed delightedly as she took Morgan's hand. "I was Hud's first foster! I'm Laura Nelson, I'm so happy to meet you. How's he doing?"

Morgan beamed back at her. "Really great! He's a wonderful guy."

"We absolutely loved him, but I had such a hard time walking him. Is it going better for you? Sydney said you're quite the dog expert."

Morgan felt twitchy about her charade, but she was in too deep to quit now. "I give Hudson all the credit. He's an excellent student."

Laura guided Morgan into the airy kitchen where groups of well-dressed women stood chatting and drinking. "Hey, everyone? This is Morgan and she's a dog pro. She's going to fix Hudson!"

Morgan shrank back. She was all too familiar with what happened when a room full of animal lovers found out what she did for a living, and "dog pro" was dangerously close to a reveal. She felt her heartbeat speed up and faked a smile as everyone's eyes swung toward her.

"Hi," she said with an awkward wave. She hadn't expected to be the center of attention and was happy she'd put some effort into her hair instead of piling it on her head.

A few people clapped, and Sydney waved back at her with both hands.

"Perfect timing," a gorgeous blonde with long smooth hair said as she placed her empty champagne glass on the table in front of her. "Why don't we get started? As you all know, I'm Abby Cogdon, gala committee president. I want to kick off tonight's meeting with reports from each of the team leads on where we stand before we get into our to-do list. Piper? Can you go first? I know our human models have been selected, but do we have confirmation on the dogs yet?"

"Working on it," a voice in the back of the room offered. "We've almost got everyone cast."

"Wonderful, that means we'll have a full house in the barking lot before and after the show," Abby said. "It's going to be so adorable!"

Everyone in the room murmured in agreement.

"We just need to make sure the play area is big enough for all the guests' dogs as well," Abby continued.

Wait, what?

"Let's move on to invitations," Abby said as she glanced down at her clipboard. "We're late as it is, thank God for the save-the-date email. Are we finally ready to mail?"

Morgan cleared her throat and took a step into the room. There was no way she was going to let the moment pass without addressing what she saw as a glaring and possibly dangerous mistake, undercover or not. "I'm sorry, but I have a quick question. Are you saying guests can bring their dogs to the event?"

"Yes," Abby answered, the shock at being questioned by the newbie registering on her face.

"And you have a play area for all the dogs?"

"Yes, of course."

"I'm not sure that's a good idea," Morgan said, shifting into her professional voice. She looked around the room to see how everyone else was reacting to her interruption, and Sydney gave her an encouraging nod. "Mixing a group of unfamiliar dogs is tough enough at a real dog park, let alone during a party when people are going to be drinking and distracted."

"Is that so?" Abby said slowly, her face shifting from displeasure at the interruption to downright anger.

"It is," Morgan answered back in a confident voice. "And people might have to leave early if their dog is having a bad time, which means you could see donor dollars walking out the door because their dog was freaking out."

"Well, that's an *interesting* viewpoint." Abby's laser eyes were at odds with the smile on her face. "I forgot to ask how you know so much about dogs. What's your background again?"

As tempting as it was to throw out the three little letters that usually made people snap to attention, she bit her tongue and met Abby's gaze. "I've worked with dogs for a long time. I'm here as Eugene Pak and Karl Reynolds's dog sitter."

One hundred percent not a lie.

Abby nodded as the corner of her mouth kicked up. "Ah, okay. You babysit dogs, got it. Thanks for your valuable insight, I'll keep it in mind."

Morgan swore Abby rolled her eyes as she looked down at her notepad. Sydney shot her an apologetic grin.

"Okay, we still have a few volunteer spots to fill," Abby continued. "Rachel needs help with print assets, Bev wants an assistant VIP handler for our high-dollar donors during the event, and we can use another dog wrangler to help out during the fashion show."

Every eye in the room turned to Morgan.

Say no. You don't need this drama in your life right now.

"Me?" she gulped. "Oh, I, uh, I'm not sure I can give it the attention it deserves. I'm so sorry."

"It's *one* night," Sydney offered in a hopeful voice. "Just a few hours on the twenty-ninth. We could really use someone like you, to keep the pups safe and happy."

It was a deadly one-two punch. Asking for a single-night commitment and mentioning dog safety. It was impossible to say no without looking like a complete asshole.

The room went uncomfortably still as everyone's gaze jumped between Sydney, Morgan, and Abby.

Trapped. There's no way out.

"Of course," Morgan finally answered, mustering up some fake enthusiasm. "I'd love to help."

The room murmured their approval and Sydney mouthed *thank you* at Morgan. She shot a glance at Abby, who looked like she was carving Morgan's name on the volunteer list with a dagger.

"I've never seen her like this," Morgan said, her eyes wide as she watched Bernadette run rings around Palmer in the backyard.

Morgan had invited Tess and Palmer over for a test playdate, and the four of them were set up near the rose-covered pergola by the pool. Hudson was blissfully unaware of the trespassers, taking his afternoon siesta in Morgan's quiet bedroom after a long training session. She'd left the stereo system tuned to white noise to keep him from hearing Bernadette's happy yips.

She smiled at the relaxing scene in front of her: the dogs frolicking in the sunshine and Tess, in her dirt-smudged "Hortensia" T-shirt and shorts, standing on the first step in the pool. The temperature was a blissful eighty degrees, the birds were chattering above them, and every so often the breeze blew something heavy and sweet her way.

Paradise.

Morgan waited for the twinge of guilt over her good fortune and felt . . . nothing. It was like the stress tentacles had packed their bags for time off too. She had no doubt they'd be back, but she relished the chance to live her life without them for a little while.

Palmer stood still with his mouth in a wide pant and watched Bernadette dash by him, clearly delighted by the senior citizen acting like a puppy. He dropped into a play bow every so often, bum up and elbows on the ground. After a few bows without any follow-through, Bernie seemed to realize that he wasn't going to use his size against her, so she kicked up the silly.

"Palmer brings out the best in other dogs," Tess said, stepping out of the pool and walking over to Morgan. "It's one of my favorite things about him. He's everyone's buddy."

"He's amazing," Morgan agreed. "How old is he again?"

"Two. But he's got the soul of an old man."

Morgan narrowed her eyes and studied Palmer.

More like the body of an old man.

She'd noticed that the few times Palmer had halfheartedly chased after Bernadette, he'd bunny-hopped instead of using his rear legs independently. And when he stood up, he kept his back legs close together in a narrow stance, which looked odd considering how big he was.

Shit. I can't not say something. Tell her.

"Does he have a hard time getting up?" Morgan asked.

Tess smiled as she watched Bernadette slide-roll to where Palmer had settled then flop around in front of him like a fish on dry land. He nosed at her belly playfully. "Yeah. Sometimes it seems like he can't get traction."

"Um-hm. And does he ever crap out during walks? Like, just lie down and refuse to keep walking?"

"Have you been spying on us?" Tess laughed. "He likes to take breaks. He'll plop down wherever, sometimes in the middle of the street. Everyone thinks it's hysterical but me. It's not like I can move him."

Morgan continued studying Palmer. "Does he ever favor his back legs?"

"He limps sometimes, but I just assumed it's when he's played or walked too much." Tess turned to Morgan, a look of realization spreading across her face. "Wait a sec. Do you think something's wrong with him?"

She quickly debated telling Tess why she was practically positive about Palmer's diagnosis, but she pulled back at the last minute. "I've had experience with hip dysplasia and he's presenting with—I mean, everything you mentioned are signs of it. X-rays are the best way to confirm it, though."

"Oh my God, really? What is that, exactly?" Her eyes went wide. "Is it bad?"

"It's an abnormal formation of the hip socket, and it can be painful if left untreated," Morgan answered gently. "Palmer's learned to compensate, and he's young so it's probably not that bad yet. But it might be why he's not as active as you would think at this age. And if it's not treated it'll get worse as he gets older."

"What's the treatment? What do I have to do?" Tess started pacing in circles. "Because I'll do anything. He's worth it."

"It depends on the severity." Morgan realized that the more

detailed her diagnosis and recommendations became, the closer she got to outing herself. "He might just need medication, or he could need something more, like surgery."

"Oh no!" Tess jogged over to Palmer and dropped to her knees beside him. "I can't believe I didn't pick up on it. I just thought he was lazy!" She wrapped her arms around his shoulders and buried her face in his fur.

Bernadette sat up and shot Morgan a concerned look.

"Just take him to your vet, get it checked out."

But I know I'm right.

"Should we leave? Is it bad for him to be doing this?" Tess sat down on the grass next to Palmer.

Morgan walked over and sat alongside them. "I think Bernie and Palmer would both be upset if you left now. He's still having fun watching her. And she seems to be enjoying showing off."

Palmer rolled onto his side and swatted the grass next to Bernadette playfully. She yipped at him and ran in a wide circle around them.

"How do you know so much about hip dysplasia?" Tess asked, leaning back on her elbows next to her dog.

Morgan's stomach twisted. The lying was still gnawing at her insides, but she also didn't know Tess well enough to tell her the truth, especially now that her dog was about to have medical needs. Once Morgan got home, she'd be ready to be the animal know-it-all again, but for now she was enjoying being just another dog enthusiast.

Who happens to know a shit-ton.

"My family dog had it. A Boston terrier, Betty. She was diagnosed really young. She had it in both hips, so she had to have a double femoral head ost—uh, an operation on both of them."

Tess's eyes bugged out again, and she reached for Palmer. "This is bad."

"I think you're both going to be fine," Morgan replied in her most comforting yet definitive voice.

"Let's talk about something else," Tess said, reaching for her glass of sparkling water on the low side table next to them. "What do you think of Nantucket so far?"

"Love it. It's beautiful, and tranquil, and everyone seems pretty cool. I expected snob city, but I haven't gotten any attitude yet."

Except Abby.

"How long have you been here?" Morgan asked.

"Ten years," Tess said, running her hand along the cropped grass as if grading the groundskeeper's skills. She'd already declared the liriope edging along the slate walkway "basic-ass," which would horrify Eugene and Karl. "I came here with a bunch of friends for a long weekend, fell in love with the island *and* a local boy, and never left."

Morgan beat back a little twinge of envy.

"That's pretty romantic."

"It was. Now it's just life," she smiled and gave Palmer's head a pat. "Cyrus works at Bartlett's Farm, I bust my ass with my business, and Palmer keeps us both sane. We live in a shack we can barely afford, but I wouldn't change a thing."

The twinge intensified.

"What about you?" Tess asked, rolling onto her side. "Job, relationship status, pets? Tell me everything."

Morgan reverted to her sin of omission. "Right now, I'm just focused on taking care of Bernie. I'm trying to be in the moment, you know? Enjoy everything Nantucket has to offer."

Totally not a lie.

Tess nodded. "Preach."

"And I'm between dogs. I, uh, lost my dog George six months ago."

For the first time, six months sounded like an awfully long span to go without one.

"But I'm getting closer," she continued. "I'm not ready yet, but I can at least envision the possibility of a new dog."

"Are you single?" Tess asked.

"I am," Morgan sighed, looking down at her bare feet. "It's for the best right now. I can't take on the drama of a relationship. Same scenario as the dog stuff. Not ready yet, but maybe someday soon."

The texts she'd exchanged with Nathan a few hours prior flitted through her mind.

"Can I ask you a gossipy question?" Morgan ventured.

It was still the friendship-courtship phase of getting to know each other, but Tess's easygoing attitude made Morgan feel like she already knew her.

"Of course. Bring it on."

"It's about Nathan Keating," Morgan offered. She felt like a middle schooler gossiping about her crush.

"Okay," Tess frowned. "What about him?"

Something in her expression made Morgan pump the brakes.

"You said he's a player. Should I watch out for him? Because he actually seems . . . nice."

Tess kept her eyes on the dogs as they flirted. "I've only run into him in passing since he's been here, so I'm not sure how he is now. People change. All I know is he was *really* douchey in high school."

It didn't make sense. Nathan *looked* like a frat boy, but he acted like everybody's best friend.

"He might be different now, who knows?" Tess said as if reading Morgan's thoughts.

I hope so because he's taking me out tonight.

chapter twelve

W ow."

The word ricocheted out of Nathan as he gave Morgan a quick once-over.

"Hi," Morgan answered, doing her best to play off the compliment even though it made her giddy. She was glad she'd put some effort into getting ready, straightening her hair and putting on makeup. It had been too long since she cared about feeling pretty.

She met Nathan on the front porch of the Pak-Reynoldses' house like they were courting in an old-timey movie, even though they were just going for a casual hang at Cisco Brewery. Nathan looked like he'd put in some effort for their night out as well, with his shaggy hair still damp from a shower and a hint of something brisk and spicy around him. His relaxed pink golf shirt looked strategically worn out, with a slightly frayed collar and a few small holes dotting the shoulder.

But he doesn't even have to try. The man could show up in jorts and a mesh tank top and still make it work.

"You sure you don't want to bring Bernadette?" he asked. "I

know Hudson is still too new to hang, but maybe she wants to come with us and Archer? He loves every dog he's ever met."

Nathan pointed over his shoulder to the bright blue vintage Chevy parked in the driveway, where a tan pit bull was hanging out the window grinning at them.

"Maybe someday. I want to check out the place before I bring her."

"Fair enough," he said with a smile. "Let's hit it, if we get there too late we won't get a table."

Archer *woo*-ed excitedly at them as they got closer to the truck, his paws dancing on the edge of the open window and his tail helicoptering.

"He likes you already." Nathan let out one of his contagious laughs. "I'm surprised he hasn't jumped out the window to meet you."

"I'm guessing he likes everyone?"

"Pretty much," he answered as he put his hand on the truck door handle. Archer started spinning in place on the seat. "You don't have any issue with pitties, do you? Because he can be a little . . . overwhelming."

"Not at all. Bring it on."

Morgan braced herself as Nathan opened the door and Archer shot out in a graceful arc. The dog didn't even look at him and instead ran wide, happy laps around Morgan, so fast that his shoulder almost touched the ground each time he circled.

"He's definitely young," she laughed as he began his up-close investigation of her feet and legs. "You're so fast, Archer!"

Morgan knelt when the dog finally came to a complete stop and looked at her with his tongue hanging out of his catfish mouth, grinning and wiggling. He danced his way closer and bumped against her leg, so she took it as an invitation and finally reached out to pet him.

"He's so soft," Morgan exclaimed as she ran her hand down the dog's khaki fur.

"Yup, my velvet hippo," Nathan said, leaning against the truck and watching them with a bemused expression.

Archer was lean and muscular, with an athlete's body and a comedian's face. The black mask around his muzzle highlighted the fact that he looked like a reverse vampire with his two lower canines jutting out in a pronounced underbite. He slid his body to the ground with a plop, then rolled onto his back and swatted at Morgan to pet his belly.

"Okay, bossy," Morgan said, reaching out to rub as instructed.

"Bro, let's *go*." Nathan laughed at his dog thrashing around in front of Morgan. "He's never going to let you stop now. Arch, c'mon."

His laughter wrapped around her like a hug. It started off as a rumble and turned into something sweeter, almost a giggle. Nathan seemed to exist in a space of ease and happiness, where delight was everywhere around him just waiting to be discovered. Morgan wanted to set up camp in his world.

Archer finally hopped up and looked at Nathan, who pointed at the truck. The dog jumped in and paced on the bench seat, quivering with excitement as they joined him. He was the perfect chaperone for their first official night out, a speed bump in between them to keep everything casual. But Nathan had asked her out on a *date* date, point-blank. There was no mention of meeting other people there, just a simple, unambiguous invitation to go to the brewery with him. She tried not to stare at his perfect profile as he chattered about the scenery during the drive.

Ten minutes later they arrived at a spot that looked like nothing more than open fields with a few cars parked along the road.

"Good, not too crowded yet," Nathan said with an approving nod as he eased his truck off the road and onto the shoulder. He snapped a thin black leather leash onto Archer and turned to Morgan. "Okay, let's drink!" He paused for a beat. "Responsibly, of course."

Cisco Brewers felt like a beer garden oasis in the middle of nowhere. A few open-front barns flanked a wide courtyard of uneven pavers dotted with adults, kids, and dogs. The pups seemed to have free rein of the place, running around untethered, but Nathan asked Morgan to hold Archer's leash while he went in to get beers for them. The vibe of the space felt like a neighborhood block party, where everyone was just a beer or two away from being best friends.

Morgan watched Archer scan the crowd, his tail wagging any time a being on two legs, or four even, glanced his way. The dog clearly had his person's happy, easygoing energy and it made her think of tightly wound Hudson and feel bad for him.

Nathan came out of a barn holding two overfilled plastic cups and scanned the crowd for her. His grin when he spotted her sent a ripple of warmth through her.

Take this for what it is. A fling and nothing more.

"Isn't it a cool spot?" he asked as he led her toward a picnic table near a guitarist playing an Amos Lee cover. "It's definitely changed since it opened, though. I came a few years back when it used to be more of an undercover local joint with just one bar, and now it's more touristy. The food trucks are newish too. Speaking of, you want grub?"

"Sure, I never say no to gourmet tater tots."

"Cool, we'll start with that, then maybe move on to a few lobster rolls." He jumped up before she had a chance to stop him. "Watch Arch for me, I'll be right back!"

The dog trotted a few steps after Nathan, then got diverted by a little dark-haired boy passing by. Archer lowered his head and wagged his entire hind end to telegraph that he wanted some attention. The boy smiled and started to reach for him, but his mother glanced down and gasped.

"Ryder, *no*! That kind of dog doesn't like kids." She jerked him away. "Don't touch it!"

Morgan glared at the woman as Archer walked back to her, dejected. He planted his blocky head in her lap.

"Don't pay attention to them. What do they know?" She ran her hand along his forehead and noticed that he shifted his head whenever she got close to his ears. "What's going on in there, mister?"

Morgan slowly massaged her way up to his floppy ear, flipped it back, and spotted the telltale dots of black deep inside.

Great. Now to find a casual, definitely-not-a-diagnosis way to mention Archer's ear infection.

She was pondering the best way to broach the topic with Nathan when a fluffy brown tornado crashed into Archer and knocked him back a few steps.

"Palmer!" Morgan exclaimed when she recognized who it was. "What are you doing here?"

Archer jumped back, startled at the abrupt introduction, but then started wagging his tail when he seemed to realize that it was a friendly accident. Palmer barely acknowledged him and seemed to only have eyes for Morgan.

A handsome guy with a tan, buzz cut, and intense brown-black eyes came running over and picked up the leash Palmer was dragging behind him.

"Sorry about that, he tugged away while we weren't paying attention. The cornhole competition is getting intense." He pointed over his shoulder with an apologetic grin.

"I know Palmer!" Morgan replied as she tried to juggle her attention between the two dogs. "I'm Morgan. Tess brought him over for a playdate with me this afternoon."

"Right, okay!" He smiled in recognition. "She mentioned how much fun you guys had. I'm Cyrus."

"Is Tess here too?" Morgan asked as she peered at the other filled picnic tables.

"Yup, we're in the back. We have friends in town, so of course we had to bring them. I'll tell Tess you're here, she'll be happy to see you."

Cyrus led a reluctant Palmer away right as Nathan came back with two heaping servings of tots.

"Okay, I got an order of parmesan chive and one with smoked queso sauce. Which sounds better?"

"Both?" she laughed as he placed them in front of her.

"Well, dig in."

Morgan took time to study Nathan as he popped tots in his mouth, one after the other. He had an ease about him, like he existed in the peaceful haze after a yoga class, mixed with the confidence of someone who knew that everyone stared at him when he passed but didn't give a shit about it. He was unlike anyone she'd ever met before, probably because most of the people she associated with were as stressed out as she was.

Nathan bobbed his head in time to the music and grinned when he caught her eye. She felt heat spread on her face that he'd caught her staring.

"So good, right?" he asked her when the set ended. "The music, the food, the vibe."

"The company," Morgan added, bolstered by liquid courage. She smiled at him.

"To the company," he said, slapping the table with one hand and raising his nearly empty cup in the air with the other.

"Canine and human," she said, knocking her cup against his. "Speaking of, where's Archer?"

Nathan pointed to a nearby picnic table, where the dog was rolling around on his back with a black Lab. "The mayor of Nantucket is greeting his constituents."

"I bet Bernadette would have fun with him too. She loved playing with my new friend's dog." Morgan swiveled her head looking for Tess. "She's here somewhere, I ran into her boyfriend."

Morgan realized that Tess hadn't stopped by to say hi yet. She scanned the crowd to try to spot her, but the courtyard had filled with bodies.

"Let's plan on getting Arch and Bernadette together soon," Nathan said. "And would you ever want to go surfing with me?"

The idea slammed the brakes on the warm fuzzies she was feeling about spending more time with Nathan.

Um, can we do anything *but surfing?*

"What's wrong?" Nathan asked, and she realized that she had zero poker face outside the clinic.

Just say yes.

Morgan had a split-second vision of falling and getting her teeth knocked out by a runaway surfboard. Or getting pulled into a vortex she couldn't escape. And what were the riptides like in Nantucket, anyway? But she wasn't going to miss any opportunities to hang out with Nathan, so she sucked it up.

She adjusted her face into a semblance of an excited expression. "Nothing's wrong, sounds fun. I'd love to."

"Excellent. Have you ever surfed?"

"Total novice," she answered before she drained the last sip of Whale's Tale Pale Ale. "But I'm a quick study. Sort of an overachiever."

"Yeah," he snort-laughed good naturedly. "I can tell. You've got that vibe."

Her brow furrowed at his accurate read. "Now why would you say that?" she asked, trying not to sound offended.

And just how transparent am I?

"I mean it as a compliment," he said, backpedaling. "You seem like the kind of person who gets shit done. Your pet-sitting business must be super successful."

A cloud settled over Morgan. Here she was thinking she was gradually morphing into the not-a-stressed-out-vet version of herself only to discover that she came across as tightly wound as ever.

"So, you can teach me to surf?" she asked, hoping to avoid further conversation about her career or personality type.

"Oh, definitely. It's kind of my thing, aside from functional beverages."

It was the first mention of anything about his real life, and she wasn't going to miss the opportunity to learn more.

"How so?"

He traced the wood grain on the table with his fingertips, and she couldn't help but stare at his long, elegant fingers. "I've been involved with a surf charity in New Jersey for the past ten years called Good Waves. We help kids that need special attention learn to love and respect the water."

Wait. What?

She'd expected him to talk about being an instructor at a posh resort somewhere tropical. Morgan could picture him fighting off swarms of bikinis pretending to want to learn to surf just to get closer to him.

"Okay, wow. What kinds of kids?"

"Any of them." His face lit up. "All of them, it doesn't matter. Our goal is to support *any* little folks that need some Zen. If they're dealing with divorce, or are facing an illness, or if they live in the city and have never touched sand, or they're on the spectrum, or they're low income . . . whatever. If they need us, we're there. It's pretty transformative. For them and us."

Nathan's face shifted as he explained the program. Pride, and the tiniest hint of melancholy. Morgan realized that given the types of kids he was involved with, he'd probably experienced his own share of sad outcomes. For the first time all evening, his blue eyes wandered away from her face and his smile faltered.

"Sounds incredible," Morgan said softly. "How does it work from a teaching standpoint? Do you mix everyone together? All ages and abilities?"

Nathan leaned forward as the music kicked up again, and she forced herself to hold his gaze without looking away. He'd moved close enough for her to see the hint of squint lines running along

the tops of his cheeks. It was the face of someone who was always turned to the sun wearing an eye-crinkling smile.

Someone who loves his life.

"The program changes depending on who we get," Nathan
replied, forcing her back into the moment before she could get
too wrapped up thinking about what it would take for her to
love *her* life. "If it's a group of kids from the city, we'll work with
them as a class. Or sometimes we buddy up one-on-one. That's
my favorite." He shrugged like what he was describing was no
big deal even though it sounded like a major time commitment.

They listened to the guitarist singing about driving with the
windows rolled down for a few minutes.

"Anyway." Nathan banged his empty cup on the table like a
gavel. "I'm talking too much. Tell me about your dog-sitting
business. What's the name of it so I can stalk you?"

Morgan's stomach seized up reflexively. She *still* hadn't fine-
tuned her cover story.

"Uh, I don't have social media for it. I keep it low profile, re-
ferral only. I take care of dogs, cats, and the occasional goldfish
or donkey." She shrugged and tried to think of a way to derail
the topic. The deeper the lies got, the worse she felt. Nathan
seemed like an open book, all she had to do was ask, and here
she was, hiding everything about her life.

But it's not like any of this is real.

Archer ran over to them and put his front paws on the bench
next to Nathan.

Perfect distraction, bud. I owe you.

Morgan pointed to the dog. "I noticed that Archer was acting funny when I was petting his head, so I peeked in his ears. I
think he's got, like, an ear infection or something?"

She wanted to kick herself for sounding like an unsure teenager even though she was positive that's what it was.

"Really? How can you tell?" Nathan reached for Archer's ear and the dog moved just out of reach.

"That," Morgan answered. "He didn't want me to touch them, so I took a quick peek and saw some buildup. My old dog used to get them all the time," she lied. George was always in perfect health, until he wasn't.

"Huh," Nathan answered. "Do you know what causes them?"

Moisture, pollen, food allergies, ear mites, foreign bodies, water…

She bit her tongue. The more decisive she was in her diagnosis, the more he'd start to lean on her for advice. It always happened, whether it was the checker at the grocery store or new neighbors next door.

"Um, I think a bunch of stuff? If he swims with you, maybe he got water in his ear and it didn't dry out?"

"Hm. Maybe. So should I take him to the vet?"

Morgan nodded. "Yeah, probably a good idea. It's an easy fix."

"Well, thanks for catching it. I'll make sure we get it taken care of. Right, bud?"

Nathan took his dog's head in his hands and kissed him on the nose. The sweetness of the gesture sent a shiver of anticipation through her.

Me next, please?

chapter thirteen

He's exhausted," Nathan said, gesturing to Archer asleep on the seat between them as he pulled into the driveway. Morgan had left the porch and yard lights blazing so the property was lit up like a public park, which didn't set the tone for a romantic moment.

If that's where this is going.

"He had a busy night. So many new friends made," Morgan agreed.

The thought of what she hoped was to come sent an anticipatory shiver through her. How long had it been since she kissed someone? Or used her hands for anything other than diagnostics? She'd barely had the energy to touch herself let alone another human. And now, the most perfect one she'd ever seen in real life was just a sleeping dog's length away from her.

We're probably going to make out. If I have anything to say about it, we definitely are.

Nathan turned off the truck and Archer didn't stir. "I'll walk you to the front door. If that's okay."

Getting him in the shadows was all she wanted.

"Sure, thanks."

They hopped out of the truck and Morgan took care not to slam her door. As much as she liked Archer, she didn't want him *aroo*-ing his way into whatever was about to happen between them.

Nathan started for the front porch, which was lit up as bright as a football stadium. Morgan stopped abruptly.

"I'm staying out back, in the pool house." She pointed to the walkway that branched off to where the lights were dimmer and more conducive for all the things she wanted to do to him.

"Off we go, then," Nathan said, taking her hand and pulling her along with him.

He laced his fingers through hers like it was something they did all the time, even though it was the first time they'd actually touched, aside from the quick introductory handshake. The sensation of his hand dwarfing hers was enough to make Morgan's heart trip out of rhythm for a second. For most people, holding hands was kindergarten-level affection, but it had always felt bigger and more meaningful to her. Even Shakespeare had said something about the foreplay of being palm to palm.

If you're feeling like this because of hand-holding, you're in deep shit.

Nathan reached for the fence door, and she jerked him back so abruptly that he stumbled.

"No, it squeaks!" she whispered like she was a high schooler trying to avoid waking her parents after curfew. "The dogs know all of the house sounds, and if they hear the fence they'll both start barking, which will wake up Archer, and then . . ." She stopped, realizing that she'd basically told him what she wanted to happen next.

"Ah, got it," Nathan said softly as he moved toward her in the darkness, his eyes locked on hers. "And then I won't be able to do this."

The next thing she knew, Morgan was caught up in his arms, her hands pressed against his chest and his beautiful face just inches away, gazing down with a look that said nothing mattered more than her. The shock of being so close to him, wrapped in his warmth, left her breathless.

Morgan shivered again.

"What's wrong? Is this okay?" Nathan asked in a hoarse whisper. His eyes roamed her face as if trying to read her thoughts. "You're trembling."

It had been ages since her body had responded to pleasure. For too long, her life had been an endless cycle of deprivation, of not enough sleep, or food, or relaxation, or *happiness*. But now, as she was getting ready to kiss a man so pretty that he didn't seem real, the exhilarating feelings came flooding back, tripping each sense until they responded like they'd been starved. Morgan cataloged every nuance of what was happening in an instant, from the pressure of his hands on her body to his suntan lotion scent.

Nathan's brow creased and he started to ease his grip on her until she finally found her voice.

"Please don't let me go," she said in a breathy exhale, letting some of the tension and nerves drain from her body. Morgan wrapped her arms behind his neck and moved closer to Nathan to prove that she wanted to kiss him more than anything in the world.

"Good," he said softly, and finally lowered his mouth to hers.

Nathan brushed his lips against hers so tenderly that it almost made her melt. It was as if he could tell that she was on the verge of sensory overload from just the hint of a kiss and held back from giving her a full hit. He allowed her a taste of what was to come, grazing her mouth with his for a moment, then slowly pulling away a few centimeters, so she could adapt to the delicious sensations. Morgan felt a numb buzz spread through her body as she waited to see how Nathan was going to beguile her next.

One of his hands was warm against her lower back and the other slid up her neck to gently cradle the back of her head. His eyes searched her face like he was looking for permission, because she was practically limp in his arms. It was the enormity of what was happening between them, the fact that she was feeling things she hadn't experienced in way too long, that was making her weak. Before meeting Nathan, Morgan had started to worry that part of her was forever dormant, like the neural pathways that triggered raw animal attraction and pleasure had been severed. She hadn't experienced as much as a crush in the time since she and Sam had broken up, but here she was in Nathan's arms feeling like just the brush of his fingertips could get her off.

She moved closer to him, squeezing her linked arms behind his head to show that she very much wanted to continue. Nathan finally slanted his mouth against hers in a way that said he wasn't going to be tentative any longer.

A noise escaped her as they kissed that sounded like she'd just tasted something delicious, and Morgan felt him grin against her mouth before deepening the kiss. The barest hint of stubble, so light that she hadn't even noticed it on his face, tickled her as their mouths and tongues explored. Morgan had to fight to keep from standing on one leg and wrapping the other around him to draw him as close to her as possible.

She wanted to slide her fingers beneath his shirt and let her hands wander along his smooth skin. But just as she unlocked her arms from behind his neck and started to pull at his shirt, he moved away, breathing heavy.

Morgan's stomach fluttered at the sight of him looking as undone as she felt. It was painful for their mouths not to be smashed together, yet here he was, maintaining an agonizingly polite six inches from her.

"We should probably say good night."

It was the most ridiculous thing she'd ever heard.

"Wait . . . what do you . . . *why*?" she managed to get out in a raspy whisper. She felt dizzy and overheated and nowhere near ready to stop what they were starting.

Nathan brought one hand up to her cheek and cupped her face. She leaned into the curve of his fingers and closed her eyes, savoring how perfectly she fit in his palm. Even if this was all they did for the rest of the night, letting their clothed body parts meld together in different configurations, it would be enough. She wanted to keep feeling all of the sleeping synapses he'd re-awakened within her. She wanted him to quench the fire he'd lit.

I want to fuck him.

He sighed as he stared into her eyes. "Because it doesn't matter how much I want you right now, I think we should take our time."

It wasn't something a player would say. A player would've been working her the whole night at Cisco, angling his way into her bed. A player would've thrown open the gate door and followed her lead into the pool house. Instead, Nathan was about to leave her feeling horny and desperate.

Morgan grabbed onto the only objection she could come up with. "Yeah, but we don't *have* a lot of time."

He leaned in and kissed her gently on the mouth again, an end-of-conversation good-night kiss that that was far sweeter than what she was craving. "We have plenty. Trust me."

chapter fourteen

"Evan and Ginny are at the beach, but he usually only lasts an hour or so before he has a meltdown, so we need to knock this out quickly. He doesn't like the way sand feels," Sydney said, placing two glasses of lemonade on the table in her pretty backyard. Violet the Frenchie was passed out next to them, panting and lying on her side on the hot bricks. The compact outdoor area was half patio and half perfectly trimmed golf-course grass, ringed by a massive wall of green hedge. Even the window boxes on the garage were overflowing with red and purple flowers.

I totally understand the anti-beach sentiment, kid.

"Plus, I've got calls this afternoon," Sydney continued. "My real job."

It was the first time Sydney had mentioned working. Morgan had just assumed she was a stay-at-home mom. But Morgan wasn't about to ask for details, in order to avoid questions about her own background.

They were sitting on outdoor furniture that was as comfortable as a living room set during this unplanned meeting, the result of a last-minute emergency call from Sydney that made it sound like there was a gala-related catastrophe going on. The event organizers needed to find a space to house the dogs leading up to their turns on the catwalk, and she wanted Morgan's unofficial input about the safety of it.

"I'm sort of disappointed that everything has to be so pink, but that's what Abby wants," Sydney said, flipping through the papers on the table in front of her. "Pink logo, pink step and repeat, pink centerpieces. She said it's good for branding."

Morgan was still in a post-Cisco haze and having trouble focusing on the details. She had to fight off a grin every time she thought about Nathan.

"Abby runs a tight ship, huh?" Morgan asked.

Her fingers itched to snag the files stacked on the table beside Sydney and take a peek, to try to find out exactly what she was in for during her one night of volunteering. Her primary exposure to fund-raisers was limited to small events run by pet charities at home, where the ticket never cost more than twenty-five dollars and the funds raised rarely topped ten grand. The Nantucket event was already on another level.

"You don't even know," Sydney answered, shaking her head so that her ponytail smacked her cheek. "But the truth is, this fund-raiser is *her* baby. She's on the board and everyone sort of tiptoes around her. Between you and me, I think we're all a little afraid of her. She loves the animals and wants what's best for them, so we let her run the show because in the end, she raises a ton of money. But the woman takes no prisoners. You'll see."

Sydney handed Morgan a sheet of paper. "That's the specs on the location. It's a privately owned home that belongs to one of the rescue's board members. We only have access to the yard, so we'll have to bring everything in. We've got an events group donating the tenting, tables, chairs, lighting, and luxury porta-johns. But here's the issue: we forgot to reserve a holding space for the dogs." She frowned. "We've got time, but I wanted you to be in on it, so that we choose the right option. We want everyone to stay safe."

The sheet showed a magnificent gray-shingled house, a sprawling thing that looked more like a hotel than a private home, with porticos, gables, dormers, and porches, plus a few outbuildings clustered near an infinity pool. The endless lawn stretched out to an inlet.

"Speaking of staying safe, did Abby give any thought to what I said at the meeting about only allowing dogs that are in the show?" Morgan asked.

Sydney pursed her lips. "She didn't directly, but you inspired a *ton* of emails among the volunteers. It seems most people didn't realize that inviting guests' dogs could be an issue, but now they get it. And let's just say that Abby is having a hard time letting go of her barking lot."

"Yikes." Morgan grimaced. "So what's next?"

"We're fighting to change the line on the invitations from 'Your furry best friend is welcome' to 'Two-legged guests only, please,'" Sydney said. "But if we can't make it happen, well . . . that's where you come in." She smoothed the papers in her lap and gave Morgan a hopeful smile.

Oh shit.

"How, exactly?" Morgan asked slowly.

"I know you're only supposed to be dealing with the dog

models backstage that night, but maybe if we wind up going through with this stupid barking lot you could also be, like, a referee in the area?"

"You want me to be the model wrangler *and* a dog cop?"

The scope of what Morgan was being asked to do shifted into focus. As much as she wanted to keep a low profile and take it easy while she was in Nantucket, there was no way she could knowingly allow dogs to be put in jeopardy. Preventable canine drama was her kryptonite. Everyone involved in the fund-raiser had their hearts in the right places, but it seemed that the people making decisions didn't know much about dog behavior.

"Why aren't the rescue people involved with planning?" Morgan asked. "I'm sure they'd have an opinion on the barking lot."

"Oh, they're *so* busy dealing with the day-to-day stuff of the rescue. We don't ask them to be a part of fund-raisers, it's sort of our gift to them. We handle everything so they can focus on the dogs."

Morgan fiddled with the tie on the edge of the cushion while she envisioned the potential canine chaos at the event.

"If I agree to it, would I be able to have some safety features included? Like, separating the big and little dogs into their own spaces, and making sure the fence is high enough so no one can jump it?"

Sydney scrunched up her face. "It makes sense to *me*, but we'd have to talk to Abby. That sounds like additional expenses."

"How about limiting the number of dogs in the area so there aren't too many at one time?"

"Abby again."

Morgan was silent as she realized what Sydney was asking of her. "Sooo . . . what you're saying is you want me to go toe-to-toe with Abby on dog safety stuff?"

"Sort of?" She gave Morgan an apologetic grin. "There's still a chance we won't have guest dogs there, so consider this an on-call situation for the moment. But I think that since you're an outsider—no offense—and you have dog knowledge, she might be more open to listening to you."

That's not how it seemed at the meeting.

Morgan shifted, the patio chair suddenly uncomfortable despite the thick navy-and-white-striped cushion on the seat. "I want to be honest with you. I'm, uh, not in a place where I want to get involved with confrontation, so if that's what you're hoping for . . ."

"Oh my God, no, of course not! Never. That's not how we roll in our little group," Sydney answered, frowning at the thought of it. "I just thought you might be willing to help keep the dogs as safe as possible, you know? Based on everything you did the first time you met Hud, I could tell you know more about dogs than the average person. You've got a way with them."

If you only knew.

Sydney's softening blows were having their intended effect. Morgan was feeling weaker by the minute. She leaned back in the chair and crossed her arms.

"I could really use your help, to be honest," Sydney continued, her tone taking on an edge of pleading. "Or should I say, the dogs could."

Before you agree to anything, set some boundaries.

Morgan shifted again, realizing that she needed to reveal

some of her true self to Sydney. "I, uh, I've been through some . . . stuff lately. I'm trying to avoid stress this summer."

"Wait a minute." Sydney's face clouded as she studied Morgan. "Are you okay? Do you want to talk about it?"

Mentioning that she was dealing with something seemed to trigger a kill switch in Sydney. She leaned toward Morgan, the stack of papers in her lap forgotten, and her excited energy calmed.

"Oh, no, I'm fine," Morgan answered quickly, waving her hand like she was fanning away cigarette smoke.

Sydney's focus intensified and Morgan suddenly felt like a pathology slide under a microscope.

"I guess I should tell you that I'm a licensed counselor," Sydney said in what was probably *her* professional voice. "And an excellent listener." She searched Morgan's face in a way that made her feel even more exposed, like her façade of in-control badass was slipping away and the scared girl with imposter syndrome was being revealed. "If you ever need to talk, just let me know."

Morgan tensed her muscles and held her breath at the thought of it. So far, Nantucket was keeping the stress tentacles paralyzed, and she wasn't about to accidentally wake them up now by discussing her life.

Talking made it worse. Talking made it real. All the animals she couldn't help, and the owners who yelled at her, blamed her, and berated her while she did her best.

That's a hard pass on the talking.

"Thank you, good to know," Morgan said in her practiced, cheerful tone. It was the same one she used on her parents and the few non-veterinary friends she managed to maintain. "So . . .

as for the volunteering stuff. If we can agree to keep it drama free, I'll do my best to help."

"As long as you're okay with it. I promise I'll have your back if you need to discuss something with Abby. You have my word." Sydney was still watching her carefully, and Morgan felt like the rawness she'd been suppressing was written all over her body. She regretted even alluding to the trouble at home.

"Okay, then, I'm in," Morgan said with a shrug. "Anything for the dogs, right?"

Sydney nodded and watched her for a second longer, then went back to thumbing through the paperwork. Morgan studied the sheet with the photo of the house.

I hope this isn't a mistake.

Violet heard something in the distance and let out a test woof. When nothing answered her call, she flopped onto the pavers, letting out an audible fart as an editorial comment.

The afternoon had turned into a scorcher and Morgan was relaxing in the shade of an oversized black umbrella next to the pool, updating Hudson's training notes. Bernadette was sleeping the day away in the main house, exhausted from her walk, and Morgan's student was panting in the grass next to her chaise lounge.

"'Stay' is a lot more work than ya realized, huh, buddy?" Morgan asked him, reaching down to scratch his head. "You're cooked!"

Hudson was acing his basic manners training in and around the house, but his leash reactivity was a case of two steps forward and one back. The sheer unpredictability of going for a walk—*Were they going to run into an unleashed dog? Would a dog on an extendable leash try to get up in his face?*—meant that progress came in fits and starts. But Morgan was seeing glimmers of greatness in between the accidental freak-outs.

She doodled in the margins of her notebook, tracing the same flowy pattern over and over. Morgan flipped back to look at how far Hudson had come in the short time they'd been together and decided that adding background about their sessions would help her remember the context of what was going on with him. She went back to each entry and added notes about the weather, and what else she'd done during the day.

Which is a lot of nothing.

But it also felt like she was keeping busy in the best possible ways: naps, reading, window-shopping, hanging out by the pool, and loving on Bernie and Hud.

Morgan's phone pinged and she grabbed for it so quickly that she almost knocked it off the table. She'd already exchanged a few quick texts with Nathan, and she was now responding like Pavlov's dog any time her phone made a noise. They'd made plans to surf the following day, and she was excited despite the whole ocean-and-chance-of-dying aspect.

She squinted at the screen and saw that it was a text from Vidya, not Nathan. Just seeing her friend's name was enough to make her heart seize up out of habit. Texts from Vidya could range from asking her to cover a day at the clinic for her to venting about a tough patient, and Morgan wasn't in the headspace to think about any of it.

Not yet. Not until I have to.

She gritted her teeth and opened the message. It was a photo of Vidya standing next to Rebecca with a baby goat in between them. They were both making heart shapes with their hands, and the accompanying text read, Miss you, hope you're good.

Just seeing the two of them in the clinic brought it all back. She could almost *smell* the photo, and her body went into an unexpected free fall. Something in her chest tightened painfully and she let out a long breath through pursed lips, like she was in a Lamaze class.

She wrestled with missing them but feeling like she was nowhere near ready to go back as Sydney's words echoed in her head.

Do you want to talk about it?

Do *I* want to talk about it?

Keeping everything stuffed inside had worked fine until it had erupted and landed her on an island in the Atlantic called The Grey Lady, caring for a last-chance rescue dog and a diabetic senior. Talking about it wouldn't change anything. Sure, she might get a little lift while she was far away from the grind in a place where every day felt better than the last, but she was still going back.

Because at the core, she loved her career.

Morgan glanced around the yard, trying to find something to focus on to keep the stress tentacles from creeping up her spine. Maybe the hydrangea bushes, heavy with clusters of blue flowers? The outdoor shower she'd yet to use that Eugene and Karl couldn't stop talking about? The ominously elegant black-bottom pool that made her nervous to wade in deeper than her thighs?

A dull pain throbbed behind her eyes, so she closed them and leaned her head back. She swiped at the tear that slid down her cheek and sniffled against the pinching sensation in her nose.

When she opened her eyes, Hudson was standing next to the chaise, staring at her.

"Hey, you," Morgan said, placing her hand on the side of his face with a sad smile.

He looked up at her with a concerned expression, his ears plastered against his head and his tongue lizarding out of his mouth. He shifted his weight, then gently hopped up so his front paws were on the chaise next to her. Before she realized what he was doing, Hudson leaned closer to gently lick her cheek, exactly where the tear had rolled down.

"Oh my God," Morgan whispered as it dawned on her. "You're worried about me?"

Hudson continued licking her cheek no matter how she moved her face away from him. It was like he needed to distract her and wipe away any tangible traces of her sadness.

"Hud, I'm okay. I'm okay," she lied as new tears of recognition welled in her eyes.

Oh my God. Hudson is a comfort dog.

Their family dog, Betty, had been one, so keyed in to offering support to the humans in her house that she could practically smell tears from a room away. Betty had been particularly helpful during Morgan's angsty teen years, seeking her out when she was feeling depressed.

After realizing that Hudson meant business and wasn't going to stop his comfort rituals, Morgan surrendered to him. She pulled him up onto the lounge, and he leaned his body against hers like a weighted blanket.

Hudson closed his eyes and panted while she massaged him. Comfort dogs took their jobs seriously, and while they were committed to their work, Morgan also knew firsthand that being an empath took a toll. Hudson would need proof that his efforts had paid off, much like search-and-rescue dogs needed to have "live finds" to keep from getting depressed.

"Hey, Hud, you did it!" she said in her happiest voice, dragging the back of her hand across her eyes to wipe the tears away and smiling widely. "Look at me, I feel *so* much better now!"

He flopped his head against her shoulder and thumped his tail on the chair.

Yeah, it worked, buddy.

For now.

chapter fifteen

I say we go for it," Nathan said. "I've got good dog sense, and worst-case scenario, I'm a fast runner."

Nathan was standing in the driveway, barefoot in the morning light, wearing a long-sleeve snug-fitting navy shirt that showed off every impressive ripple from shoulders to abs and a pair of yellow-and-red Hawaiian floral board shorts. Morgan couldn't believe that she was going to strip off her own shorts and T-shirt in a few minutes and be half-naked with him.

She'd told Nathan that she was worried about Eugene and Karl arriving home that afternoon, unsure how Hudson was going to take to them after spending time with just her. Nathan had offered to be a volunteer victim, to allow her to work through the reintroduction protocols to check for any weak spots, and based on what she'd seen of his dog sense, she knew that he'd be a stable first intro for Hudson.

"Are you sure you don't mind? It would be a huge help."

"Totally. Plus, I really want to meet that dude." He grinned at her and she felt a flutter in her chest. "Just tell me the dos and don'ts."

"It's easy, let's head to the backyard."

He fell in step beside her, and she could smell the beachy coconut scent of sunblock. It triggered a sense memory that made her jittery, but she comforted herself that if she was going to drown, at least she'd have a nice view as she disappeared beneath the waves.

"I like your fanny pack," he said, gesturing to the black treat bag she never seemed to take off.

"All the cool kids are wearing them." She laughed as she opened the creaky wood gate to the backyard. "Okay, your job is to sit in a chair, avoid staring at him, and toss him treats when I tell you to." She took a handful of cubed chicken from the treat bag clipped to her cutoffs and handed it to him. "If he comes over to you, don't reach for him, just let him investigate you first. He probably won't want you to pet him, but you can feed him treats."

"What's his deal? Has he bitten anyone? Because this all sounds very bomb-squad-y." Nathan looked more concerned about Hudson's welfare than worried about the possibility of a bite.

Morgan shook her head. "Nope, and we want to keep it that way. I'm pretty sure this is overkill, but it doesn't hurt to be cautious."

"Got it," he said with a nod. Nathan scanned the backyard. "Hey, nice place."

"It's incredible, and so are the owners." Morgan went out on a limb. "You'll probably meet them at some point."

"I'd like that," he said, holding her gaze, causing the flutter to turn into a full-fledged gallop.

Why does it feel like we're talking about meeting my parents?

"Sit at the head of the table." She pointed at a chair. "Ready?"

"Ready." He sat down and saluted her. "At your service."

Morgan jogged to the pool house and slid the door open. She kept Hudson gated in the bathroom when she wasn't around, but it was like he had a surveillance camera on the property and already knew something was up. By the time she reached him, he was on high alert about the presence in the backyard. He wagged at her, then looked toward the door with a concerned expression.

"Yeah, I know, there's someone here," she said as she clipped the orange-and-navy-striped leash to his collar and knelt in front of him. "There's a guy outside and I think you're going to like him. Because between you and me, I already do. Be nice, please."

It felt safe admitting it to Hudson. He wasn't likely to tell anyone, and she hoped that letting the canine empath in on the secret might make him more willing to accept Nathan.

Hudson shot her a look when they stepped outside. He wasn't used to being on leash in the yard, and the change in their usual pattern made him even more suspicious. She led him to his pee spot, then meandered around, a safe distance from Nathan.

Morgan peeked at Nathan and saw that he was frozen in his seat with a lovesick expression on his face while he watched Hudson nose around. Then, as if the dog could feel the weight of Nathan's gaze, Hudson snapped to attention and glared at him. His hackles went up between his shoulder blades.

"Yup!" Morgan chirped, using the marker word that meant that Hud was about to get paid. The initial stages of the training were simple; pair something scary (Nathan) with something wonderful (food). Hudson stared at Nathan for a second longer, then finally tore his eyes away to look up at Morgan for his treat. When he realized that she was using chicken, he threw a half-hearted glance back at Nathan, then moved closer to her to ask for more, as if he realized that a distant stranger didn't pose a threat and the chicken was one hundred percent more important.

"This is good. We're going to walk around a bit, but don't move or say anything," she instructed. Nathan seemed to be taking her advice to heart; he was statue-still.

She closed the distance between them gradually, zigzagging across the yard and sweet-talking Hudson for being brave. She ended up at the far end of the long table, feeding the dog a steady stream of small treats.

"He seems fine with you, so I'm going to drop the leash now. Just ignore him."

Nathan nodded and kept his eyes fixed on the distance.

The man knows how to take direction.

Morgan took a breath and let go.

Hudson sniffed around her feet looking for chicken crumbs, then glued his nose to the ground and headed to where Nathan was sitting. He examined the grass around his bare feet, then snuffled his way up to his ankles, calves, then knees. Morgan openly admired Nathan's tan skin and the white-blond hair that dusted his legs without having to worry about being caught.

She watched Hudson's body language and was relieved that he'd loosened up a little. "Throw a piece of chicken away from you, so he has to chase after it. Running away from you to get a goody is a little tension breaker."

Nathan did as he was told, moving for the pile of chicken on the table in slow motion. He cranked his arm back and catapulted a piece across the yard, and Hudson immediately took off after it.

"That was a bit much, but okay." Morgan laughed at him. "Throw the next one about five feet away instead of all the way to Madaket."

Hudson came running back to Nathan with his tail wagging, ready for the game to continue. He arced another cube of chicken so it landed on the concrete near the pool, and Hudson raced to grab it, then ran back and plopped into a sit in front of Nathan.

"He's a really good boy," Nathan whispered out of the corner of his mouth.

Morgan realized that he was still avoiding looking at the dog. She laughed again. "Sorry, you can say hi to him now!"

He finally exhaled and relaxed. "I was so nervous! I didn't want to fuck it up."

"You're doing great," she said. "And so is he."

Hudson stood in front of Nathan, shifting his weight from paw to paw in anticipation of more chicken.

"Give him a treat from your hand this time."

Nathan took a cube, then held his open palm out in front of him. Hudson snatched it but didn't move away, his tail wagging. When Nathan didn't immediately grab another treat, Hudson went into a sit position, then slid into a down.

"Are you kidding me, mister?" Nathan exclaimed in awe, a smile cracking his face as he quickly grabbed a piece of chicken. "Did that pretty lady over there teach you how to do that?"

Morgan blushed at the compliment. She started to give more instructions but kept quiet when she saw what was about to happen.

Hudson moved closer to Nathan and planted his head on his leg, looking up at him with puppy-dog eyes.

Nathan rolled his head back in surrender. "He just murdered me with cuteness."

"Pet him, please!" Morgan said, swooning over the new bromance. "He's dying for you."

As she watched Nathan massage Hudson's head, she felt heat rush to her face for the second time.

And Hudson's not the only one.

chapter sixteen

You ready to learn how to rip?" Nathan asked, beaming at her as he unpacked the surfboards from the back of his truck.

"Yup. A little nervous, but I think I can handle it."

Are my hands shaking? Why are my hands shaking?

"Leave your flip-flops in the car. Easier that way," he instructed as she started to follow him through the small parking lot.

It was early, long before the beach was warm enough to fill with vacationers and a few hours before Nathan was due at his Peachy post on Straight Wharf. The sky was still shifting from the pinks and yellows of the sunrise to another bright blue day. Morgan spotted a couple with an off-leash dog in the distance and made a mental note to look into bringing Hudson and Bernadette at some point.

"Isn't the water going to be freezing?" she asked, fearful she already knew the answer. Morgan was wearing a long-sleeve pink Nantucket T-shirt and the wind was slicing through it.

"Totally. But we're not going hard-core today. I always keep my intro lessons short, so you get the bug but none of the begin-ner frustration."

Yeah, I wouldn't be so sure about that.

Nathan placed the boards on sand and pointed to the longer of the two. "This one is yours. Much more buoyant. Grab it and let's get in there."

Morgan froze in place, her arms crossed over her chest. "Wait . . . what? Aren't you supposed to leave it on the sand, and we practice jumping on top, like they do in the movies? We're going right in?"

Just a little more time, please . . .

"You know it," he crowed. "That's the way I do it with the kids, to get them excited. They love it. I want you to feel how the board reacts in water first. Get comfortable with it in the shal-lows, you know? Just some belly-boarding today, then we'll worry about pop-ups next time." He paused and scanned her. "You look strong, I think you're going to do really well."

Morgan straightened her back and blushed at the compli-ment. It was probably what he said to the kids in his classes to encourage them, but it was exactly what she needed to hear.

"Thanks."

"You've boogie-boarded before, right? When you were little?"

She shook her head. She'd always spent her time on their infrequent family beach trips under the umbrella reading or playing right at the water's edge with Mack. She knew how to swim, she just didn't enjoy being in open water. The lack of con-trol, being tossed around with the briny taste of water in the back of her throat just didn't seem fun to her. As she got older, she'd blamed her hair's tendency to frizz in salt water as her excuse to avoid getting in.

The combination of sand, wind, and stress triggered a sudden sense memory that stopped her in her tracks. The beach trip with her family, playing with Mack and her father in the shallow surf. She'd felt safe standing next to her dad until he turned to swish Mack through the water. What felt like a hurricane-force wave knocked her off her feet and trapped her under the surface, forcing Morgan to fight against the frantic feeling of water rushing up her nose. She remembered not being able to tell which way was up and wishing someone would notice that she was drowning. Then the relief she felt when her father's strong hand fished her out, and how she clung to him, trying not to cry as he told her she was okay. She could still feel the burning in her nose as she sniffled and agreed that she was fine.

Excellent timing, repressed memory. Thanks, brain.

Morgan hugged herself tighter and shivered.

"You can keep your shirt on," Nathan said as he gave her a quick once-over that made her shiver for a completely different reason. "It'll get heavy, but we're not standing today so it won't matter. I'll let you borrow one of my rash guards next time. But the jorts gotta go." He pointed at her jean shorts, then sliced the air with his thumb and made a raspy whistling noise.

Morgan managed a casual-sounding laugh, popped the button, and wriggled out of them, thankful that the T-shirt hit the bottom of her butt. If he got to remain half-dressed in knee-length board shorts and rash guard, then she should be allowed to hide her bikini.

"Onward!" he said, picking up his board and tucking it under his arm.

The maneuver wasn't as easy for Morgan. Her board was longer than Nathan's, and the thing teeter-tottered awkwardly until she figured out how to brace it against her body.

Nathan looked back at her. "All good? You need help?"

"Nope, I got it."

Story of my life.

They paused where the dry sand turned a shade darker from the moisture, the water lapping toward them from a few feet away.

"Here's what we're gonna do. It's simple, I promise." He shot her another devastating smile and she believed him.

The guy keeps packs of kids alive in the water, he knows how to handle a newbie. Relax.

"As you walk out, keep the nose of the board up, so the waves crash under it. We're not going deep. Let's hit it."

He strode into the water without hesitating, so she followed behind him, convinced that it must be one of those situations where the cold air makes the water feel bathtub warm. The moment a wave lapped over her toes, she discovered how wrong she was.

Morgan danced in place, trying to levitate above the surf as goose bumps zipped up her legs. "Oh my *God*! It's freezing!"

Can I get a pass on this, please?

Nathan was already in up to his knees. "You'll get used to it, I promise! Come on, catch up to me."

It all came down to that moment: stay safe on the sand or follow Nathan out. But there really was no choice. Morgan didn't fail. Ever. Morgan Pearce rose to challenges and swallowed her fears. Morgan Pearce was a winner.

Go.

She jogged awkwardly to reach him, her teeth chattering for a million different reasons as the water splashed up her legs.

"You're a natural!" he enthused when she reached him. "You're not fighting the waves. That's a great sign."

The compliment combined with his smile was enough to make her forget about the icy water numbing her from the waist down.

"Remember, always keep the nose of the board pointed to the beach. We're looking for nice little foamy, mushy waves to start off, okay? We're going to ride them in."

Morgan nodded even though she had no idea what a mushy wave looked like. A decidedly un-mushy one rolled by and nearly knocked her off-balance even though her feet were planted firmly on the ocean floor. She tasted salt water on her tongue as she struggled to hold on to the board, feeling awkward, uncoordinated, and nervous as hell.

"Once we spot one, you're going to hop on so that your feet are kind of hooked and hanging off the back, like this." Nathan grasped the edges of his board and slipped on in a fluid motion so that his belly was on it, his wet shirt clinging to the well-defined planes of his back.

Yup, that helps. Definitely feeling warmer.

"When the wave is about six feet away, start paddling," he continued. "Like this. Long strokes, cupped hands, kicky feet."

Nathan demonstrated a few strokes and Morgan swallowed hard as the muscles in his shoulders and legs flexed.

He has to be part merman. He looks so at home in the water.

"Once you feel the wave connecting with you and carrying you, stop paddling and hold on to the rails." He moved his hands to the sides of the board. "Then, just relax and enjoy the ride." He slid off the board, so he was standing in the water and grinning at her. "Make sense?"

I didn't hear a word you just said.

She nodded and tried to figure out if the buzzy feeling inside was fear or horniness.

"Excellent. Now let's watch for some waves. I'm gonna quiz you." He floated his surfboard closer to where she was standing.

The water was still, so they stood side-by-side in silence for a few seconds, staring out at the vast horizon, waiting for the perfect combination of current, wind, and magic. She watched Nathan out of the corner of her eye, waiting for him to give her more instruction. His expression was serene as he scanned the water, almost like he was meditating.

I want to feel that way.

He turned abruptly and caught her staring.

"Hey, you okay?" He frowned. "You look worried."

He waded closer to her and studied her face, and Morgan felt a confusing mixture of embarrassment and relief that he might call the whole thing off.

"Yeah, just cold," she managed with a convincing shiver. "Plus, I'm more of a pool person, so, you know . . ." She shrugged and gestured to the vastness around them.

"Oh shit," Nathan murmured as he scanned her. "You're scared. Morgan, *fuck*. I didn't know! I'm so sorry I didn't take it slower. C'mon, let's go in, you don't have to do this today."

Morgan wasn't sure if her fear was written all over her face or if Nathan's time working with kids had helped him hone his observation skills; all she knew was that she'd never felt more seen. He strode through the water until he was right beside her, the tips of their surfboards bouncing like bumper cars.

"It's okay, we can work up to this part," Nathan said softly. "Or we can skip it completely and just sit on the beach and make out."

Morgan was so busy warring with herself to be brave that the comment sailed right over her head.

"No," she finally managed. "I can do it. I'm fine, I swear."

Nathan studied her silently for a few seconds, his blue eyes boring into hers. "You sure? There's no shame in taking it slow."

She nodded and swallowed hard. "I'm not a quitter."

A baby wave moved through them, but Morgan didn't break off eye contact.

"I can tell," he said, his expression finally softening. "Okay. Just remember that I'll be right here. You're not alone. You're safe with me, Morgan."

If it was possible to hug someone with words, Nathan had just done it. Suddenly the water felt a little less cold.

Then, as if he sensed that she needed an extra dose of encouragement, he leaned across her surfboard and placed a soft, salty kiss on her lips. It was quick, too quick for her liking, but it was enough to leave her with a goofy grin when he pulled away.

"That's better." Nathan nodded and gazed back at the horizon, shielding his eyes. "Okay, how does that one look?" He pointed at an approaching blue-green swell. "Think we can ride it?"

Morgan turned and saw a nonthreatening bubbling white mass in the distance and took a guess. "Looks mushy to me?"

"Exactly, you've got this," Nathan cheered. "Now, get in position. Nose toward the beach."

He slipped onto his surfboard in a graceful leap, landing

smack in the middle of it on his belly. Morgan attempted the same move but wound up flopping awkwardly to one side of the board and almost falling off. The thing was wobblier than she expected given how huge it was, and she felt her core engage while she struggled to stay on top of it. Her heavy wet shirt was draggy and didn't help her balance. She realized that she didn't remember a thing he'd told her and was now on a floating mattress with a wave, albeit a small one, barreling toward her. Morgan looked at Nathan for feedback with wide eyes.

"Quick, hook your feet off the end," he yelled encouragingly. "Then paddle, paddle, paddle. You're gonna do this!"

He started moving into position, looking back over his shoulder at the approaching wave, then at her. "You got this, Morgan. Come on!"

Her dog paddle looked nothing like the long, elegant slices Nathan was doing, but they were enough to move her along as the wave got closer. She felt like she was fighting the water, and the muscles across her back tensed, bracing for the embarrassing wipeout that was about to happen.

She could hear the wave coming, so she paddled faster, convinced that Nathan was wrong, and it would be better to outrun it than get caught up in it. Everything inside her turned to jelly as the energy of the water reached her toes. She felt like a spring pulled taut, trembling with fear as the wave enveloped her.

And then.

Everything shifted. Her movements stopped mattering as the frothy wave overtook her. She felt the locomotion of the current all around her as the water lifted the surfboard and carried her along.

All she had to do was hold on.

Morgan's tension melted into a full-bodied laugh as the wave pushed her closer to shore, to where Nathan was watching her. She could feel the ride coming to an end too soon.

Again, again, again!

"You *owned* that thing," Nathan yelled, beaming with pride. "What did you think? You okay?"

Morgan slid off the board and stood in the knee-deep water. She felt the cold seeping back into her bones.

I did it!

She'd tried meditation, but monkey-mind was a way of life for her. It was impossible to quiet herself and focus, but what she'd just experienced on the surfboard changed everything. For ten glorious seconds, nothing else mattered but becoming one with the water.

Nathan was glowing in the morning sun, squinting and smiling in a way that made her toes curl into the sand.

"I think I'm hooked," she called back to him.

And you're my gateway drug.

chapter seventeen

What a *love*," Eugene said as he stroked Hudson under the chin. "He seems so relaxed compared to the first time we met him. You've got the magic touch."

"It's all him," Morgan replied, focused on Hudson's body language to make sure he was enjoying the petting. "He's a solid dog. Quirky, yes. But perfect at the core."

They were sitting in the backyard in the late-afternoon sun, discussing how the first leg of the launch had gone while Hudson and Bernadette got used to sharing the same space. The carefully orchestrated meeting with the human and canine Pak-Reynoldses had gone perfectly, but Morgan remained vigilant about the dogs' interactions while she sipped an Aperol Spritz.

The first moments of the dog meetup after she got back from surfing had nearly given her a heart attack. Despite giving Karl strict instructions to keep a firm grip on Bernadette's leash, he'd managed to drop it as soon as she'd come out with Hudson. The little dog had trotted over to the corner where she and Hudson were standing, sized him up from a distance, then

walked over to squat and pee a few feet away from him. Bernadette seemed to understand that Hudson needed a few seconds
before they met noses-to-butts, so she sniffed around in the
flower beds with one eye on him. Morgan walked Hud over to
Bernie's pee mail and let him get fresh intel on his housemate.
The fact that they'd been orbiting each other for a few weeks,
smelling their markings in the yard and hearing their barks,
seemed like enough to broker a pre-meeting peace treaty, and
within minutes, Bernadette and Hudson were shoulder to shoulder, strolling around the yard finding things to explore together.
Bernadette didn't have the same playful vibe with Hudson that
she had with Palmer, but Morgan preferred a bland yard hang to
a death match any day.

"Are you happy with how the launch went?" Morgan asked,
tucking her leg beneath her and settling back against the chair.

"One hundred percent. It was *amazing*," Karl replied. He
looked happy to be sprawled on the outdoor couch in relaxed
linen pants with Bernadette in his lap and Eugene beside him
after playing host at Target stores up and down the East Coast.
"We're thrilled. Great crowds."

Morgan nodded. "I saw all the Insta updates. Your team did
a great job posting everything."

"I won't be truly happy until we get the numbers," Karl added,
ever the realist. He reached down to give Hudson a scratch behind the ears and the dog leaned into it. "But at face value, yes, it
was a solid launch. One down, fourteen more to go."

"Solid?" Eugene snorted. "He's such a pessimist. We sold out
of nearly everything. The faux bois mugs are hot." He tipped his
head back and drained the rest of his red wine. "Have you been
having a good time so far?"

"Yup." Morgan blushed unexpectedly and glanced between them. "Really good. I went surfing for the first time this morning."

And I have the bruises to prove it.

"Is that a fact?" Karl asked. "With whom?"

The blush intensified, as she thought about her quick kiss with Nathan in the water and again when he'd dropped her off.

"His name is Nathan. We're just hanging out, no big deal."

Eugene tapped Karl's arm. "That's code for something, right? Like Netflix and chill?"

"Oh yes, definitely young-person-speak." He nodded knowingly. "Do tell, Dr. Pearce."

Morgan ignored the clench in her stomach at hearing her title for the first time in weeks. "It's nothing, I swear. He's just a nice guy who sells fancy soda on Straight Wharf."

He's already more than that, stop lying.

"Oh, hold on," Karl said, snapping his fingers. "I think I know who you're talking about. That blond guy . . . What's his stuff called again?"

"Peachy."

"Yes, right. It's good! *Nantucket Magazine* did a story about him, and he's not just drop-dead gorgeous, he's got hustle too. Good work on that one."

Hustle? Mr. Laid-Back?

She'd meant to creep on him online, but part of her wanted to keep what was happening between them pure. If she got too deep into his background, she might discover that Tess was right about him and feel weird about the fact that she was going to keep hanging out with him anyway. And the truth was it didn't really matter what he was like out in the real world, what was happening between them was a no-strings vacation fling.

"How so?" Morgan tried to sound casual.

"He's trying to grow the drink business into something that's attractive to one of the big beverage companies," Karl answered, ever the voice for all things numbers related. "He didn't come out and say it in the article, but that's the impression I got."

"Huh."

It didn't make sense. Sure, Nathan seemed devoted to his business, and he'd developed a cool brand, but to Morgan it seemed like a small idea. She stifled a giggle as she tried to picture Nathan in a corporate boardroom, wooing potential buyers in flip-flops.

Morgan watched Eugene and Karl coo over Hudson and noticed Bernadette giving him side-eye from her perch on Karl's lap.

"I want to take Bernie for a walk, I feel like she needs some personal attention away from her new housemate." Morgan stood up and whistled for Hudson so she could give him a break in the pool house. He shot her a disappointed look from where he was sitting at Eugene's feet.

"You can leave him with us," Eugene said, massaging Hudson's ears. The dog's eyes closed in ecstasy. "I think I'm falling in love with this guy."

"And we're not going anywhere," Karl added. He pointed at the crowded tabletop beside him. "Wine? Check. Snacks? Check. Travel-induced inertia? Double check."

Morgan weighed the possible outcomes of leaving Hudson alone with them. Could they handle him if he got nervous? Would he try to chase after her? She watched them fuss over the dog and it hit her.

They could adopt Hudson!

It was perfect. Eugene and Karl's schedules would calm down by the end of the summer, which would perfectly coincide with the end of her time on Nantucket.

"Okay, I think he'll be fine hanging out with you. Just text me if anything gets weird."

"Take your time," Eugene answered as Hud swatted his hand for more pats. "We're good."

Bernadette sensed her boyfriend Palmer's presence before Morgan had a clue he was nearby. Their walk to town had been uneventful except for the little dog's tendency to stop and sniff every lamppost, railing, and mailbox. They started to cross Centre Street and Bernadette stopped in the middle of it with her nose twitching up in the air, ignoring the UPS truck barreling toward them. She used all twelve pounds to drag Morgan down the sidewalk to where Palmer was sprawled out in the shade next to an inn, sound asleep even though someone was using an edger nearby.

Morgan paused. She hadn't heard from Tess, and the fact that she'd avoided her at Cisco Brewers stung even though she'd probably been busy entertaining her friends.

But still. Not even a wave hello from a distance?

It felt weird, and Morgan was doing everything in her power to avoid weirdness while on Nantucket. Except for the fact that she was lying about her background, had been roped into fostering a dog, and was getting involved with a guy who may or may not be a player.

"We're going to keep walking, Bernie. Leave him alone, he's sleeping."

Morgan tried to move her along, but Bernadette planted her feet and barked impatiently at the brown lump in the distance. The sound was shrill enough to carry over the noise of the edger, and Palmer sat up with a jolt, then looked around in a daze.

"Shit," Morgan muttered, scanning the sidewalk for Tess. "Bernie, I'm not in the mood for awkward small talk."

She winced as she watched Palmer lumber to a stand and head down the sidewalk toward them. He was too young to look so old. She hoped Tess had gotten him in for an exam.

Bernadette danced on her back legs as he got closer and dropped to a play bow when he was a few feet away. Palmer did a halfhearted juke, then walked over to lower his shoulder next to her. She wagged her tail and did coquettish spins in front of him.

"Palmer, bud, it's not safe for you to wander like this," Morgan said to him when she realized that he wasn't on leash. "C'mon, let's go back."

She headed for the spot where he'd been resting, hoping that she wouldn't run into Tess, but the edger had turned off.

"Palmer?" her panicked voice called out. "Palmer?!"

"Don't worry, I've got him," Morgan yelled back as they got closer. "He wanted to see Bernadette."

Tess popped out from behind a hedge. "Oh, hey. Sorry about that, he knows better than to run up to people."

There was a coolness to her tone that confirmed Morgan's suspicion. Something had changed between them. Tess let herself out of the gated yard and narrowed her eyes at Palmer as they got closer.

"That was naughty, Palm."

"I guess Bernie's irresistible," Morgan answered, fiddling with the leash. "Didn't mean to interrupt, it looks like you're busy."

Tess nodded and frowned. "Two people called out today, so yeah, things are nuts, which is why I'm still working this late. The last thing I need is to worry about this guy."

"Understood. We'll get out of your way." Morgan bobbed her head. "Nice to see you." She waved and turned to walk away, feeling awkward.

Sometimes people are weird. Don't worry about it and move on.

"Hey, do you have a sec?" Tess's voice rang out behind Morgan.

She stopped walking and Bernadette took the opportunity to run back to where Palmer was standing.

"I do."

Tess let go of Palmer's collar and took off her gloves, then shoved them in the back pocket of her shorts.

"I saw you at Cisco the other night. With Nathan."

Uh-oh . . .

"Yeah, I met Cyrus while I was there," Morgan answered in her fake cheerful tone. "He seemed nice."

"I meant to come over and say hi, but the truth is, there's more to the Nathan stuff." She paused. "I didn't tell you everything about him."

Morgan's heart dropped, but she tried to keep her expression neutral.

"Okay . . ."

The jingling of dog tags filled the awkward silence.

"It feels stupid saying it out loud," Tess continued, popping her knuckles and fidgeting. "I mean, I'm embarrassed that it still bothers me, but I guess it does. It was so long ago." She sighed and looked down at the sidewalk. "When we were in high school he asked me out, then stood me up. See? Stupid."

The worry clawing at Morgan faded.

We all did stupid stuff in high school.

"Well, that was . . . shitty of him," she offered.

Tess shot her a sheepish look. "He probably doesn't even remember. *I* shouldn't remember, but it's one of those cringey teenage things that I can't get past. My whole school knew who he was because, well, he looked like that back in high school too. When he asked me out I told *everyone*. Dating someone from the rival school was Romeo and Juliet–level back then. It was a big deal. And then he didn't show."

"Okay, I get it." Morgan wrinkled her nose. "So, you never found out why? You guys didn't run into each other?"

She shook her head. "We didn't hang in the same circles." Tess barked out a laugh. "I guess my grudges last longer than I realized. But I heard I wasn't the only girl he did it to, so I just assumed he was a dick. It caught me off guard when Cyrus said you were at Cisco with him."

"Yeah, that makes sense. But he seems different now, if that helps." Morgan studied Tess, trying to gauge if her feelings for Nathan hovered in unrequited territory. "I mean, the guy volunteers with kids."

Palmer rolled onto his back and let Bernadette nip at his ears.

"Yeah, it was a million years ago. I'm sure he grew up. Hey, I was a little goth girl in high school who never set a foot outside. Look at me now." She laughed and gestured to her dirt-streaked T-shirt.

And I was exactly the same from grade school to vet school. Most likely to succeed.

"Anyway, I hope we can hang out again. I think these two would be bummed if we didn't." Tess pointed at the dog scrum.

"Of course, I'd love that. Let's do it soon," Morgan replied, feeling a little weird about what she'd learned about Nathan. "I should let you get back to work. But I'm glad we talked."

"Same." Tess started to walk away but stopped abruptly. "Oh, I forgot to tell you! I took your advice and Palmer has an appointment for X-rays. My vet agrees it's probably hip dysplasia, though. Thanks for noticing it."

Morgan felt a wave of relief wash through her. The surgery and recovery process wasn't going to be easy for either end of the leash, but Palmer would be a changed dog after it.

"Happy I could help."

This was why she got into veterinary medicine. To make life better for animals.

She made a kissy noise and Bernadette reluctantly untangled herself from Palmer.

chapter eighteen

T he choices were overwhelming.

It was her third scouting trip into town in as many weeks, specifically to decide on a keepsake option. The T-shirts and hoodies she was accumulating were fine, but she wanted something special that would bring her back every time she looked at it.

A talisman. A touchstone. A reminder of when life was as sweet and easy as jelly on toast.

It seemed like every boutique had its own endless selection of Nantucket-themed jewelry, from diamond-studded outlines of the island on gold to simple silver bangles stamped with the island's coordinates. The more options Morgan saw, the tougher the decision became.

Bernadette was always a willing copilot for excursions into town, and nearly every store was dog friendly. She hoped that eventually Hudson would feel confident at the far edges of town, if not the bustling center.

Morgan stopped into an ivy-covered shop off the main drag called Mercy Mercantile and quickly realized that if a candle

from the store could set her back sixty-five dollars, she was un-
likely to find a bracelet or necklace within her budget. She was
heading out when someone called her name.

"Morgan and Bernadette! Over here." Sydney peeked out
from behind a rolling rack of earth-tone dresses and waved at
her. "Big gala dress decision going on." She pointed behind her
and rolled her eyes.

"Ooh, can I see?"

Morgan walked to where Sydney was standing and stopped
short when she saw Abby scrutinizing a dress laid out on the
counter.

Oh shit.

But it was too late. She was spotted. Abby managed a tight
smile while she eyed Morgan like she was a Miss Corn Husk-
ers contestant who'd accidentally bumbled her way into Miss
America.

"Sorry," Sydney said to Morgan under her breath as she
stooped to pet Bernadette.

They walked over to the counter where Abby and a pretty
brunette were hovering over a pool of fabric that dripped off the
edge of the counter.

"Why don't we let Morgan vote on it too?" Sydney asked in
an overly cheerful voice.

"Oh, perfect, we can always use an *outsider's* perspective,"
Abby said.

Morgan ignored the jab and focused on the dress, a whisper-
thin pale pink silk confection with dustings of tiny iridescent
paillettes on the bottom that looked like pixie dust.

"Wow, I love it," Morgan said, reaching out to touch the delicate fabric.

Abby cleared her throat in a way that made it obvious she was annoyed that Morgan was there. "It's really pretty, yes, but I wanted more of a statement piece. Morgan, do you actually know anything about fashion, or do you only care about dogs?"

Morgan looked down at the emerald-green-romper she'd worn that she'd *thought* was cute until Abby managed to dismiss it with a drag queen's precision.

"You know, I don't, actually," she answered, giving Abby her fakest smile. "Sorry, I'm just a dog babysitter." She shrugged apologetically, then winked at Sydney, who looked mortified.

"Well, that settles it then. We won't be going with this one after all," Abby said, pushing the pile of fabric toward the woman behind the counter. "Let's move on to our other options."

"She's *pissed*," Sydney whispered once they were out on the sidewalk watching Abby walk away.

Morgan frowned. "Why? She got what she wanted."

"No, I didn't tell you we vetoed the barking lot and we're not allowing guests' dogs at the event! Everyone came together at the very last second and rallied to skip it based on your recommendation. We literally had to call the printer and do a stop-the-presses on the invitations."

Morgan's mouth dropped open in shock. "So, I'm off the hook? I don't have to fight with Abby about it?"

"Nope, and you don't have to be a dog cop either," Sydney replied. "We never considered that it could've been a PR nightmare. Plus, we don't want people to get distracted from opening their wallets."

"Well, guess I need to steer clear of Abby during the event."

"Trust me, you'll be plenty busy dealing with all the dogs backstage." Sydney looked at her phone. "Evan's at adventure school until two, wanna grab lunch?"

"But what about . . ." Morgan pointed at Bernadette, who was fixated on a shaggy dog heading toward them.

"Outdoor seating is dog friendly. *Everywhere* is dog friendly here, you should know that by now," Sydney teased. "Don't make me beg, let's have lunch. I'll take you somewhere touristy for a lobster roll, it'll be fun."

"You said the magic words: lobster roll. I still haven't had one," Morgan replied. "I'm in."

They threaded through the crowds on the uneven brick sidewalk and stopped at the restaurant that opened into Harbor Square near Straight Wharf, where groups of people sat waiting for the fast ferry with rolling suitcases and glum expressions. Morgan peered beyond them and spotted Nathan's umbrella.

So close, but so far away.

She realized that it was going to be hard to eat knowing he was just a quick walk down the dock.

"It doesn't get much more touristy than the Tavern, but I'm starving, and you need to hit all of the tourist traps to get the full experience," Sydney said as she led Morgan to the host stand.

He brought them to a prime corner table, where there was enough room for Bernadette to settle underneath on the little roll-up mat Morgan had in her bag. It was the perfect spot for people watching, plus Morgan had a line-drive view of Nathan's cart. She could see his tall outline every time the crowds parted.

"What's down there? What are you looking at?" Sydney asked, leaning forward to follow Morgan's sight line. "Ohhh, *him.* The drink dude. Yeah, he's been the talk of the town since he got here."

Morgan played dumb. "How so?"

"Have you seen him up close? He's hot!"

She blushed and grinned. "He's teaching me to surf. We've been hanging out."

"Seriously?" Sydney's eyes went wide. "Well, well. Look at you!"

"I'm just having fun." She shrugged, staring at the menu and still smiling.

"I'm happy you've got a little diversion," Sydney replied, rearranging the condiments on the side of the table. "It's not my place to say anything, but based on what you told me at my house, you could use some fun. It's a good first step for getting past . . . your rough stuff."

Morgan froze. She'd forgotten she'd been so candid with Sydney. After the conversation, she'd done what she always did with things that made her hurt or feel uncomfortable: boxed up the conversation and shoved it away.

"Oh, it's okay. I'm fine," she replied quickly as a dull pain started to throb in her chest. Was she too young for a heart attack? Morgan looked around for the waiter to derail the conversation.

"Mm-hmm," Sydney replied, not sounding at all convinced as her eyes jumped from the menu to her face. "We're all works in progress, there's no shame in that. I can tell you're a striver, Morgan. I bet you work hard to keep your shit together."

"Don't we all?" Morgan asked with a hollow laugh, running her finger down the condensation on her water glass as stress started to bubble up inside her.

"Well, we all *try*, but not all of us succeed. Take me, for example. I have a problem with negative self-talk, and I can really beat myself up if I don't stay ahead of it. Any time I find myself slipping into 'you' talk I hit pause."

Sydney studied Morgan as if she was gauging how the comment landed.

Okay, okay. Fine, I'll bite.

"What's that?" Morgan asked.

Sydney leaned closer. "If we use the word 'you' when we talk to ourselves it can sound accusatory, like we're standing outside ourselves and judging. I picture my negative 'you' voice like a miniature version of me on my shoulder wagging a finger at me. She says blame-y stuff like 'You're a shitty mom' or 'You're so forgetful.' Obviously it's not helpful."

Morgan paused to consider her own inner voice. "What if it's both 'you' and 'I'?"

"That's normal," Sydney nodded. "My point is we need to be aware of which voice is louder. If it's the judgy one, it's worthwhile diving into why that is and doing some work to recalibrate."

The waiter interrupted them before Morgan had a chance to start dissecting who had the upper hand in her head.

Sydney leaned closer to Morgan and lowered her voice. "I know I'm repeating myself, but any time you want to talk, just let me know. Nothing official, of course. Just consider me a good listener."

The way Sydney was pushing Morgan to open up was embarrassing. "Do I seem like . . . I don't know, broken or something? Is that why you're offering?"

Sydney's face fell. "Oh my God, *no*! Not at all, and I didn't mean to imply that. You seem incredibly strong, Morgan. But you said you were going through something, and I know first-hand how hard it can be for strong people to work their way through stuff." She paused. "Sometimes powering through isn't the best option, you know?"

The comment nearly cracked her open.

Morgan felt embarrassingly transparent, like everything she thought she'd been camouflaging was written on her body for Sydney to read. But she also felt . . . *seen*. It was the first time in a long time that someone had tuned in to her enough to pick up on what was simmering just below the surface. The fact that Sydney barely knew her spoke to her powers of observation. Morgan was shocked that the woman had managed to figure her out in just a few quick meetings.

But then again, it's her job. Just like I can diagnose hip dyspla-sia and an ear infection on the fly.

The thought of confiding in Sydney felt safe. In a few weeks she'd be gone, and they'd never see each other again. Maybe clearing out some of the trauma luggage she kept storing away would help her get ready to go back to the daily grind?

She glanced around the restaurant as her heart raced. She had two hurdles to clear before she started unpacking: first, swearing Sydney to silence about what she did for a living, and second, admitting . . . admitting *what*? Just how deep did she want to go into her shaky mental state sitting in an outdoor restaurant with a beer sweating on the table in front of her?

Sydney reached out and gave Morgan's hand a quick squeeze, which made her realize that her inner conflict was probably oozing out of her. Again.

"Hey, no pressure, okay? We can gossip about Abby instead."

Morgan shook her head. "No, actually there's something I want to tell you. A few things. But you have to promise to keep it between us, okay?"

"Of course. *Nothing* will go beyond this table, you have my word."

The way she said it, with such care in her voice and concern in her eyes, made Morgan realize that talking to Sydney would be . . . okay.

"You know how I said I'm a dog walker?"

Sydney nodded.

"Well, that's not exactly true."

chapter nineteen

Therapy?
   Like, real, in-an-office therapy?

Morgan had intended to walk down to see Nathan after lunch with a belly full of lobster roll and a healthy buzz, but instead her head was spinning with cold hard truths.

When Morgan had finally revealed that she was a veterinarian, Sydney looked like everything was snapping into place, like a detective who'd just puzzled out the last clue in a tough case. She'd immediately rattled off stats about Morgan's job, like the punishing hours, the crippling debt-to-income ratio, and work-life balance issues, saying her sessions with physicians had given her insight into what veterinarians go through as well.

"I want you to make it official," Sydney had said to Morgan, worry creasing her face. "You need to talk to a neutral person. Support from friends and family isn't enough, you need a safe space to work through everything."

"Neutral person" means therapist.

Morgan hated the thought of it. Her time away was supposed to be enough to reset her. Then once she got home, all she had to do was work a little harder and a little smarter and she'd be fine.

Sydney had given her a phone number of someone she knew on island, a licensed clinical social worker who she thought would be a good fit. There was almost pleading in her voice when she told Morgan to reach out to the woman.

"We both know the statistics, Morgan, but I'll say it anyway: veterinarians are more likely to die by suicide than the general population."

Talking about it with Sydney had made it all so . . . real. It was one of the most uncomfortable conversations Morgan had ever had, because Sydney knew enough to call her on her bullshit. Nantucket was nothing more than a Band-Aid. A beautiful, sunny, romantic temporary fix that wouldn't be enough to keep her from eventually crashing again.

Bernadette stopped to pee next to a signpost, and Morgan finally refocused on the world around her instead of the hurricane in her head. She was still far enough away from Nathan's cart to spy, so she paused to watch him do his thing from the cover of a crowd of senior citizens in matching red T-shirts.

He was talking to a woman who looked pretty, even at a distance. Morgan squinted. She was wearing oversized black sunglasses and minuscule khaki shorts, and she kept smiling and touching him on the arm. Every time Morgan saw Nathan laugh or make the woman giggle at him, she felt something black bubble up inside her.

Jealousy. Down, girl.

The ferry crowd started depositing their suitcases on the luggage carts and lining up to board, and Morgan realized that she was exposed. All it would take was for Nathan to finally pry his eyes away from the MILF goddess and glance down the side-walk to see her, but it seemed impossible for him to do it.

He was *flirting* and it was obvious even at a distance.

"Whatever," Morgan muttered under her breath to Berna-dette, feeling even bleaker. "We're out of here. Let's go."

She chewed on what she'd just witnessed as she walked away. Maybe she'd been wrong about Nathan, and Tess was right? Was it possible that he was still a player and hiding it from her?

But you said it didn't matter.

She stayed close to the little freestanding shops that lined the sidewalk as she headed back toward Main Street, peeking between them to watch the people coming back from fishing charters and cleaning the catch of the day on tables at the edge of the dock. Maybe she needed to try fishing before she left?

"Morgan!"

Nathan's voice rang out so loudly that she instinctively cringed. The *last* thing she needed was to have to fake her way through a smiley conversation.

She turned around and saw that Nathan was staring at her, and the woman had left. Morgan realized how stupid it would look to continue walking away, so she reluctantly headed over to Nathan's cart.

"Hey. I wasn't expecting to see you today." Nathan squatted to greet Bernadette and beamed up at her as if he hadn't just been flirting with someone.

I bet you weren't.

"Bernadette insisted on it," Morgan replied, gesturing to the little dog with a shrug as if she had no control of the situation and would've opted out if given a choice.

"I always knew she was a smart dog."

Morgan fought the question forming in her mouth, which was aided by three comfort beers, but spat it out before she could stop herself. "Who was that you were talking to?"

"Sarah?" He tipped his head and gestured over his shoulder. "She's the mom of one of my surfers. It took a few seconds before we could place each other. I loved her kid, total daredevil. She's here with her husband celebrating their tenth anniversary."

Morgan shrank down a few vertebrae. "Wow, small world."

"It totally is." He paused a beat and his eyes skimmed over her. "You look amazing, by the way. I'm happy to see that green is your color."

"Why is that?"

A couple walked over and stood in between them, reading the sign on the side of his cart, forcing a pause in their conversation.

"Hey, folks, let me know if you have any questions or if you want a sample." Nathan gave them his full attention and high-wattage smile before turning back to Morgan. "Tomorrow morning looks perfect for surf lesson number two. You still in?"

"One hundred percent. I've been watching video tutorials and visualizing the process, so I think you might be surprised by my hanging of ten."

Nathan laughed at her. "You really are an overachiever, aren't you?"

She shrugged. "If the resources are there, why not use them? I like learning stuff."

The couple started debating the merits of Great Fruit over Watermelon Mint.

"I better let you work," Morgan said, sliding her eyes toward them.

Nathan nodded. "Before you go, I have a present for you."

He walked to the basket on the front of the bike, pulled out a small rumpled black shopping bag, and held it out to her with a proud smile. Bernadette did a few halfhearted jumps as if she thought that it was something for her, and settled in the shade next to the cart when she realized that it wasn't food.

Morgan squinted at him as she took the bag, her heart thumping wildly at the unexpected gesture. "What? A *present*?"

"It's nothing, honestly. It's more of a necessity than a present. Seriously, it's not a big deal." He shuffled and looked down at his flip-flops, then ran his hand through his messy but still adorable hair.

The bag had a sticker on it that said "Hover" in a simple silver font, bisected by a surfboard. She peeked inside, then pulled out a ball of apple-green fabric and let it unfurl.

"A rash guard, just for you," he said proudly as she held it up. "So you don't have to borrow one of mine tomorrow. You'll be more comfortable in something that actually fits you. And I thought the color would look great on you." He ducked his head after he said it, as if picking colors was something to be embarrassed about.

The shirt could've been puddle-brown and she still would've loved it. And the fact that Nathan was worried about her comfort made it a sweeter gesture than a bouquet of roses.

"Thank you!" Morgan said, unable to put her gratitude into something more eloquent.

She stood on her tiptoes to give him a quick kiss on the cheek while the people bickered about whether they should share or get their own bottles, and he turned his head so that her mouth landed on his lips instead. In the bright sunlight and surrounded by people, Nathan had just taken their summer fling to the next level.

It's middle-of-the-day PDA-official now.

Morgan held on to the kiss, keeping her lips pressed to Nathan's until she could feel the weight of two sets of eyes on them.

"Excuse me, can we get some of the watermelon stuff?" the man asked in a snappish voice. "We got a ferry to catch."

"Sorry, of course you can," Nathan said, jumping away from Morgan like she'd scalded him. Once they were rung up and blissing out on his concoction, Nathan turned back to her.

"Just a heads-up, I'm dealing with some pineapple co-packer stuff and there's a slight chance I might have to postpone our surf date tomorrow. I'll know more at the end of the day."

Morgan was about to ask him what a co-packer was when her phone sounded off in her bag.

"My brother, gracing me with a call. Excuse me for a sec," Morgan said, a mix of excitement and nerves that their weekend together was getting closer.

"Tell my best-friend-to-be that I say 'howdy,'" he called after her.

Morgan laughed as she headed for the narrow strip of dock facing the boat slips.

"Hey."

"Hey," he replied. "You haven't answered any of my texts about visiting, so I thought I'd try calling for a change."

She frowned. "What are you talking about? I didn't get any texts." Morgan felt her blood pressure rising just from the tone in his voice. It was typical for Mack to "forget" to plan and then find a way to blame any resulting problems on someone else.

"Whatever, it's cool. Anyway, Elle and I have a date I wanted to run by you."

Morgan paced on the dock by the charter fishing boats with Bernadette high-stepping along, dodging the day-trippers. She waited for him to keep talking, but the silence broke her first. "Okay, what is it?"

"The weekend of the twenty-eighth. It's basically the only one that works for both of us, so I hope it's doable on your end."

Of all of the weekends, he had to pick the same one as the gala. She opened her mouth to try to negotiate another date or opt out of the trip altogether but realized that it felt like their one chance to make things right, or at least to make things righter than they had been for years. And it wasn't like the fundraiser would take up her whole weekend; she'd have plenty of time to entertain them. Hell, they'd probably want to go to the event considering the type of people attending.

"I have a volunteer event that Saturday night, a fund-raiser for the local animal rescue. If you don't mind going to it, then that weekend works for me. Or you two can do your own thing that night. Whatever you want."

"Dope, I'm always down to throw some money at homeless dogs. Done. Did you get a chance to find some inns for us?"

Do I look like your personal assistant?

She sighed and parked herself on a bench. Bernadette plopped down in the shade beneath it.

"I really don't think you have to do that. I told you there's plenty of space where I'm staying. The owners are fine with you guys being there, they're used to having tons of visitors. They *literally* wrote the book on entertaining, you'll be very comfortable."

"Really?"

"Really. I can send you photos of the room choices if that'll help convince you. Or you can check the feature they did in *Architectural Digest* a few years ago, your choice."

"Damn. Well, okay then. Sounds great."

It was still hard for her to believe that they were organizing a visit. They hadn't hung out without their parents in forever.

"Check the ferry schedule and let me know what time you think you'll get here. And don't forget to factor in traffic on the way to Hyannis, because the entire state of Connecticut is always a mess. Make sure to take the Steamship Authority ferry, it's a great way to start your trip," she said, echoing the advice she'd gotten from Eugene.

"Yeah, that's not happening." Mack laughed dismissively. "We're flying in. We looked into driving and taking the ferry and it takes too long."

Morgan's shoulders slumped. It was like Mack to choose the destination over the journey. She'd hoped that he'd have the same experience that she did, the slow unfurling of tension as the lighthouse came into view in the distance. The understanding that the spot they were heading toward was unlike anyplace else. Instead, Mack and Elle were going to go from airport to airport quickly and efficiently without any sort of emotional downshift into vacation mode.

"That's fine," she answered, trying to keep the frustration out of her voice. "Keep me posted on your arrival time."

She started to say she was looking forward to his visit but stopped short. Morgan had the sneaking suspicion that the visit was less about mending fences and more about Mack showing off.

The line went silent for a beat.

"Will do." Mack paused. "You know what? I can't wait to see you, Morgie. Been too long."

A tiny chunk of her anger broke away.

No matter how much had changed between them and how different they'd become, they were blood. They owed it to each other to at least try to find their way back to a version of what they used to be, especially with a wedding on the horizon. Morgan wanted to start things off on the right foot with her sister-in-law-to-be. Even if she couldn't find her way with Mack, at least she could build a bridge with Elle.

Morgan felt a little weepy, no doubt partially due to all the beer and heavy conversation at lunch. "Me too, Mackie."

She hung up and felt a tickle in her nose, and the faintest glimmer of hope, which was enough to propel her to do the thing that she never thought she'd want to do. Morgan looked around to make sure no one was close to her, scrolled to the text Sydney had sent her with the phone number, and dialed before she could second-guess herself.

chapter twenty

It was the earliest Morgan had been up since arriving on Nantucket. Despite being awake with the roosters at home, it was like her body had undergone a time zone shift the moment the ferry left the dock in Hyannis. Setting her alarm to meet Tess and Palmer for a seven a.m. walk on the beach felt ridiculous.

The lack of hills or cobblestones made the three-mile bike ride to Dionis Beach easier than she'd expected. Her body was slowly adjusting to the twinges and aches that came along with riding everywhere around the island, to the point where she considered buying a bike when she got home. It was a hopeful thought, the idea that she'd have the time and inclination to ride it.

Bernadette had also gotten used to spending more time in the basket on the handlebars with the wind in her fur. She was blossoming in ways Morgan hadn't anticipated, making it clear that she enjoyed her new life *off* the leash. She made sure to send photos to Eugene and Karl of all of the adventures they were having, hoping that they were getting the hint that the little dog was a badass who could hold her own no matter where they went or who they met. She hoped that in time, Hudson would be able to do the same.

Morgan was happy for the morning diversion. Nathan had been called away to deal with his co-packing issue after all and was spending the night at home in New Jersey, so she was doing everything possible to fill the day before it was time for . . . it.

The appointment.

Tess was just unloading Palmer from their Subaru as Morgan rode up to the parking area. She was surprised to see Cyrus come around the side of the car, looking scruffy-handsome in a hoodie, board shorts, and baseball cap. They were both in similar colors, khaki on the bottom and navy on top, in the adorable accidental twinning way that long-term couples seemed to adopt.

"He's crashing our party," Tess said to her, pointing at Cyrus.

"The more the merrier," Morgan said, taking a quivering Bernadette out of the basket so she could run over to greet her massive brown boyfriend.

They made their way down the path between the seagrass-covered dunes, and Morgan could see the vast expanse of blue in the distance. She felt a twinge that she wasn't with Nathan, but she pushed thoughts of him out of her head and tried to be in the moment. There was still plenty of time to be with him.

Palmer led the way, doing his usual loping walk-jog down the path, with Bernadette at his side taking five running steps for every one of his. The big dog was off leash, but Morgan wasn't willing to take the risk with Bernadette, so Bernie had to deal with fake freedom on a thin fifteen-foot leash.

"Perfect day," Cyrus said as they stepped onto the beach. He kicked off his sneakers and Morgan followed his lead.

She closed her eyes and inhaled the sea air and dug her toes into the sand. She let the sound of the pounding surf lull her for a few seconds.

Am I turning into a beach person?

She opened her eyes reluctantly and scanned the shoreline, realizing that they were alone except for a man walking with a black Lab in the distance.

Beaches at home were always crowded with bodies and vibrating with energy and sound. There was nothing relaxing about a day at the Jersey Shore. Morgan hadn't visited a Nantucket beach at midday yet, but she couldn't imagine that they'd match the towel-to-towel chaos of beaches in her adopted home state.

Morgan noticed that the dog was off leash and way ahead of the guy, and she instinctively tensed up as it ran toward where they were standing. Bernadette kept her eye on the dog as well, but Palmer was oblivious, sniffing something invisible in the sand.

As the dog got closer, Morgan saw that he was carrying a piece of driftwood like it was a trophy, head up at an awkward angle to compensate for the weight of it. It was a beautiful black Lab, its coat wet with salt water. She relaxed when she realized that the dog hadn't even noticed they were there, so focused on the joy of kicking up sand that nothing else mattered. It was the essence of dog happiness distilled to a moment, and Morgan's heart pinched when she realized it was a pleasure that Hudson couldn't experience.

Yet. Someday he's going to be able to race down the beach with wet fur and a smile on his face, carrying a piece of driftwood with a buddy like they're running a relay race.

The man followed behind the dog and waved at them.

When he was a safe distance down the beach they started toward the water.

"Does she swim?" Cyrus asked, pointing at Bernadette.

Morgan considered it. "I'm not sure, but I'm thinking no. Eugene and Karl have a pool that she avoids, and I can guarantee they don't take her to the beach."

"Well, this is a good spot to test it out," Tess answered as she zipped her hoodie up. "Water's nice and calm."

They headed down the narrow strip of beach to the rocky sand at the water's edge. Palmer didn't hesitate to walk in, grinning back at them as he waded. Bernadette watched him forlornly from the sand.

"Probably feels good," Morgan mused as Palmer started swimming. "Less load on the joints, plus swimming can improve his gait as he recovers from surgery."

Whoa, back off on the diagnostics.

She was enjoying the purity of the new friendship with Tess, and now Cyrus. She didn't have to worry that the only reason they were hanging out with her was to pick her brain about Palmer's surgery and recovery. She could offer advice when she wanted, not on demand.

"That's right, Tess told me you picked up on his hip dysplasia," Cyrus said, watching Palmer. "We really appreciate that you figured it out. How do you know so much about dogs?"

Morgan bit the inside of her cheek.

Damn it.

"I guess dogs are just my thing," she said, smiling and shrugging like a Disney Channel teen.

Bernadette scolded Palmer from the shore and ran up to the water as if she was ready to swim out to him. A lazy wave rolled in and touched her paws, causing her to run backward like it was lava.

Foamy, mushy waves.

It wasn't like Morgan knew anything about surfing other than what she'd learned during her brief lesson with Nathan and the few instructional videos she'd watched, but she could tell that the gentle rolls heading to the shore would be perfect for her initial pop-up lessons. She still couldn't believe that her mistrust of the ocean had transformed within a span of thirty minutes thanks to Nathan. Not like she wanted to take up scuba diving or anything, but at least she wasn't petrified of going under.

"How's Nathan?" Tess asked, as if reading Morgan's thoughts.

"You talking about Nathan the juice dude?" Cyrus asked.

"It's Nathan the *functional beverage* guy," Morgan said with a smile. "There's a difference."

"Morgan's been hanging out with him," Tess continued.

"He's good," she answered. "He's back in New Jersey dealing with some pineapple issue. He'll be back tomorrow."

"I like him," Cyrus mused. "He came to the farm to talk about sourcing strawberries from us. Turns out it's not feasible for him, but at least he tried. Did Tess tell you he broke her teenage heart and she still isn't over it?"

He crashed his shoulder into Tess as they walked.

"Would you stop it!" Tess smacked him with the droopy sleeve of her sweatshirt. "It's ancient history."

They walked in silence as a surprise gust of wind buffeted

them. Bernadette put her head back and closed her eyes, inhaling the new scents in the air.

Palmer trotted out of the water and headed up the sand toward them. Bernadette ran over to him, barking a frenzied greeting as if he was her sailor truelove coming home from a voyage. Morgan could almost see the wheels turning in Bernadette's head as she watched him. He took a few more steps toward the surf, then play bowed an invitation for her to follow.

"You can do it, Bernie," Morgan encouraged. "I'll walk to the water with you."

"You're a brave pup," Tess called to Bernadette. "And don't worry, Palmer's part Newf. He can save you if you start to drown."

Morgan let Bernadette lead the way down to the water's edge, murmuring encouragement and praise as she edged closer. Palmer waited patiently in the water, his belly fur dripping each time the waves receded.

The little dog looked up at Morgan.

"Your choice, my friend," she said. "No pressure. Swim, don't swim, it's all good."

Palmer barked his encouragement, and it seemed to do the trick. Bernadette paused and waited for a moment when the water was calm, then ventured in so her paws were covered. Once she seemed to realize that the water wasn't so scary after all, she waded out until she was belly deep.

Tess and Cyrus clapped and cheered from the beach as Palmer bounded over to her.

"You did it!" Morgan exclaimed. "See? It's fun!"

The two dogs sprinted through the water together, their joy as bright as the sunshine.

. . .

"The hard part is over, Morgan," Cynthia Fielder said, placing her pen down on top of her notepad. "You found the courage to make the call and you got yourself here. *That's* when your therapy began, when you picked up the phone. I think it's wonderful."

Morgan fidgeted in her chair as a combination of pride and embarrassment tripped through her. "Thank you."

Twenty-four hours prior, she never would've imagined that she'd be sitting in a cozy office mapping out her vital stats to a stranger. When Cynthia had opened the door to welcome her into the bright, plant-filled space, Morgan had felt the jarring sensation that she knew her from somewhere. For the first ten minutes of the session, she kept trying to place the woman until it hit her: Meryl Streep. Cynthia had the same light hair, delicate bone structure, and elegant nose as the actress, and it instantly put Morgan at ease.

Who doesn't love Meryl Streep?

"Believe it or not, we're finished for today," she continued in a comforting tone.

Morgan looked around the office with wide eyes, trying to spot a clock since her phone was turned off and buried in her purse. "No way. Really? That was easy!"

"Glad to hear it," Cynthia said with a beatific Meryl-y smile. "I want to be honest with you, though. It's not always like this. We have a lot to cover, and some of it will feel uncomfortable for you. The first session is about getting your history; next time we'll start going a little deeper."

The thought of "going deeper" was like a record scratch in

her head. Then it dawned on her: therapy was a trap. You sit down on a comfy couch and talk about your parents' happy marriage, and who's the older sibling, like you're chatting with someone at a party who's curious about you, and the next thing you know you're being forced to relive the time you lost a dog due to septic abdomen.

"Now as for the next session," Cynthia continued. "You mentioned that you've got a couple of four-legged friends with you for the summer. Would you like to bring one of them along?"

"Really?"

"Of course. I don't have a dog at the moment, so I get my fix here in the office." She smiled mischievously and pulled her relaxed cream cardigan tighter across her chest. "No pressure, I just wanted to put it out there."

"Yeah, maybe I will. It'll be a chance to expose Hudson to a new environment."

Morgan hoped that she wouldn't end up crying with the dog in the office, since he'd step up to provide his own form of therapy.

"I don't give much homework as a rule," Cynthia said, "but I do have a simple assignment for you as we begin our journey." She fixed her gaze on Morgan. "Tell me, what's the one thing that makes you lose yourself? I'm talking about an activity where time doesn't seem to exist."

"Non-work-related?"

The corner of Cynthia's mouth turned up in a gentle smirk. "Obviously."

"Then, surfing. I'm brand new at it but it's like nothing I've ever done. It's . . . magical."

And the guy teaching me how to do it was pretty damn magical too.

"Okay, so your homework is go surfing and bliss out, at least once. Put *all* your focus on that, and let everything else fall away. Can you make that happen?"

"Definitely."

Surfing and bringing a dog along is therapy? I'm gonna ace this.

chapter twenty-one

Mack said he was going to talk to you about specific dates for his visit. Has he called you recently?"

Morgan was on the phone with her mom, sitting on the couch in the pool house with the glass doors wide open, watching raindrops ripple the pool water. Hudson was taking up space on the couch next to her, stretched out like he was the rightful owner, and Bernadette was dozing on the ottoman across from them. The drizzly, moody afternoon, combined with the aftershocks of going to her first therapy appointment, had her feeling melancholy, and hearing her mom's voice only intensified it.

"Yup, we've got a date nailed down."

Hudson adjusted his position so that his head was resting on Morgan's feet.

"Oh, honey, that makes me so happy. You're going to have a wonderful time together. And you're going to love Elle. What a fun trio you'll be!"

"Well, actually . . . I've sort of been hanging out with a guy, so maybe we'll be a foursome," Morgan finally admitted, plucking at the edge of her Nantucket-red T-shirt.

"Well, that's nice, but I hope you're not taking on too much," her mother said in the quiet, concerned voice that usually signaled a pending pep talk. "You need to look out for you, do you hear me? Don't get all wrapped up in some guy and forget about why you're there," she scolded gently.

As if I could.

"I'm okay, Mom. Just being away from the practice for a little while is helping. But I do miss it." She paused. "Well, most of it."

"I'm already worried about your *reentry*," her mother said. "How are you going to cope once you get back? Have you thought about it? Because I won't have you go through . . . *that* . . . again."

In all of their conversations since she'd fainted at work, her parents had never given a real name to what had happened to Morgan. It was an "episode," a "touch of anxiety," a "rough patch." Morgan herself wasn't quite sure what to call it when she allowed her thoughts to wander close to that day. It wasn't that anyone wanted to minimize the severity of what she'd been through, but the act of naming it would make it . . . *big*. Something to be treated.

Which is exactly what I'm doing.

She debated telling her mom that she'd seen a therapist. Morgan knew she'd be thrilled, but telling her would trigger a drawn-out conversation about the mechanics of "fixing" her, and how quickly it could happen.

"I'm going to do yoga more often, that's for sure," she lied. "And get to bed earlier. Eat better. You know, that sort of stuff."

"Okay, good, honey." Her mom's relief practically oozed through the phone. All she wanted was for her children to be happy and healthy. "That's wonderful. I like to hear that you're making concrete plans."

The line went quiet as they both tried to come up with acceptable topics of conversation after raising the specter of her breakdown.

"Are you having fun, honey?"

It seemed like a simple question, but it was clear that Jean wasn't ready to move on from Morgan's mental state. She smiled into the phone.

"I am, Mom. I really am. Each day is better than the one before."

The text woke Morgan from her post-pasta, pre-bed nap on the couch. She'd made a quick dinner for herself in the kitchenette, and the dirty bowl sat on the coffee table next to the untouched novel she'd bought at Mitchell's Book Corner. As much as she wanted to read, it had been impossible to resist the draw of a nap under the light-weave blanket with the soundtrack of the rain outside. Hudson made a groany noise at her feet as she reached for the phone.

Hey, I'm back early, the text from Nathan read. I know it's last minute, but do you wanna frappe tonight?

Her happiness at the unexpected text from Nathan turned to confusion. Morgan quickly ran through her mental Urban Dictionary trying to figure out what he meant by "frappe." It sounded nasty. Was Tess right about him after all? Would a dick pic follow?

Welcome back! Not sure what you mean.

She frowned at her phone as she waited for his response.

You haven't had a frappe from the pharmacy yet?
That changes tonight. Want me to pick you up?

Pharmacy?

Still not following.

Forgot you're a newbie. It's a milkshake from the
Nantucket Pharmacy. They serve food. Best
grilled cheese around if you want dinner.

Morgan breathed a sigh of relief. Nantucket's quirks revealed themselves slowly, from the roadside, postage-stamp homes that cost over a million dollars, to the woven baskets that did double duty as purses, to a Main Street pharmacy that filled prescriptions and served grilled cheese sandwiches too.

I'm in. The rain stopped, so I can walk there to
meet you.

Great. See you in 30?

Morgan turned on her camera and snorted when she saw her reflection. She had pillow creases pressed into the side of her face and her hair hung down in stringy tendrils.

Yup! she texted back.

A pit-crew-style overhaul, potty break for Hudson, and speed-walk to town later, and Morgan was more than ready for a milkshake. She rounded the corner onto Main expecting to find the usual crowds, but the misty weather seemed to be keeping most people at home. She felt a smile spread across her face when she spied Nathan sitting on a bench in front of the pharmacy, reaching down to pet a beagle-esque dog leashed to a nearby streetlamp. He was in a white T-shirt, rolled-up ripped jeans that looked like they'd been through the laundry a million times, and his usual flip-flops.

She watched him pet the dog gently and murmur to it. They were equally focused on each other and nothing else around them seemed to matter. Morgan knew that unattended leashed dogs could be dicey, since most of them were nervous about being left alone. They usually preferred to be ignored by passing strangers so they could stress out and look for their people, but as he leaned into Nathan, she could tell this dog was an exception.

Or it could be that he's got the magic touch.

"Looks like you made a friend," she said, plopping on the bench next to him. She scanned the panting dog quickly.

Middle-aged, slightly overweight, some tartar buildup, but in good shape overall.

"Hey there," he exclaimed, sounding like she'd startled him. "Hi!"

"Hi back," Morgan answered shyly as she soaked up his approving gaze.

The flicker in his eyes still shocked her. It was a split-second microexpression of appreciation, a nonverbal *Damn, girl* that made her feel like a goddess even though she hadn't washed her hair in two days.

Nathan leaned over and gave her a quick kiss like it was their standard greeting. Like they were a *couple* couple.

"You ready for something delicious?"

Her eyes landed on his mouth.

Yes, I'd definitely like another taste.

"I never say no to dessert," she managed.

He nodded and gave the dog one last scratch under the chin. "Bye, Brando. See ya later."

"Do you know all of the dogs on Nantucket?" Morgan laughed as they headed for the pharmacy.

"Most. No, hold on. Since I met Hudson, I can safely say that, yes, I know *all* of the dogs on Nantucket. Every last one of 'em." He held the screen door open for her. "Let's frappe."

Morgan hadn't bothered to stop in the pharmacy because she'd had no need to, but once inside she realized that it wasn't anything close to a CVS. It felt like stepping back in time.

The front quarter of the narrow building was dominated by a traditional lunch counter, complete with black vinyl-topped swivel stools bolted to the ground in front of it. The menu was printed on a series of chalkboards mounted high above a mirror on the wall facing the seats. The aisles toward the back were close together and overflowing with merchandise. Morgan spotted a display of a premium skin care line and realized that even though the pharmacy looked old-fashioned, it knew how to cater to its audience.

"Check it out," Nathan said, pointing at the glass-front refrigerator just beyond the door, next to a shelf crowded with sunscreen. "They carry Peachy!"

"I'm impressed," Morgan said as she checked out the full line of his drinks next to bottled water and sodas. "Speaking of, you need to tell me what happened with your pineapple emergency."

His face went grim. "Yeah, that. Anyway, let's order. We're lucky it's rainy, otherwise we'd be fighting the crowds."

"What do you recommend?" she asked him.

"I always go for a coffee frappe, but there's no bad choice."

Morgan scanned the menu as the teen behind the counter stared at her. "I'll try a chocolate peanut butter frappe, please."

They sat on the stools while the young woman behind the counter made their drinks.

"I like this place. It's not what I expected." Morgan couldn't stop herself from spinning on the stool while they waited.

"Welcome to Nantucket." Nathan grinned at her. "There's a lot of that. Do you want to drink it here, or walk?"

The girl placed an overflowing cup in front of Morgan.

"I'll definitely need to walk that off."

After Nathan paid, they headed out into the crisp evening air. There were a few people strolling but it still felt like they had the street to themselves compared to the usual crowds. Morgan took a long drag on the straw in her frappe and swooned.

"Delicious! I needed this."

"Same," Nathan answered. "I love my Peachy, but sometimes you just need the hard stuff."

Morgan laughed.

"Let's go down to Straight Wharf."

"Are you sure? That's sort of like going to your office."

Nathan smiled at her. "I never thought of it like that, but I guess you're right. I happen to love my job, so it's all good."

They walked in silence past the dark storefronts and crowded restaurants.

"What was the pineapple emergency?" Morgan asked, chewing on the straw to keep from downing the whole thing in five gulps.

Nathan made a frustrated noise. "Almost a disaster. I use a co-packer to do my high-pressure processing because those machines are *expensive*. It's a good way to get a feel for the business without investing in the heavy equipment, you know? I had a huge shipment of pineapples ready for a test bev and I got booted off their production line. One of their big customers took my spot, so I had to go there and fight to make sure they scheduled me in. I got the pineapples at a discount because they were about to turn, which means they couldn't sit. Not only would it have been a financial loss, but it would've been a waste, and I hate waste. It goes against everything I'm about. I mean, the money is important, but I wasn't about to stand by and lose all of that beautiful pineapple."

Suddenly the idea of a pineapple emergency made sense.

"Did they fit you in?"

"You know it," he said proudly. "I wasn't a dick or anything, but I made it clear that even though I'm small, I'm still consistent and I pay on time. Plus, it's a lot harder to say no to someone in person."

Yeah, especially to someone who looks like you.

They strolled past a bar in a vintage train car as the sound of laughter drifted out. They continued past the spot where Nathan set up his cart every day and beyond the crowded Instaready restaurant where the docks began. The air was colder by the water, and she hugged her arms to her chest. Morgan wished she'd worn something other than the boxy, cropped yellow sweater that left a sliver of midriff exposed to the air.

"Let's sit," he said, pointing to the bench that was quickly becoming one of her favorite places on the island. "I realized that I know next to nothing about your daily life. Tell me how you got into the dog-walking game. And I still don't know the name of your business."

Shit, shit, shit.

"Uh," Morgan choked on her frappe and coughed to clear her throat. "It's 'Like Family,'" she replied quickly, stealing the name of another dog-walking business in town.

He tipped his head and considered it. "Cute. You must love it, huh? Spending your days hanging out with animals. What a great gig."

Okay, the lying is starting to get weird now.

A tentacle flicked at her spine as Morgan quickly weighed her options. Telling Nathan the truth about what she did for a living would mean swearing him to secrecy for the remainder of her stay. She'd already let Sydney in, why not Nathan too?

No.

She told Sydney because it felt like she didn't have a choice. Sydney was too perceptive and had almost goaded her into spilling the secret. But her time with Nathan was simple, and easy, and fun, and there was no need to burden whatever they were doing together with real-world stress.

"Yeah, I guess I'm lucky," she replied as the image of a red-faced man yelling at her for being late for his appointment flashed through her mind. "What about you? How did you get into the beverage business?"

"Totally tripped into it. I've always been into food and cooking—both of my parents are chefs—but I knew that I didn't want to spend my life in the kitchen. I know firsthand how tough it is. I was a food science major and I've always wanted to create my own products. I tinkered around and came up with Peachy." He shrugged. "That's my origin story."

"Any plans to hire minions to help out this summer?" she

asked, hoping he would be able to drag himself away from the cart if he did.

Nathan shook his head as he took a long sip, and Morgan tried not to focus on the way his lips wrapped around the straw. "Nope. I won't be doing that for a while. But I've got big plans. I'm going to scale up slowly, but eventually you'll be seeing Peachy in grocery stores across the country."

"Seriously?"

"Yup. Dream big, right? We steer where we stare, and I'm looking directly at big-time growth." He extended his hand in front of him and closed one eye like he was navigating into the black water.

A twinge spread in Morgan's chest. Was it envy? Nathan had his plan all mapped out, and here she was, an anxiety-riddled mess in therapy. She forced herself not to think about it. Sitting in the dark with Nathan was *definitely* not the time.

"Kicked it," Nathan said, shaking his empty cup at her.

Morgan filled the air with the sound of sucking out the last drops of her frappe. "Same."

He took her cup and walked it to the barrel-shaped garbage can. When he turned and headed back to her, she caught her breath.

He was just *so* damn handsome, especially when he was smiling at her. For her. Because of her?

"Let's walk to the end," Nathan said, pointing down the dock.

Morgan jumped when his fingers threaded through hers. Nathan's hand was warm, and he gave hers a gentle squeeze as if to offer her some of his heat. She looked up at him and smiled.

"Your fingertips are freezing," he said.

"I'm always cold, especially when the weather can't make up its mind."

He brought their joined hands up to his chest and rubbed the back of hers. Then, as if it was the most natural thing in the world, he raised their entwined hands and kissed her knuckles.

It didn't matter that it was a sweet gesture, the sensation of his lips on her skin was enough to make her catch her breath. Her body was still responding like it had been starved for physical affection, as if even the most innocent contact was the equivalent of a hand wandering up her thigh or a finger teasing a bra strap off her shoulder. She glanced around to see if anyone was nearby, to make sure there would be no witnesses when she jumped him.

"I really like spending time with you, Morgan."

Warmth flooded through her as Nathan searched her face, like he was trying to gauge how his confession had landed. How was this happening? Morgan felt like a rom-com scriptwriter was pulling the strings.

She nodded, her eyes locked on his like she was hypnotized. "Same. It's easy being with you. It feels . . . natural."

And horny. Don't forget that part.

He let go of her hand, then moved a step closer and cupped her face, one thumb gently stroking her cheek. A shiver rolled through her despite the warmth of his palm against her skin. Morgan swore she could still smell a hint of coconut in the air around him, like the sunscreen he used was fused into his DNA.

"I like doing this too," he murmured, sliding his fingers beneath her chin, then tilting her face up. He studied her, wearing a smile that bordered on naughty. Morgan closed her eyes as Nathan dropped his mouth to hers.

She shivered and felt the synapses within her spark to life, each part of her body waking up and responding to his touch as they kissed. His lips were slow and lazy against hers, teasing her with the faintest pressure. His hand moved from her cheek down her throat, then slowly slid to the back of her neck and rested there, scorching her. Once again she was shocked at her urgency and absolute *need* to get as close to him as she could. Morgan fought to keep her desperate hands from wandering along his body, considering they were in public. People walked down the dock constantly, but it just so happened that in this moment, under a hazy moon, they were alone.

"Hey, Soda Boy, get a room!"

The voice bellowed down the dock, causing Morgan to bounce away from Nathan. They both squinted toward the sound.

"It's Brooks," the voice echoed to them.

"Shit," Nathan said under his breath.

"Who?" Morgan frowned as she touched her hand to her still tingling lips, feeling like she'd just eaten a jalapeño.

"The guy that owns *Her Madgesty*, that huge yacht. He'll want us to party with him."

"Is that a bad thing?" she whispered, watching him zigzag down the dock toward them.

"No, he's great, I'm just not in the mood tonight, you know?" The corner of his mouth kicked up in a secret smile.

The wobbly beach ball of a man stumbled to a stop in front of them. The blue sweater that had probably been nattily knotted around his shoulders at the beginning of the night was hanging across his chest like a pageant sash.

"Soda Boy, good to see you! Who's your friend?" he slurred, his eyes squinty.

"Hey, Brooks, this is Morgan. Morgan, meet Brooks."

The man held his hand out and when Morgan extended hers, he grabbed it and snaked it to his mouth, giving it a dry kiss.

"Aren't you lovely? Pleasure is mine, m'lady."

Between the public intoxication, sexist greeting, and floating mansion, all signs pointed to Morgan instantly hating him, but there was something about Brooks that was strangely charming.

"Why don't you two join me for a nightcap?" he asked, his unsteady frame listing toward the end of the dock. There was an air of pleading in the invitation.

"We'd love to, but we need to take a rain check." Nathan said. "Dogs need their nightly walk. Soon, though, okay?"

"Imma hold you to that," Brooks slurred, shooting him with finger guns. "Nice to meet you, Maryann."

Morgan bit back a smile and watched him trip away.

"Yikes."

"Brooks," Nathan exhaled, shaking his head. "He's a good guy, super smart businessman, but he parties way too hard. Obviously."

"He seems to like you."

"I hope so," Nathan said quietly.

"Huh?"

A crowd of rowdy, red-faced guys in khakis and dress shirts in various shades of gingham came barreling down the dock.

"Watch out, Chads on the loose," Nathan said, pulling her

close and tucking her against his body. "Brooks probably invited them over and forgot."

They walked down the dock pressed together, their footsteps in perfect rhythm.

Remember, it's a summer fling, nothing more.

She hoped her heart had gotten the memo.

chapter twenty-two

Tonight's the night.

Morgan grinned into the darkness and felt like she was levitating her way up the crushed-shell driveway. She'd had enough of their horny kissing in public; it was time to take whatever they were doing together to the next level.

"I had fun tonight. Thanks for coming out on short notice," Nathan said as they paused in front of the house.

"Yeah, I'm lucky Hudson let me leave. He had me pinned on the couch." Morgan laughed.

"Not a bad plan, if you ask me."

Nathan gave her a stare that sent goose bumps skipping up her arms.

Oh yeah, tonight's definitely the night.

She reached out for his hand and started pulling him toward the gate to the backyard. Nathan gave her a questioning look, and she nodded at him. In the brief, wordless exchange they both knew exactly what was about to happen.

He swept her into a kiss as they walked, and she moved backward in rhythm with him like they were dancing with their bodies pressed together. It was a hungry kiss, and Morgan was almost embarrassed by the little noises she made. She let her hands dip below his waist, then realized with a start that they were perfectly framed in the surveillance cameras, about to give Eugene and Karl a free show if they opted to check the footage. Nathan pulled away at almost the exact same moment and stared toward the backyard.

"We're being watched." He pointed behind her and Morgan looked over her shoulder at the house, expecting to see Eugene peeping at them from behind the trellis.

"Where?" She backed away from him reluctantly and scanned the yard.

"There," Nathan answered, pointing at the gate that led to the backyard, where two glowing eyes hovered just above the fence line.

"*Hudson?* How did you get out?"

She untangled from Nathan and jogged to the dog while he danced with his front paws up on the gate, overjoyed to see her. Nathan joined her and Hudson wagged harder, but his eyes darted around wildly and his panting was exaggerated despite the cool night.

"Bud, this isn't good! Maybe the guys came back early and let him out?" Morgan leaned over the fence to peer into the yard. "Karl? Eugene? Are you back there?"

The only sound that answered her was Hudson's heavy breathing.

"Looks like you've got a jailbreaker. Want me to help round him up?" Nathan asked.

Morgan thought about the two of them going into the yard, and Hudson's slightly panicked body language, and realized that even though Hudson liked Nathan, seeing him might stress him out even more.

"I think it's better if I handle this by myself. He's never done this." Hudson whined and paced on the other side of the fence. "Shh, it's fine, you're okay."

"Maybe not," Nathan said, pointing into the yard.

Morgan looked closer and saw the remnants of one of the patio cushions in a few million pieces and spread everywhere. She squinted and saw one of the couch pillows from her little house floating in the pool.

"*Shiiiiit*," Morgan whispered. "Hudson! What did you do?"

"Whoops," Nathan said softly.

Hudson let out a head-shaking squealy yawn.

"I hope this isn't separation anxiety," Morgan said, glancing down at the nervous dog. "That's the last thing either of us needs."

Morgan felt queasy as she surveyed the damage she could see and worried about what else might be waiting for her in the pool house. Separation anxiety was the canine equivalent of a panic disorder, and if it was bad enough, it could require medication to treat.

Had she been in such a rush to leave that she forgot to secure the baby gate in the doorway of the bathroom? And how had Hudson managed to open the sliding glass door? The thing was so heavy she had to use two hands to tug it open.

"I need to deal with this. I hope Karl and Eugene don't kill me. Or him."

"Hey, it can't be that bad," Nathan replied in a comforting voice. "He's in one piece, and everything else is fixable."

Tell that to some of the separation-anxiety dogs I've seen come through the clinic. Let's hope he didn't swallow anything.

"You sure you don't want my help?" he asked, his eyes darting between the dog, Morgan, and the yard.

"No, thanks. I can handle it," she replied, nervous about what she was about to face. Had Hudson chewed holes in the drywall? Pooped all over the pool house?

"Well, my offer stands," Nathan said. "And I'm pretty handy, so if he got into mischief inside, I can probably fix it."

"I hope I don't have to take you up on it," she replied glumly.

"Hey," Nathan said, grasping Morgan's forearms and pulling her close. The heat of his palms reminded her of what they were going to miss out on that night. "It's going to be okay, I promise. And if it isn't, we'll *make* it okay."

There was something comforting about the way Nathan acted like he could wave a magic wand and make all of her troubles disappear. Maybe that was the way things worked in his life, but it wasn't anything she was used to. Stress and drama? *That* was her reality.

He was still holding on to her, and he pulled her close and brushed his lips over hers in the kind of kiss that made Morgan believe that maybe Nathan *could* make everything better. For a few seconds everything else around them faded.

He pulled back a few inches and studied her face. "You're going to be okay. Got it?"

She nodded as if in a trance, her eyes focused on his mouth.

"Just call if you need me."

Nathan gave her one last quick kiss, then jogged off, leaving Morgan swaying in the darkness. Hudson hopped up on the fence and whined as he disappeared into the black of the driveway.

"I know, bud," she said, reaching over to pet him. "Me too."

· · ·

The on-site event meeting with Sydney, Abby, and the party planner the next day was a necessary evil, but at least it had been quick. The property was perfection, with a long, wide carpet of grass that ended in Polpis Harbor, but since they were holding the gala in what amounted to an open field, it meant that they had to import everything they'd need, from the lighting to the bathrooms to the shrimp forks. Morgan was happy she'd only been called on to supervise where the dog-holding area needed to be set up, because Abby couldn't stop murdering her with her eyes the whole time.

When she got home she was happy to find Karl and Eugene relaxing on the couch by the pool with Bernadette dozing next to them. Morgan wondered if they noticed the missing cushion. She half expected to see Hudson outside with them since he'd clearly learned how to escape his hangout spot.

"Welcome home, guys," Morgan said, plopping onto a chair across from them. "How was it?"

"Hi, Miss Morgan. Good to be back. As for how it went, I have one word: Kansas," Eugene sneered.

"Please don't crap on Kansas," Karl scolded. "It turns out we had some competition from the county fair, so we didn't have the crowds we've come to expect. But all the other stops were phenomenal. How about you? What have you been up to?"

"Lots, but first I need to tell you what happened last night."

Her stomach twisted. For all she knew, the throw pillows from the pool house and the porch cushion were made from discontinued fabric hand-sewed by nuns in Italy.

"You look positively green. What in the world is going on?" Karl asked.

"So last night I went out with Nathan—"

Eugene made a check mark in the air. "Score one for our girl."

She stifled a smile. "*Anyway*, I guess Hudson was feeling a little . . . left out . . . and he—"

"Oh, we know what happened," Karl said matter-of-factly. "We saw it on the footage."

Morgan's eyes went wide. "Wait . . . do you guys *watch* the surveillance cameras?"

"Why, is there something you don't want us to see?" Eugene asked, wiggling his eyebrows at her. He pulled his phone out of his pocket. "Because I've got it all right here."

"Stop it." Karl laughed and leaned over to smack Eugene. "Morgan, no, we do not make a habit of watching it. But last night the motion-sensitive lights in the backyard kept triggering over and over, and we got an alert about suspicious activity, so we popped it on. We saw Hudson having a blast with the pillows."

"We were in the middle of a dinner with some of the Target people, otherwise we would've called. But we figured you were on top of it."

"I'm so sorry it happened, I had no clue he could get out. He jumped on the vanity and parkoured over the baby gate, but I still haven't figured out how he opened the sliding door. I'll pay for the damaged stuff. It was four pillows from the pool house and . . ." She trailed off and pointed to the naked chaise lounge.

"Morgan, please. You do not have to pay for a thing. The pillows were literally trials from our line that didn't make the cut—"

"Good riddance," Eugene added. "The patterns were basic."

"And the lounge cushion was all mildewy on the bottom. Hudson did us a favor, we needed to have that one replaced anyway."

She let out a sigh of relief. "Thank you. Again, I'm so sorry."

Eugene waved his hand at her. "Please. Do you have any idea how much we appreciate you being here? I mean, you brought Bernie to the beach! Look." He turned his phone around and the lock screen was one of the photos she'd sent them, of Bernadette with her head back and eyes closed with the ocean in the background. "You owe us *nothing*. Hell, he could've shit on the dining room table and we wouldn't care."

She laughed. "Thanks, but I'll make sure *that* doesn't happen."

"Hold on, hold on. I just thought of a penance you can do," Karl said with a sly grin.

"Tell me," Morgan said. "Anything."

"Use the damn outdoor shower." He pointed across the lawn to it with a demanding finger. "It will change your life, woman. Do it and report back to us."

She rolled her eyes. "Oh my God, what is it about that thing? Both of you keep bringing it up!"

"Just try it and you'll be a convert," Eugene said. "We're heading out for the afternoon, so you'll have the whole yard to yourself. But it's totally private either way."

A few hours later, Morgan gathered the fancy new soap she'd bought in town, shampoo, and a towel and trudged to the shower to atone for Hudson's sins. Unlike the rest of the house, the thing was an unremarkable slatted wood structure just off the mudroom door. She hung her towel on the vintage-y hook on the post next to it and stepped in.

The interior of the shower was big enough that she could turn on the water and stand huddled off to the side with her arms crossed over her chest until it warmed up. She felt vulnerable being naked outside, like at any second someone could peek over the edge. Within a few seconds, the water from the oversized black shower head started steaming and Morgan stepped beneath the spray.

Wow . . . they were right.

The combination of the hot water rushing over her, the crisp summer air, the sunshine, and the sound of birdsong turned the shower into a Zen experience. It wasn't even something she could put into words, the outdoor shower just felt . . . *better.*

Just like everything about her summer so far.

chapter twenty-three

"Go potty, go potty," Morgan chanted to Hudson in a cheerful voice.

They were in the shady back corner of the yard and Hudson was too interested in investigating every dewy blade of grass to pee. Morgan was running late and hoping that a quick pee trip would suffice until she could give him a long training walk after her rescheduled surf lesson with Nathan.

She peered across the yard to the house and could see Bernadette through the sliding glass doors, already stretched out on the couch for her morning nap. While the two dogs were tolerating each other beautifully, there was no way Morgan trusted leaving them alone together yet. Plus, she didn't want to push her luck with Hudson by giving him free rein and risking any more ripped-up pillows.

"Hurry, hurry," she said in a voice that verged on pleading. "C'mon, bud, he's going to be here any minute!"

Sure enough, right as Hudson finally lifted his leg, she heard the crunching of tires on the driveway. Hudson perked up as he finished his deposit and strained to see who was pulling in, but the driveway wasn't visible from the back.

"Nice work, bud!" She praised him and gave him a little treat.

Morgan whistled for Hudson and headed for the pool house, but he ran toward the gate, and two seconds later Nathan appeared around the corner.

"Well, hello, good-looking!" he said to Hudson, leaning over the fence to pet him while the dog snuffled his hands and forearms.

"I thought you were talking to me," Morgan said with a laugh as she walked over to meet him.

Nathan let himself into the yard and squatted to pet Hudson. "If I were talking to you, I'd have said 'Hello, *gorgeous*.' The rash guard looks great on you. Fits you perfectly."

Morgan looked down and tugged at the snug waist. "It's a little tighter than what I usually wear, but I guess that's on purpose?"

"Yeah, you don't want to have a draggy shirt in the water. You ready? I've got Archer in the truck, he wanted to come. He's gonna coach from the shore."

Suddenly, Hudson's close investigation of Nathan's hands made sense.

"Yup, let me just get him settled—" She broke off and looked past Nathan when she heard the sound of jingling dog tags. Hudson stopped wagging and alerted to the sound as well, stiff and expectant.

Before Morgan even realized what was happening, a khaki streak sprinted around the corner and pushed through the unlatched fence into the yard.

"Archer!" Nathan exclaimed as his dog ran past him. "No, sir!" But it was too late.

The dogs stood facing each other, statue-still, tails up, weight forward, and in Hudson's case, hackles raised. Archer looked like he outweighed Hud by at least twenty pounds. Based on the body language, there was nothing positive about the introduction going down between them.

"Shit-shit-shit," Morgan said under her breath as she watched the drama unfold, powerless to stop it.

Hudson and little Bernadette's growing friendship wasn't an indication of his feelings for *all* dogs, especially given that Bernie was a calm, confident senior and Archer was a goofy teen.

Morgan could hear her heartbeat pounding in her ears as she realized that there was no easy way to separate them if they decided to fight. She held her breath knowing that she needed to try to keep the mood relaxed even though her insides were twisting with stress. She made a kissy noise and opened the treat bag at her waist.

"Hey, Hud, want a treat?" Her voice trembled as she spoke. She waved the hunk of cheese in the air, hoping the scent would waft over to either dog and cause them to disengage from the standoff.

Hudson was immobile, glancing at Archer out of the corner of his eyes, then looking away. His mouth was clenched shut even though he'd been panting happily with Nathan a few minutes prior. The bigger, younger dog stood still, facing Hudson and licking his lips repeatedly. Archer's tail quivered over his back.

"Hey, Arch, let's go," Nathan said, clapping and walking toward the gate. "C'mon, bud."

The sound of his voice seemed to jolt Archer from his trance, and he glanced at Nathan, then dipped into a surprisingly goofy play bow next to Hudson.

Okay, that's a really good sign.

Archer gave Hudson a hopeful tail wag, still in the play position.

"I can vouch for Arch, he loves every dog he's ever met," Nathan said in a worried voice, "but it looks like Hudson wants nothing to do with him."

Morgan checked to see how Hudson responded to Archer's playful change in attitude, but he seemed literally unmoved, still frozen in his ready stance. Archer seemed like a youngster trying to tease the grown-up into playing, and Hudson was having none of it. He padded toward Hudson's rear and took a drive-by sniff.

"That's a good boy, Hud," Morgan said, praising him for not flipping out at the breach of etiquette. As the older, resident dog, Hudson should've gotten first dibs on the butt examination. Archer was being a pushy guest, but he wasn't doing anything outwardly aggressive. Much of how the rest of the interaction would go rested on Hudson's tense shoulders.

Archer seemed to be feeling more confident, sniffing around Hudson even though Hud was giving zero indication that he was cool with the up-close examination. A more seasoned, dog-smart dog would've taken the hint and backed off, but Archer was oblivious that Hudson wasn't enjoying his attention.

Morgan panicked as she noticed Hud's mouth trembling into a grimace while Archer poked his head up in his undercarriage, an even bigger breach. If she didn't intervene, things were going to head south *fast*.

"Hey, Hud, let's walk!" she singsonged. "Come with me, my friend."

The dog shot her a glance but didn't move.

Archer wuffed at Hudson with the oblivious swagger of the young and dumb. He faked a shoulder bump, which caused Hudson to finally move, an abrupt, powerful, full-body jerk toward the bigger dog. There was nothing cheerful about the move, but it didn't seem to dawn on Archer that Hudson wasn't playing for fun, he was playing for keeps. Archer play-bowed again, then nose-punched Hudson in the ribs.

It was all Hudson could take.

The next move seemed to unfold in slow motion. In one hideously graceful takedown Hudson leapt toward the pit bull, grabbed him by the neck, and pinned him to the ground. He then stood over Archer with his teeth displayed, growling like he was about to rip his throat out. Archer looked half the size he normally was, curled up beneath Hudson with his ears pinned tight to his head and his paws drawn against his chest for protection.

"*Hudson!*" Morgan yelled despite herself. "Let's go!"

"Hudson, knock it off," Nathan yelled at the same time.

She knew there was no way she could safely grab for either dog, and doing so could trigger things to get even worse, so she watched helplessly while he postured on top of Archer.

In this moment it all came down to how the younger dog reacted. If Archer was game for a fight, there was bound to be blood. Morgan got into position behind Hudson. The only safe way to separate them would be to grab his hind legs at the hips and pull him away wheelbarrow-style.

"How do we stop this?" Nathan asked in a panic. "What do we do?"

"Nothing right now," Morgan answered in a quiet voice, hedging her bets that things weren't going to escalate.

The shift between the dogs was almost imperceptible, but she was close enough to see it happen. Hudson's face relaxed as if satisfied by the younger dog's deference, and he moved his head up away from Archer's face. He remained hovering over the nervous dog, but the tension eased from his body, and then he got off him, shook off, and trotted away. Archer leapt to his feet and shook off too, then ran to Nathan.

The entire exchange only lasted about a minute, but Morgan felt like she'd aged ten years. Her whole body was shaking, like she was about to give a presentation that she wasn't prepared for. She jogged to where Hudson was sniffing along the grass as if he hadn't just delivered an Olympic beatdown and gently grasped his collar.

"C'mon, bud," she said softly. Morgan led him back to the pool house and called to Nathan. "I'll be right back. Check his face and neck to make sure Hud didn't break skin."

She contemplated what the fight would do to Hudson's chances of being adopted. They already knew that he didn't skew dog friendly, but the interaction showed that he could also be dog *inappropriate*. Archer's goofiness was rude, sure, but Hudson's punishment didn't fit the crime. A simple corrective growl probably would've been enough to get Archer to stand down, but he'd opted to go for the literal jugular instead. Morgan shuddered to envision what might have happened if things hadn't gone so smoothly with little Bernie during their intro.

After Hudson took a long drink and had a few minutes to cool down, Morgan headed back outside still feeling queasy.

Nathan was on his knees with Archer lying on the ground in front of him, leaning in close and running his hands along his fur.

"Is he okay?" Morgan asked, her heart in her throat.

He looked up at her with a frown. "Hudson got him, right on the cheek below the eye. He's bleeding a little."

One of the worst spots.

She shifted into undercover doctor mode. Archer's tail thumped on the grass as she jogged over to them.

"Let me take a look."

Nathan pointed to the spot and sure enough, there was a dime-sized jagged red cut marring his light brown face.

Morgan ran her fingertips along his muzzle and the wet fur on his neck, looking for blood. The wound near his eye was more of a scrape, which suggested that Hudson hadn't bitten and held on, it was more of a tooth graze on thin skin as he took Archer down. Even though the dog was still probably pumping with nervous adrenaline, Archer let her examine all along his muzzle and neck without fidgeting.

"Good boy," Morgan said softly as she finished up her exam. She realized too late how official it must have looked, but she didn't care. Her number one priority was making sure Archer was okay. "It's not a bad bite, but I still think you should go to your vet for antibiotics, just in case. It's a sensitive spot. But it could've been so much worse," Morgan said, trying to ease some of the tension. "He didn't *bite* bite, it's more of a graze."

"Yeah, I guess," Nathan answered, not looking up from Archer. "But it looked pretty bad to me. Arch just stopped shaking."

Did I imagine it or was that accusatory?

"I'm really sorry it happened. It was a crappy accident. He must've jumped out of your window, and the gate wasn't latched so . . . here we are." She ran her hand down Archer's side. "But you came on really strong, mister. How are you going to make friends when you act all pushy like that?"

"Hold on a sec," Nathan said, sounding upset *and* pissed off. "Don't blame Archer. He's never been in a dog fight. And you said yourself that Hudson is dog aggressive."

Morgan leapt to Hudson's defense. "No, I never said that. I was said Hudson was *reactive*. Big difference."

"He sure looked aggressive to me when he pinned my dog to the ground," Nathan shot back.

"Well, what do you expect?" she snapped. "Hudson did over-react, but Archer came barging into his yard and got all up in his face."

"He's never had a problem with any other dogs, so you tell me who's to blame."

It was as if the stress hormones from the dog fight lingered in the air and turned the humans combative as well.

"It was an accident due to a bad intro, simple as that." Morgan finally said, leaning back against her heels. "Again, I'm sorry it happened."

He finally looked up at her and met her eyes. "I hope this fight doesn't trigger something in him. Every dog experience he's had so far has been super positive. And now he's been at-tacked." Nathan rubbed Archer's belly.

She'd never seen him look so upset.

"I don't think you have to worry. I've seen how he is in public, he was great with every dog at Cisco. You did the work and socialized him when he was younger. As long as you keep him interacting with dog-friendly dogs, he'll be fine."

Which means we won't be able to have any happy dog hangs with Hudson.

"You really think I need to take him to the vet?" He took Archer's muzzle in his hands and scrutinized the cut again.

Morgan felt herself answering before he'd even finished asking the question, but she forced herself to give a CliffsNotes version of a diagnosis. "Dog mouths are filled with bacteria, so even a little scrape like this one can get infected and lead to bigger issues. It's a smart thing to do."

She held back mentioning the potential for a localized abscess or cellulitis if the wound wasn't treated.

True to the canine code of "shake it off and move on," Archer didn't seem fazed by the confrontation. But Nathan was quiet as he scrolled through his phone to check on the vet office hours.

Shut up, don't say it, don't say it . . .

"Do you want me to come with you to your vet?"

Morgan knew how triggering it would be to go into a clinic, even an unfamiliar one. The smells, the sounds, the pace . . . it would only take a few seconds of exposure before the tranquility she'd found since arriving on Nantucket would start to drain away.

"No, it's easier if we go alone. Thanks. I'll head over there now and see if they can squeeze us in."

He stood up abruptly and Archer leapt to his feet, tail wagging as if he hadn't just been through a battle.

"I'll pay for it," Morgan said hurriedly.

"No, it was an accident. Don't worry about it."

Nathan's feel-good vibe was gone, replaced by a furrowed forehead.

"He'll be fine, I promise," Morgan said, worrying that she might've scared him with the snap diagnosis. "A quick course of antibiotics and that scrape will be just a memory."

"Yeah, the cut will heal, but it's the fight I'm worried about. I'll let you know how it goes."

Morgan jumped up as Nathan headed for the gate, hoping he'd kiss her goodbye, but he only had eyes for Archer.

chapter twenty-four

Morgan had walked into Cynthia's office with Hudson, determined to use the second session to talk about her relationship with her brother. She figured she could tease out some of the weirdness with him and fix it prior to his visit.

So why did the conversation keep going back to her job?

"Have you ever thought about the fact that you're in a customer service profession?" Cynthia asked after Morgan told a story about a bad online review that she totally didn't deserve.

She chuckled, then realized that Cynthia wasn't kidding.

"Everything you do is based on empathy and giving," Cynthia continued. "You're trying to make things right for the animals *and* their people. And you have to take a lot of crap because of it."

"Do I ever." Morgan reached to pet Hudson, who was finally settling into a comfortable napping position. He'd been wary of the office and the stranger in it at first, but the calming effects of both seemed to work on him as well.

"It's a one-sided dynamic," Cynthia said. "You're giving *way* more than you're receiving, and after a while you're bound to get depleted. That's why recharging is so vital. I can't even imagine what you face every day."

Morgan shifted on the couch, feeling the tentacle flick along her spine.

"Is this making you uncomfortable?" Cynthia asked.

"A little," she answered in a small voice.

"Can you tell me why?"

Morgan picked at a jagged edge on her thumbnail. "This was my dream job. Being a vet was all I ever wanted. I have no right to feel this way."

"All feelings are valid, Morgan. You're *allowed* to feel overwhelmed because your workload is intense. You're *allowed* to feel sad because you deal with unfortunate outcomes. Denying yourself the right to those emotions is unhealthy. Yes, you're lucky enough to be doing the job you've always wanted, but that doesn't negate the challenges that come with it."

Morgan waited for Cynthia to continue, hoping that she could focus on her soothing voice and not the weepiness she felt welling up inside. Hudson kept glancing up at her as if he could also sense what was bubbling just below the surface.

"Does that make sense?" Cynthia asked.

Morgan nodded.

"Is there something else going on with you right now?"

She managed a smile. "How are you in my head?"

"Oh, I'm not, don't you worry about that. I just sense that you've got something more . . . topical . . . on your mind."

Nathan.

In the two days since the great yard beatdown, she'd only heard from him twice. Once to let her know that the vet visit had gone well and he'd gotten antibiotics, and a second time, to blame bad weather for canceling their next surf lesson. She'd asked him point-blank if he was angry at her for what happened and he'd said he wasn't, but his lack of communication suggested otherwise.

"I've been spending time with a guy here, and Hudson had a scuffle with his dog, Archer. His dog ended up with a cut under his eye, and I sort of blamed Archer for starting the fight. I think he's upset I said that. He was also worried about the cut, but I told him it wasn't a big deal."

Cynthia adjusted her glasses. "Having a veterinarian reassure him that his dog would be fine helped, no?"

"Oh, he doesn't know what I do for a living."

Morgan said it matter-of-factly, but as soon as the words were out of her mouth, she realized how odd it sounded. She watched to see if Cynthia's expression would change to shock, but realized that her training probably prevented her from making any expression other than a placid poker face.

"And why is that?" Cynthia asked, tipping her head.

Morgan didn't feel like she was being judged. Instead, Cynthia seemed like she was genuinely curious.

"I haven't told anyone here that I'm a veterinarian. Except for Sydney, of course."

"Okay, why don't we talk a little more about that decision?"

"It's something I decided to do before I got here. Lots of veterinarians keep their profession a secret in public." Morgan sighed and reached down to pet Hudson, who was napping with his head on top of her feet. "Once people know what I do, it's like that's *all* I am. They ask me for advice about their dogs' illnesses and injuries. And they talk about putting their dogs and cats to sleep. Like I want to hear about that when I'm trying to pay for my groceries."

"Of course, understood. So you decided that while you're on Nantucket, you'll tell people you're a . . ." She gestured to Morgan and waited for her to fill in the blank.

"A dog walker. Just a person who loves animals."

"Mm-hmm. So this guy you're dating—"

"We're just hanging out together," Morgan corrected quickly.

"Excuse me, this guy you're hanging out with. Do you feel like he would do the same thing if you told him? Start treating you like a resource?"

Morgan considered it.

"No . . ." she answered slowly. "I don't."

"Okay. And would you say that you trust him?"

This time she didn't have to think about it.

"I do." Morgan smiled shyly and leaned down to rub Hudson's ear between her fingertips. "Yeah, I actually do."

Cynthia sat back in her chair and said nothing. The silence in the room went from companionable to awkward as the seconds ticked on.

Morgan felt herself smiling as she thought about her time with Nathan. The way he made her feel safe and cared for. The way he looked at her. Kissed her.

"Oh my God," Morgan said as the realization dawned on her. "You're saying I should tell him, aren't you? That if I trust him, I should let him in."

"I didn't say a word, Morgan. *You* just came to that conclusion on your own."

Her heart raced at the thought of it. "But what if it makes

him even more upset with me? Because I haven't been honest with him?"

"That's a possibility."

Morgan wanted Cynthia to say more, to give her advice, or better yet, map out exactly what she needed to do.

"So, I should just . . . tell him?"

"If you're comfortable with that decision, then yes," Cynthia said in a quiet voice. "How does the thought of it make you feel?"

Morgan mulled over how the conversation would go and let out a shallow breath. "Nervous. Really nervous."

"And does feeling that way make you want to change your mind about telling him?"

Morgan pictured Nathan's smiling face.

"No."

"It sounds like you have a few things to talk over with him. His feelings about the dog fight, and the secret you've been keeping from him. When do you think you'll be ready to have that conversation?"

There was no need to wait.

"Now."

Trying to navigate the Pak-Reynoldses' Jeep on the narrow, crowded streets in town made Morgan's palms sweat. Even though it had only been a few weeks since she'd driven, she felt like a beginner in a new country. A man crossing the street with newspapers clutched under his arm screamed at her when she drove past him, forgetting that pedestrians have the right of way.

After she parked in a stroke-of-good-luck spot in the harbor Stop & Shop parking lot, she twisted the rearview mirror to check her face. The hollows under her eyes were less noticeable than usual, even without concealer, and she had color in her cheeks that was a mix of sun and a steady diet of real food. She ran her hand over the top of her head to tame the flyaways and gave herself a pep talk.

It's going to be fine. You can do this.

She headed for Straight Wharf feeling hopeful, smiling stupidly at everyone she passed. It was the end of the day and she knew he'd be wrapping up soon.

Nathan's back was to her as he wooed yet another customer, a guy in khakis and a backpack. Morgan paused to watch Nathan. How was it possible to miss someone she'd only known for a few weeks?

She waited for him to run the guy's credit card and felt an unexpected sense of dread come over her as she walked up to him.

What if you're wrong? What if he thinks it's weird that you didn't tell him?

No, life was different on Nantucket. Good things happened to her. She walked up behind Nathan and mustered up her courage, then pushed her sunglasses on top of her head.

"Hi," she said softly.

He turned to her and she watched his face, hoping to see something in it that told her she'd done the right thing by showing up.

He was already smiling, probably expecting another customer. His expression shifted when he saw that it was her, like she was a parking meter attendant about to ticket his cart. Morgan felt sweat beading along the back of her neck.

"Oh, hey," he said, finally managing a halfhearted smile. "How are you?"

"I'm okay. Do you have a minute to talk? Is this an okay time? I figured you were almost done for the day."

He checked his phone and looked around to survey the foot traffic.

"Yeah, sure, I'm done. What's up?"

There was an edge to his voice she'd never heard before.

"Could we take a walk?"

Nathan looked slightly annoyed but nodded and locked up his bike and cart.

She felt jumpy as they started off. He was obviously pissed about the dog fight, but how would he react to the fact that she'd been lying to him too?

"Let's go this way," she said, pointing to a quieter side street away from the bustle. Nathan followed along silently, keeping his distance from Morgan, seemingly waiting for her to begin talking.

"First, I wanted to talk about the Hudson and Archer . . . uh, meeting." Morgan didn't want to say the word *fight*. "I still feel really bad about it. Obviously because it was an awful way for them to meet, but also because I said that Archer started it. I'm sorry, that wasn't fair."

Nathan let out a long breath. "Thanks. That means a lot. I guess I'm overly sensitive about it, but pit bull discrimination is real. I thought your hidden anti-pit feelings were coming out. That's sort of a deal-breaker for me."

Morgan whirled to him in shock.

"Oh my God, no! Didn't I tell you my dog George was part pit?"

He shook his head. "I don't think so, I would've remembered. Trust me, I keep track of who's pro and who's anti."

The change in his expression slowed her speeding heartbeat.

The tension around his eyes was finally gone. "Yeah, been there. I totally get it. With any other dog, meeting like that probably would've been fine, but Hudson's still working through some stuff."

"But he's a great guy," Nathan offered.

"He really is. How's Archer's cheek?" she asked.

"Totally fine."

She could see Nathan's defenses falling as they talked, and it gave her hope.

"I'm glad," Morgan said, pleased that she'd cleared the first hurdle so effortlessly. "There's something else I wanted to talk to you about." She took a deep breath and Nathan watched her warily, as if he sensed that something bigger was coming. "I haven't been completely honest with you."

She watched his face fall, but pushed on.

chapter twenty-five

"Oh yeah? What about?"

Her pulse sped to triple time as she tried to organize her thoughts. "I'm not a dog walker."

He chuckled. "What are you then? A dog concierge? A dog... nanny?"

She stopped walking and turned to him so she could watch his expression. "I'm actually a veterinarian. And a pretty good one."

She smiled, hoping that Nathan would smile back at her, but his face screwed up with confusion.

"Wait, *what*?"

"I know it's weird that I didn't tell you, and I'm sorry for not being honest. But I can explain."

They were stopped on the sidewalk facing each other, and Morgan was doing her best not to fidget under his confused scrutiny.

"Okay, this is a little weird," Nathan finally said. "You've been lying to me about your job. Why? Are you embarrassed?"

"No, not at all! I love my job but . . . well, let me give you a little background."

She felt like she needed to keep moving so she beckoned him to walk with her again.

"I grew up knowing I was going to be a veterinarian. It wasn't even a choice, really. It was just . . . fact. I was *always* going to be a veterinarian." She paused as something shaky rolled through her. Usually when she told people about her path to vet medicine it was met with smiles, but Nathan seemed unmoved. She pressed on. "I love my patients. They're the reason I do what I do. There's no better feeling than helping a pet stay healthy or a sick one get better."

Talking about what she loved about her job was easy. They continued walking in silence for a few moments while Morgan tried to find a way to explain the next part.

"But what I deal with is . . . layered. On a typical day I can go from performing CPR on a nonresponsive dog, to vaccinating a puppy, to euthanizing a senior cat in kidney failure while his person is crying right next to me. Add in long hours, the strain of working with animals of all sizes, the on-the-job injuries that I have to shrug off and it's . . . hard. And dirty. Blood, poop, pus, anal gland fluid, I've been covered in all of it."

"Yikes," Nathan said, finally softening a little.

"Don't forget about the quotas and patients-per-day goals I have to worry about too. And worse, I see animals that are suffering at the hands of the people who are supposed to care for them. I treat pets that are on my table because of their people's bad decisions. I have to try to help animals that are abused and neglected. And I have to be cordial to people who are indifferent to their pets' pain, because otherwise they'll destroy me and the practice on Yelp."

Nathan let out a long breath.

"But it gets even worse," Morgan said, her voice breaking a little. "There's more about the human side of the table. The people who don't listen to my advice even though I've spent years and hundreds of thousands of dollars learning how to treat their pet. People that scream at the front desk staff and vet techs, then act sweet as can be to me. Or the ones who treat *everyone* like we're their personal support staff. The conspiracy theory people who do stupid shit like putting their little carnivores on a vegetarian diet. Then there are the ones who expect me to be a miracle worker and freak out when I'm not able to magically fix their obese dog's osteoarthritis."

She sniffled and Nathan reached for her hand. "Morgan, I'm sorry. I—"

She pulled away from him, unwilling to fall into his arms before telling him every detail. She'd scratched the surface of what she went through with Sydney and had begun to get into the day-to-day of it with Cynthia, but telling Nathan was dredging up the *bleakness* of what she went through. The stuff she'd been suppressing.

"There's more," she said, her heart heavy. "Worst of all, out of everything I've told you . . . there's . . . there's the emotional blackmail clients, the ones who say stuff like 'If you really cared about animals, you'd treat my pet for free.'"

The dam finally opened at the thought of it, and Morgan put her head down to let the tears flow. Nathan pulled her close and draped his arms around her while she buried her head against his chest and tried to stop crying.

"That one kills me, you know?" She leaned away from him and wiped her nose with the back of her hand. "Saying that I don't care about animals when I'm dedicating my life to them.

I literally can't sleep at night because I'm worried about my patients. Like, did I make the wrong call? Could I have done something faster?" She was seconds away from ugly, hiccupping sobs, but the feeling of Nathan's arms wrapped around her helped calm her down a little. He stroked her back and seemed to recognize that just holding her was enough in that moment.

It didn't matter that the sun was blazing down on them, she craved Nathan's warmth. When she finally felt strong enough to talk again, she pulled away from him reluctantly.

"All that brings me to why I'm here. I had an . . . episode. At work. I'm not sure what it was. A breakdown, a panic attack. *Something*. I fainted. I knew that if I didn't take some time away it would be . . . bad. Like, 'lock up the phenobarbital' bad." She mashed her palms against her wet eyes and rubbed, not caring what it was doing to her makeup.

It was the most honest she'd been with anyone about the way she'd been feeling, and she immediately doubted herself for being so open about her struggles. No one knew that she'd had moments when she'd been low enough to consider what Sophia had gone through with. She'd barely admitted it to herself. Summer fling aside, Nathan needed to know that parts of her were fragile before they went any further.

"Wait, hold on. Are you saying you were . . ." He trailed off as the realization hit him, his eyes boring into Morgan's.

"No, I wasn't at that point." She shook her head vigorously. "But things were pretty dark for a while. Don't worry, I'm talking to someone now," she added quickly. "I'm learning some coping strategies and it's helping."

Nathan looked like he was trying to find the right words to comfort her, his face ashen. Morgan suddenly felt itchy and needed to get away from the space on the sidewalk that felt contaminated by what she'd told him.

"Let's go."

They started off again with Morgan staring at the bricks and Nathan staring at her.

"Morgan, I get it," Nathan said. "I mean, obviously there's no way I can truly understand what you've been through, but I can see why you'd want to hide away from all of that for a while."

"Thanks," she sniffled. "Whenever someone finds out what I do for a living I go from normal person to Ms. Fix-It. I met a woman at the gym, back when I had the bandwidth to go to the gym, who I thought could be a new friend. Turns out all she wanted to do any time we hung out was get advice about her dog's Cushing's Disease. Doesn't matter if I'm holding a full cocktail and a plate of apps, I'm Dr. Pearce, ready to solve every pet problem you can throw at me. I needed a *break*. Just for a little while. That's where the dog-walker stuff came from."

"I understand now." He nodded and reached for her hand.

"I need you to know that I wasn't being dishonest with you because I didn't trust you, Nathan. That's not it at all. I was protecting *me*."

He put his arm around her and pulled her closer.

"I hope from now on you'll let me help with that," he murmured. "Protecting you."

He pressed his lips on the top of her head, and for a moment the stone in her chest felt a little lighter.

chapter twenty-six

'm flying!

After a morning of failure, Morgan was finally, *finally* standing on top of her surfboard on unsteady legs as the world's tiniest wave propelled her toward the beach.

All of the advice Nathan had given her echoed in her head, about making sure the stringer bisected her feet and pointing her front arm in the direction she wanted to travel and keeping her head up despite the urge to look at the swell bubbling under her feet. Her dozen embarrassing falls faded from memory. All that mattered was that in this moment, she and the wave were one.

She could feel Nathan watching her, but she refused to look away from her sight line to scan the horizon for him. She'd learned the hard way what happened when she lost her focus, and she'd probably have the bruises to show for it the next day. She tried to remember to breathe as the locomotion of the wave slowed and she realized that her first flight was ending. Morgan felt like she was riding a bike too slowly and was about to face-plant if she didn't take decisive action.

What am I supposed to do now? Fall on purpose? Step off?

Nathan had neglected to tell her how to end her first ride, probably because he wasn't expecting her to do it. The truth was, neither was she. Despite her ability to excel at nearly everything she tried, surfing made her look like a flailing drunk.

Until she nailed it.

She calculated how deep the water was relative to how far she was from shore. She'd managed to maintain her balance almost all the way in, but now the wave was barely pushing her, so she stepped off the surfboard gracefully, like she was at the end of a moving walkway at the airport.

The second her feet hit the sand, she raised her arms in victory and screamed. She knew Nathan could tell how frustrated she'd been getting, and as he ran over, his expression was a mixture of joy and relief. He whooped as he splashed through the shallow water to where she was standing, then swept her into a bone-crushing hug.

With soaked, slippery bodies and only a millimeter of fabric between them, the hug was basically foreplay. Nathan gripped her tightly and increased the clench ever so slightly when she shifted in his arms, like he wasn't ready to let go yet.

Morgan slammed her mouth against his, not caring that there was an older couple walking their dog and watching them like they were on beach patrol. Within a few seconds, she was overwhelmed by the hot-cold sensation of their wet bodies pressed together. She drew her legs up and locked them around his waist, making Nathan smile against her mouth. Every kiss was a promise of what was to come, and she was making it abundantly clear to Nathan on a public beach that she'd been waiting for too long. He squeezed her thighs, his fingertips just inches away from the fabric of her bikini bottom, causing her to arch against him. She finally broke away when she realized they were putting on a show.

"You were amazing out there. What did you think?" he asked, breathless and looking at her like he'd rather be kissing her again.

Morgan struggled to put the feeling into words as they walked back to the beach, surfboards clutched under their arms. "I felt like I was riding the wind. Like I was falling off a cliff but still in complete control. Does that make sense?"

He nodded. "Totally. One of my students said he felt like he was riding a hummingbird and that's probably the best description I've ever heard."

"Yeah, *that*," she exclaimed. "It's this . . . flying one-ness, you know? Connection. Focus. Nothing else mattered while I was up there."

Nathan threw his head back and laughed at her. "Oh, wow, you've got it bad already."

"I do! How much longer do we have?"

He peered at his waterproof watch. "We gotta leave now, actually. It's late. But it's great to end a session on a high. It'll keep you excited for next time."

There was no longer any doubt or worry about whether there would be a next time. Morgan knew in her bones that she and Nathan were going to spend the rest of her time on Nantucket together.

They gathered their things and trudged back to the parking lot. The bruise-y sensation of stress-tensing her muscles for too long strained along her shoulders as she lifted the surfboard into the back of his truck.

Worth it. Worth every bit of discomfort to feel the way I do on that board.

"You busy tonight?" Nathan asked as they got into the truck.

"I have a hot date with a grumpy blond on the couch, but I can probably reschedule if you have a better offer."

"Competition, huh?" He frowned, keeping his eyes on the road. "Well, has he cooked you dinner yet? Because that's what I was thinking. *If* you can tear yourself away from him."

"He has not cooked for me yet, so that settles it. Yes, to dinner with you tonight."

"Okay, so I can swing by and pick you up—"

"No, stop," Morgan cut him off. "If you're cooking for me you don't have to drop everything to come and get me. You've earned plenty of chivalry points already. Just give me your address and I'll drive myself over."

"Well, okay then, thank you. You can ride your bike, it's not too far from where you're staying. That means I can upgrade from grilling to making something I can devote some time to. Any food sensitivities I need to be aware of?"

That's right. This man has chef blood in his veins.

"None. Go crazy, I'm an adventurous eater."

"Okay, got it," he said with a nod. "I'm already planning."

Morgan wrapped the damp beach towel around her a little tighter, hopeful that the next time they kissed, they wouldn't have to stop.

"You really are the smartest, aren't you?"

Morgan was teaching Hudson to go to his bed on cue, and he'd figured out the initial steps within a few repetitions. Bernadette was relaxing in the sun on the other side of a baby gate after her morning play session, so she wouldn't try to interrupt Hudson's time in the spotlight. Morgan was doing her best to stay busy before her evening with Nathan. Every time she thought about spending time alone with him, she felt a tremor of anticipation pulse through her. Tonight was *finally* going to be the night.

Glad I packed my good underwear.

Her phone pinged and she pulled it from her back pocket hoping it was him.

Hi there, great news, read the text from Sydney. We have a couple interested in Hudson. They're going to submit an app.

Morgan felt her hackles go up as she glanced down at his sweet face.

He's not ready yet!

Sure, he was improving, but she was anticipating another month's worth of practice with him so he'd head off to his forever family on the right paw. Was it smart to send him off only halfway through his rehab?

She watched Hudson walk back to her with his tail wagging. He diverted at the last second and jumped onto his bed, doing a jig on it as he waited for her to deliver his goody.

"Best boy," Morgan said, smiling at him. She tossed him a treat.

She refocused on her phone and frowned as she typed out a response. Do they know he's got issues?

They do. They said they're fine with it and are willing to work with him.

She frowned.

Okay.

Morgan glanced at Hudson. He was in an expectant sphinx-style down on the bed, waiting patiently for his next treat.

"Hey, Hudson, are you ready for your happily-ever-after?"

He plopped his head down on top of his paws and gazed up at Morgan with giant Disney eyes like he was looking at his one truelove.

"Nope. No sir. Don't pull that cute act on me, mister. I think you're amazing, but I'm *not* going to wind up a statistic."

Morgan had heard the words frequently throughout her career: foster failure. The people who brought dogs or cats into their homes thinking they were just temporary lodgers, only to discover that there was no way they could say goodbye. It was the sweetest way to fail at something, but Morgan had entered into the foster situation with Hudson knowing she was one hundred percent immune. She didn't have the headspace to dedicate to a dog like Hudson once she was back in the real world.

The muscles in the back of her neck tightened and a familiar ache spread in her chest when she thought about going back to the clinic.

I'm not ready.

Morgan missed her fellow doctors, her sweet patients, and the clients who appreciated her work, she really did. There were days, hell, sometimes *weeks* when she felt like the luckiest person in the world to be able to help so many animals. But those good times were always punctuated by the grumps and bullies. The people who took Dr. Google's advice over hers. Morgan felt herself getting spun up and focusing on the negative. She shuddered and let out a staccato breath.

The appointments with Cynthia would hopefully help take the edge off.

At least I hope so.

When Morgan opened her eyes again, she realized that Hudson was at her feet with his ears back and his lizard tongue flicking around his mouth.

"Am I *that* obvious?" she asked, dropping to the ground so he could do his comfort dog thing. "Or are you just that good?"

Hudson dove into her lap like he was heading for home plate and flipped onto his back so she could pet his belly. He swatted her hand when she didn't get to it quickly enough.

"Yes, you're making me feel better. It's working, bud, it's working."

Her phone rang and she stretched to reach it on the counter without jostling Hudson from her lap.

Nathan?

Calling instead of texting was weird.

"Hey, you okay?" she asked.

"Yup, all good. I figured it's easier to talk. I ran into a couple of friends who happen to be in town for the weekend, and I thought maybe I could have them over for dinner tonight as well. I think you'd like them, they're in your industry."

"My industry?"

Yikes. I thought we weren't going to go there.

"Yeah, dog stuff. They're launching some food start-up, but I won't tell them about your background, I promise. Would you mind if I invited them?"

So much for the good underwear.

"Please do. The more the merrier." She felt like it was the un-official slogan of her time on the island.

"Excellent. This'll be fun. Seven work?"

"It does. Can I bring anything?"

"No, not really. I've got everything covered. Making meals is sort of my jam. You'll see."

"Can't wait."

Morgan hung up and tried not to feel disappointed about the change in plans. She was still seeing him, she just wouldn't be able to make him the appetizer.

Hudson swatted her hand again.

"Right. Sorry about that."

chapter twenty-seven

Morgan had seen enough of Nantucket to know that the house where Nathan was staying in town for the summer was prime real estate. It was on India Street, close to where she'd run into him on her second day, in one of the stately original homes that lined the narrow road. She loved the newer construction she'd seen, like Eugene and Karl's and Sydney's homes, but she was eager to see the inside one of the grand dames of the Grey Lady.

She could hear the sound of laughter echoing out the windows as she turned her bike onto the thin brick driveway. Morgan realized she hadn't asked how many people would be there or even if they were guys or girls. She spotted his Peachy cart taking up space near a quaint storage shed in the weedy back corner of the yard.

Rather than climbing the steps to the formal front door, she opted to follow the chatter down the driveway, feeling preemptively jittery.

"There she is!" Nathan's voice sounded off from inside, and

she turned to see him beaming out a small window at her. "Come in."

Her heart stutter-stepped at the sight of him framed in the small window.

She waved and slid the backpack she'd worn off her shoulder. Jean had taught her never to show up to a dinner party empty-handed, so she'd dashed into town to pick up two bottles of wine at the corner liquor store.

A preppy-looking guy with curly dark hair in a black checked shirt opened the kitchen door and stepped back to let her in. "You must be Amanda! We've heard so much about you."

"Oh, come on, don't start, Shep," Nathan growled from where he stood at the sink. He looked over at her and winked. "Hey, Morgan, welcome to Peachy's Nantucket headquarters."

She looked around the kitchen and saw cases of various bottles stacked neatly in the corner. While the house was impressive from the outside, the interior looked like it had been renovated in the 1980s and not touched since. Everything was outdated and stuffy compared to the relaxed vibes in the other homes she'd been in.

Nathan was literally up to his elbows in fish, a half-intact *something* that he was expertly slicing through, placing pink slabs on a cutting board next to the sink. There was no awkwardness of whether to greet him with a kiss in front of his friends since he was covered in guts.

"Hey there, I brought wine." She held up the backpack.

"You didn't have to do that, but thank you so much." He jerked his head to the guy who'd let her in. "That asshole is Shepherd Mansard, and Kit Donnelly is using the facilities at the moment, he should be right back."

"Sorry, that was rude of me," Shepherd said. "I was totally kidding."

"I could tell," Morgan answered with a laugh, but part of her worried that she was going to be subjected to guy humor all night. She wished they'd followed the original plan and it was just the two of them getting ready to enjoy whatever feast he was cooking up, and then each other.

A short, bearded redhead in a "Whale's Tale Pale Ale" T-shirt walked into the room, tipping back the last of his beer. He made a beeline for Morgan the second he spotted her.

"Hi, I'm Kit," he said, reaching out to her. "You must be Morgan."

"Nice to meet you," she answered as they shook hands. "So how do you guys know each other?"

"Before we get into that story, Shep, could you get Morgan a drink since I'm gross?" Nathan asked.

"Wine? Beer? White Claw?" Shepherd asked.

"We're having fish and I have a fantastic Pinot in the fridge if pairings matter to you," Nathan added.

"Wine is great, thanks." Morgan walked over to where Nathan was finishing up cleaning what she realized was salmon. She peeked in the sink and could only identify the intestines in the mess. She was happy the fish guts didn't flip her into doctor mode.

He met her eyes as he leaned over and bumped his shoulder into hers.

"Get over here," he growled softly at her. "I've been waiting."

She grinned and gave him a quick kiss.

"What can I do to help?"

"Sit for now. You can be on cleanup crew after we eat. I hate that part. Anyway, this is a super easy meal; pan-seared salmon on sautéed Swiss chard with acini di pepe pasta and fresh vegetables."

Morgan's eyes widened as she perched on a stool nearby. "Seriously?"

"It's nothing." Nathan laughed as he rinsed his hands off. "I'll teach you how to make it."

She saw a flash of his body draped over hers on top of the counter while a pot boiled on the burner and decided that she couldn't wait for her lesson.

Shepherd handed Morgan an overfilled glass of wine.

"So what's the deal with this place? Are they selling?" Kit asked as he helped himself to another beer from the fridge. "Renovating it? Because it needs it."

Nathan shrugged and put a pan on the stove. "I don't think the family knows yet. Their grandmother, the matriarch of the family, just died a few months ago, so they're still processing. They've never rented it out so they're not sure if that's the direction they want to go. It's a sad scenario, but me being here works for all of us. I'm a free caretaker for the summer while they figure it out."

"Dude, then you better start taking care of that yard," Shepherd snorted. "They're going to throw you off the island if you let those weeds get any taller."

He frowned. "Yeah, I know, I need to find someone to do it. The guy the grandma used is basically an antique who went MIA."

Could I force an olive branch and suggest Tess? Should I?

Morgan noticed a half dozen little bowls of herbs all chopped up and ready to go sitting by the stove. She couldn't remember the last time someone had taken such care to cook for her, aside from her parents, and the gesture felt meaningful. It didn't matter that Shepherd and Kit were also there, Nathan was going to make dinner for her regardless, and cooking was caring.

"This is a totally new side of you," Kit said with awe in his voice as Nathan threw garlic and shallots into the pan, filling the room with the delicious smells of a holiday meal. "I had no clue you could cook like this."

Nathan stirred with a spatula and smiled. "I've done my time in the kitchen, trust me. My parents didn't give me much choice."

He moved around the room like a pro, joking with the guys as he put the finishing touches on the meal. Morgan didn't know if he'd measured everything out beforehand or opted to cook intuitively, because he never once referred to a recipe. Morgan suddenly understood why celebrity chefs had fan clubs, even if they wore orange Crocs. The way Nathan managed to sear the salmon while simultaneously tending to the oven-roasted vegetables made her mind wander to what other kinds of multitasking he could do.

I could get used to this.

The rich aroma made Morgan hungry in a way she hadn't felt in ages. She was ready to slow down and experience every morsel of the feast Nathan was preparing.

"Can I at least set the table?" Morgan asked as he pulled the tray of sizzling tomatoes and zucchini from the oven.

"It's done," Nathan answered, nodding toward a swinging door.

She walked over, pushed the door open, and stifled a giggle. The dining room, complete with a miles-long mahogany table and Oriental rug, was set for a formal dinner for four, with blue patterned china and a lit candelabra in the center.

"I'm cooking a *meal*, damn it!" Nathan yelled from the kitchen. "We're gonna act like it."

Morgan had envisioned sitting in the yard, juggling plates and glasses on their laps, but Nathan obviously had other plans for their evening. She loved the contradictions she kept discovering in him, the scruffy surfer dude who knew his way around a kitchen and how to set an elegant table. Nathan was a puzzle she loved piecing together.

The fancy dining room looked decidedly less so post-meal. The table was littered with dirty plates and empty bottles, and the four of them were pushed back and slumped in their high-backed chairs. Morgan felt deliciously full, like she knew she'd eaten too much but was comforted by the fact that everything was good for her.

And that it was made with love. Or, at least with deep summer-fling affection.

"You missed your calling," Shepherd said, patting his stomach. "You belong in a restaurant."

Nathan shook his head vigorously. "No way. I've seen what that's like firsthand."

"How's the beverage business anyway?" Kit asked.

"Really good. I'm getting amazing market research and a bunch of new restaurant accounts here. I'll be ready to scale up by the time I get home."

"And then when you sell Peachy to Coke, you'll be able to retire and head back to Australia to surf for the rest of your life," Shepherd said, polishing off the last of his beer.

Terrible idea. Absolutely awful.

"Gold Coast, man. Those were the days." He looked at Morgan. "That's where we all met, surfing in Australia. Figures I travel halfway around the world and end up hanging with two dorks from Boston."

"You love us and you know it." Kit laughed.

"Tell us about your new dog gig, guys," Nathan said, pouring himself another glass of wine.

He glanced at Morgan, his eyes soft and understanding. Her secret was safe with him.

"Yeah, we're really excited about it. I'll give you our pitch-meeting version," Shepherd said, sitting up straight and clearing his throat. "The idea for A Dog's Dinner came about because my dog Clarence kept suffering from allergies. My wife and I tried every commercial kibble available, and nothing seemed to help. Our vet suggested that we try home-cooking for a while, and we noticed an immediate improvement in not only his skin and coat but his overall *vibe*. But home-cooking human-grade meals is time consuming, plus you need to make sure the food is balanced and complete. That's not easy! So, I called up my buddy Kit from Wharton and pitched the idea that we turn our little home-cooking idea into a real, scalable business."

Kit leaned forward, ready for his part of the sales pitch. "And the rest is history. A Dog's Dinner is now available in thirty states throughout the country, and we're growing every day. At A Dog's Dinner, we've got nutrition to go." He paused. "That's our official elevator pitch. Throw in a few slide decks with cute pictures of our dogs, and that's how we found our investors."

Morgan had heard good things about fresh frozen dog foods, but she knew that the quality didn't come cheap.

"We're growing like crazy. I feel like all we're doing is hiring lately." Shepherd turned to Morgan. "Nathan said you're in the dog biz too, so what do you do, Morgan?"

She coughed. "I'm, uh, I'm here as a dog sitter this summer. Geriatric dog with diabetes."

"And she's fostering," Nathan added, giving her an encouraging smile. "A work-in-progress dog."

"Well, if you've got friends in Boston looking for jobs, let me know. We've got like seven open spots right now, from customer support to software engineers." Shepherd continued, "And we're desperate for another veterinarian. We've already got our vet nutritionist, but we need someone who can bridge the science for the general public. Not easy to find."

For a moment she considered slipping off the Clark Kent glasses, revealing her true identity, and telling them that she knew half a dozen veterinarians in Massachusetts who would jump at the chance to work for the start-up. But then she'd be back on duty, since Shepherd and Kit seemed like the kind of guys who loved talking shop. She wanted to enjoy her wine instead of answering questions about the effects of fiber on impacted anal glands.

"I'll keep that in mind."

Morgan realized that once she got back, she could reach out to her Boston friends and let them know about the opportunity. She liked the way the guys complemented each other, and since they had Nathan's seal of approval it seemed like a solid company.

The conversation moved on to the best surfing spots in the area, and Morgan realized that it was like the three of them shared another language. But when they talked about how they felt when they were surfing, *that* she understood. Freedom, peace, unity with nature.

Morgan perked up when the conversation turned to their plans for the following day. Were Kit and Shepherd leaving? Would she finally be able to throw herself at Nathan after drooling over him from across the room the whole night? She checked her phone. Bernadette would need her final injection of the day within the hour, so they'd have to make it quick.

As much as she loved the idea of pouncing on him the minute Shepherd and Kit left, she didn't want their first time together to be quick. After the buildup, they deserved an hours-long, full-body, head-to-toe exploration of each other.

Morgan sighed. There was something to be said for waiting. Building anticipation, enjoying the journey and all that.

But when we reach the destination . . . watch out.

chapter twenty-eight

Morgan shrieked and ran out of the water carrying her surfboard as the surprise rain pelted her.

"Where did this storm come from?" she laughed to Nathan as they quickly gathered their things on the beach.

"Totally wasn't expecting this," he replied as he threw his stuff in his bag, then helped her grab hers. "Come on!"

They ran up the deserted beach to his truck, their feet sinking into the wet sand, laughing as the rain came down harder. By the time they jumped into the truck, the rain was pouring like someone had turned on a faucet, obliterating everything beyond the windshield. Morgan shivered and pulled Nathan's giant white sweatshirt out of his bag and onto her wet body. Her hair hung in soaked tendrils down her back.

"Whoa," Morgan said, still breathing hard. "So much for our session today. Maybe Mother Nature saw how hard I was ripping and didn't want me to get a big ego."

Nathan's laugh rumbled around the truck. "I can't believe how good you've gotten. You're basically a prodigy."

Morgan was happy she'd stopped drinking early at Nathan's

dinner the night before, since surfing with a hangover would've been impossible. In the weeks since her first lesson, Morgan had graduated from knee-shaking stands to a comfort on top of the board that made her never want to stop. The accidental sun-burn, sore ribs, and surf rashes were a small price to pay for the peace she felt when she nailed a perfect pop-up and rode a tiny wave all the way to shore.

"All thanks to my teacher. And I think I owe him a favor."

She moved their stuff piled on the seat out of the way and crawled over to him with a naughty smile.

"Is this going to turn into a creepy teacher-student fetish thing?" he asked, narrowing his eyes and moving his head away before she could reach him. He hadn't shaved and she wanted to stroke his golden stubble.

"Ugh, gross, absolutely not," she murmured as she got closer to him, her eyes focused on his mouth.

The rain pounded hard on the truck, obscuring their sur-roundings and making it feel like they were protected from view by a veil. Morgan climbed into Nathan's lap slowly, easing her thigh over his legs so that she ended up facing him with the steering wheel pressed against her back. Nathan adjusted be-neath her, never taking his eyes off hers. A warmth unfurled between them, starting from their fused laps.

"Hi," she whispered, linking her arms behind his neck. She trailed her thumb in lazy circles at the base of his hairline and felt him shudder.

"Hi."

He stirred, adjusting his hips like he was uncomfortable.

"What? Am I too heavy for you?"

He licked his bottom lip and shook his head, never taking his eyes off her. "Absolutely not. I love the way you feel on top of me," he rumbled softly.

Every time Nathan lowered his voice it sent tingles from her scalp to her toes.

He put his hands on her hips and pulled her closer. There was no longer a question of how he felt with Morgan straddling him; the evidence was right there, straining against her.

Nathan leaned toward her and took her face in one hand, his thumb against her chin and his fingers branding her cheek. Morgan expected him to pull her into a kiss, but he turned her head slowly to expose her neck, like he was a vampire scouting out her jugular. Morgan closed her eyes as his lips landed on the delicate skin, first in a kiss but then slowly parting to suck gently, his tongue making slow, rhythmic strokes that made her squirm on his lap.

Morgan's head lolled to her shoulder, surrendering to the pulses rolling along her spine until she came to her senses and realized what he was doing.

"You're giving me a hickey!" she gasped, using all of her resolve to pull just out of his reach. She leaned back against the steering wheel and accidentally honked the horn.

He looked at her with a wicked grin. "We're making out in a truck, isn't someone ending up with a hickey required by law? I mean, we even got the windows steamy."

Nathan traced his finger through the condensation, making a heart.

"Maybe we should go somewhere more private?" she suggested.

They both knew it was time. The nonstop kissing and groping with no grand finale was getting ridiculous.

"Your place or mine?" he asked, raising a rakish eyebrow at her.

"Karl and Eugene are home and even though it shouldn't matter, I'd feel weird about it."

"My place it is," he answered, pulling her into a final toe-curling kiss that made her wish they could teleport to India Street.

The rain didn't stop on the short drive to the house, so Nathan pulled his truck all the way up the driveway and they raced in through the backyard. He caught her up in a kiss the minute he closed the door behind them.

It felt as sexy as kissing at her grandmother's house, like she had to keep one eye on the swinging door to keep from getting caught. Morgan didn't want to stop what they'd finally started, but she'd hoped, given the beauty all around them on the island, their first time would be somewhere special. She didn't want to fuck in a museum.

"Let's go," Nathan murmured against her mouth.

They tripped their way upstairs, kissing and pawing at each other. He stripped off the sweatshirt she'd stolen from him, and her rash guard felt like it was glued to her skin, the thin fabric as good as a chastity belt. They kissed and tripped over one another on their way to what she assumed was Nathan's room at the end of a long, wallpapered hallway. He opened the door and abruptly stopped kissing her.

"No way. Not happening."

The ancient wooden four-poster bed with carved pineapples on the top of each spire managed to look massive and rickety at the same time.

"What's wrong?" she asked, her arms still wrapped around his neck.

"That bed squeaks if you look at it funny. The only thing I want to hear is *you*. Let's go."

He jogged to the nightstand next to the bed, opened the top drawer and grabbed a condom, then took her hand and dragged her down the hallway to a small white door and led her up the narrow steps behind it.

They crested the stairs into an attic space that was nothing like the rest of the fussy house. It was a bright white oasis under a sharply slanted roof, with a sturdy daybed tucked in between the windowed eaves. The rain pounded around them like they were trapped in the clouds.

Nathan pulled Morgan against him abruptly like they were beginning a tango. He gazed down at her, his blue eyes stormy with need. Then he took a step back and pulled his rash guard off, leaving him gloriously shirtless in the dim attic light.

Morgan nearly gasped at the sight of him. He was perfect, from the strong sweep of his shoulders to the barely visible sandy blond happy trail that disappeared into his swim trunks. Morgan appreciated that his stomach was flat but without over-the-top ab definition. Sure, he had the cuts on the sides from surfing, but it was the stomach of someone who knew how to enjoy a meal without needing to atone for it at the gym afterward. A man who devoured all the pleasures of life. She took a few steps closer to him and ran her fingertips down it, making him tremble.

"Now you," he whispered, the sound of the rain pounding on the roof nearly drowning him out.

Morgan didn't hesitate and pulled off her green rash guard, letting it fall to the ground in a wet pile. Nathan took her in, his eyes trailing hungrily down her body even though she was still wearing her bikini.

"May I?" he asked, moving behind her and placing his hand on the tie behind her neck.

Morgan nodded and reflexively reached up to help him, but he gently moved her hand away.

"Let me," he murmured with his lips pressed against her ear, then traced a line of kisses down the side of her neck, igniting tingles of anticipation in every spot his mouth touched. He turned her around so her back was to him and gently swept her wet hair out of the way, his fingers working the knot as he planted kisses along her neck and shoulders. He untied the bottom strap of her bikini top and gently pulled it off, then turned her around to face him again.

Nathan exhaled in awe as he took her in. "You are *incredible*. How did I get so lucky?"

"I ask myself the same question every time I look at you," Morgan breathed, stepping closer so she could finally press her bare skin against his and feel his angles melding against her curves. Their lips crushed together in a heated rush, devouring each other as if they'd been waiting years and not weeks for the moment. She couldn't get close enough to him, so she arched into him, almost moving him backward toward the daybed with the force of her kisses. His hands skimmed down her body to the curve of her waist and hooked on the edges of her bikini bottom, as he paused to draw his mouth slightly away from hers. Morgan nodded and hungrily reached to pull his lips back to hers. He pushed the scrap of fabric down until it landed on the floor, leaving her naked in the dim light. The warm ache inside her intensified as his hands slid to explore the curve of her ass.

Morgan reached for the front of his shorts, her fingertips barely cresting the edge before he dropped to his knees in front of her. She gasped in shock and pleasure as his lips pressed against the gentle slope of her low stomach, then lower still. Nathan's mouth moved agonizingly slowly, planting little kisses on her inner thighs. Morgan shivered in anticipation of the moment when he stopped teasing her and reached her heat. She whimpered when his tongue finally made contact between her legs. Little sparks went off behind her closed eyes and she felt herself twitch against his tongue. Morgan realized that she'd wound one hand into his hair and was gripping him for stability as he caressed her with his mouth, gently at first, then with more urgency as he sensed her edging closer to release. For a few agonizing seconds she found herself paralyzed by pleasure, barely able to remain upright but unable to stop him.

She was shocked when the orgasm started building within her after only a few minutes, but for a change she wasn't stuck in her head, overthinking everything. Morgan allowed herself to surrender completely to the moment, and him, and experience every sensation he unlocked within her. Nathan was ending a years-long dry spell that had Morgan tensed up like a coiled spring. She tried to delay the moment because each second of his tongue exploring her made her feel reckless and alive, but he inched her closer with his mouth until she unraveled.

Nathan steadied her as the orgasm ripped through her. Morgan let out a cry that bordered on a scream, her eyes squeezed shut and her head thrown back. The attic went silent again except for the sound of the rain, until Morgan finally opened her eyes and laughed softly.

"Thank you," she said softly, still smiling down at him. "Thank you. But you're not done."

She pulled him up off the floor and started walking backwards toward the daybed. She struggled with his tented shorts, trying to kiss him while at the same time deal with the reinforced Velcro and corset lacing the things seemed to have. Nathan swatted her hand away with a laugh and stripped them off himself while Morgan settled back against the bed, admiring him. Nathan looked better naked than she ever could have imagined, an artist model's example of a man. She finally managed to stop staring when he reached for the condom and put it on his impressive length.

Nathan climbed onto the bed and slowly lowered himself on top of her, fitting himself between her legs. He pushed into her and let out a low rumbly groan that made her want to scrape her nails down his back. He paused and stared into her eyes.

"Do you feel good?" he asked in a shaky whisper.

Morgan bit her lip and nodded.

Nathan leaned down to kiss her, then started moving against her. They rocked together to the rhythm of the rain, knowing that they had nothing to worry about but making each other feel alive until the sun went down.

chapter twenty-nine

It felt like she was getting ready to pick up a date.

The jittery feelings in her stomach, the rushing around to get ready . . . it wasn't normal to be so on edge just to see her brother. But it would be the first time in over six months they'd been together, and it had been years since they'd had to do it without their parents around to referee. Morgan had splurged on a cute green-striped sundress in town, and just for the occasion she had broken out her white Tory Burch sandals that always gave her blisters. She wanted to feel cute for the inspection to come, since Mack's once-overs were legendary.

The countdown to his visit had passed in a blur thanks to Nathan. They'd barely been apart since the rainy day in the attic, spending their days surfing in the morning and making love all night. Morgan kept herself busy while he worked, finding new spaces to explore on the island, relaxing by the pool with Bernie and Hud, and adding pages and pages of notes to the journal that had started off as Hudson's training records and morphed into more of a diary as she'd suspected it might.

And then there were the sessions with Cynthia that were

raw, deep, painful, and revealing in equal measure. She dreaded the lead-up to each session but appreciated the relief she felt afterward.

Morgan parked in the small airport lot just as a crowd of people filed out. She strained to find Mack among them. He was hard to miss at the tail end of the line, in aviators and a slim-cut gray golf shirt, holding Elle's hand.

She felt warmth spread in her chest when she saw Mack looking so happy. He and Elle seemed . . . effortless. Like they belonged on Nantucket even though neither one had set foot on the island before. Her brother looked better in person than in his most carefully filtered photos, his height and confidence drawing stares from the women around him. He'd let his stubble come in and his dark hair was longer than she'd ever seen it. Elle was a beacon of blonde in the sunlight, laughing at something Mack had said. Her sleeveless white tank showed off the definition in her arms, and Morgan wondered if they worked out together.

She hopped out of the Jeep and jogged to them, waving both hands above her head. "Hey, guys!"

"Morgie!"

She could see the happiness in Mack's face even with the sunglasses on, and for a second it felt like the old M&M sibs were back. He dropped his carry-on and spread his arms and Morgan crashed against her brother for a real hug.

He held on to her as something unspoken passed between them, and Morgan squeezed him back a little harder.

This is the beginning of a new era.

Mack pushed his sunglasses up on his head and studied her. "You look incredible. I guess this place agrees with you."

And the sex. All of the orgasms help.

When Mack finally released her, he pointed to Elle with a flourish. "You remember my lovely fiancée."

Elle beamed at them and reached out to Morgan for her own hug. "Nice to see you again!"

Morgan still couldn't get over the fact that out of all of the enhanced, perfect Insta-models her brother had dated, someone so naturally pretty had won his heart. Elle was absolutely stunning, of course, but it was in an outdoorsy, girl-next-door sort of way. Her wide-set brown eyes and Julia Roberts–smile made her seem like everybody's bestie.

"I'm so happy you're here," Morgan answered as they embraced. "Congrats on your engagement. Mack lucked out."

"Please, I'm the lucky one. Look at what your brother did!" Elle said as they pulled apart, thrusting her hand toward Morgan.

The ring was yet another surprise. It was an impressive emerald-cut diamond with two smaller stones flanking it, but it wasn't the knuckle-grazer she'd expected. The band was white gold without any extra bling.

"It's gorgeous." She turned to Mack. "You did a great job."

"I didn't help at all," Elle said, looking at Mack with an adorably lovesick expression. "He knows me so well."

Mack's grin went lopsided, and Morgan felt like she was intruding on a moment between the two of them.

"Let's load up. Should we grab some brunch? You guys hungry?"

Mack glanced at his massive silver Rolex as they headed for the Jeep. "Yeah, I could eat. Elle's been reading up on the restaurants and it sounds like there are a ton to choose from. I want to try that place called the Crew Walk."

It wasn't a surprise that Mack had locked on to the most Instagrammable restaurant on Straight Wharf, the one just a few steps away from where Nathan set up shop every day.

"I'll see if we can get a reservation tonight." Morgan paused as they climbed into the car. "For four."

Mack jerked toward her. "Hold up. What?"

"Ooh," Elle exclaimed, leaning forward from the rear seat. "Sounds like someone's got a summer romance going on!"

Mack squinted his eyes at Morgan. He'd never paid much attention to who she dated, but she assumed his own change in relationship status was making him reconsider who Morgan might be hanging with.

"Are you seeing someone?"

"Yeah," Morgan's lips twitched into a grin. "I am. He's great. He taught me to surf."

Mack gave her a playful punch to the shoulder. "You found yourself a trust fund surfer dude. Nice."

"No, Nathan works," Morgan replied as she eased onto the road. "He's launching a new venture. Functional beverages."

"Wow, he's in a super trendy category," Elle said. "Love it."

Morgan glanced at her in the rearview mirror. "Maybe you two can talk marketing? His business is called Peachy. The drinks are delicious."

"Totally, I need a new challenge," Elle replied. "I hate to say it, but I'm *over* the fitness industry. There's only so many ways to spin 'Our at-home interactive biking system is better than Peloton, please buy one.'"

"Yeah, but Sector Bikes won't be number two for much longer," Mack said, reaching back to squeeze her leg. He glanced at Morgan. "Elle could hook you up with one at cost, Morgie. It's an incredible system, you'd love it because you can squeeze in a workout whenever. I know you're super busy back home."

It was the first time he'd ever acknowledged the demands of her job. Mack usually cracked jokes that all she had to do was play with puppies and kittens all day. Morgan wondered if her mom had been more candid than usual about the price she'd had to pay to earn her ticket to Nantucket.

Morgan gripped the steering wheel a little tighter as she thought about her typical end-of-day collapse after work. "That's really sweet of you to offer. Maybe!"

There's no way I'd do an at-home workout.

The line outside Black-Eyed Susan's was surprisingly short for a change, and within a few minutes, they were seated at one of the elbow-to-elbow tables in the tiny space. It was a modest restaurant that looked more suited to locals than vacationers with its basic décor and open kitchen area. Mack glanced around and wrinkled his nose.

"What?" Morgan asked, slipping back into their shorthand.

"Nothing," he answered. "It's just so . . . *quaint.*"

The way he said it made Morgan realize that she'd made her first misstep of the visit. Mack was probably expecting see-and-be-seen locations, and she'd started them off at one of Nantucket's homiest spots.

"I know, I love it," Elle said. "I read about this place, I'm surprised we were able to get a table so quickly! It's super popular."

Morgan wanted to hug her. Elle was like conversational antacid, neutralizing tensions with just a few words and a smile.

The couple at the table next to them collected their things and left, and Morgan watched Mack check them out as they walked out. His old habit of sizing up everyone seemed to be as strong as ever. He caught her watching him and smiled guiltily.

"What?"

She rolled her eyes at him and went back to studying the menu.

"Someone left their wallet," Mack exclaimed as he reached over to grab it off the chair beside him.

"Maybe they'll come back for it?" Morgan said. "You can give it to the hostess."

He was already jogging toward the door when he answered. "No, I bet I can catch them. Order the huevos rancheros for me, please."

Elle watched him with a moony smile. "That's just like him. Always out to save the day."

"Mack?"

It burst out of her before Morgan could stop herself.

Elle's face screwed up in confusion. "Yeah, why? Hasn't he always been like that?"

"Uh." Morgan bit her tongue to keep from saying something wiseass. "Yeah, he definitely was when we were kids."

When they were younger he was always by her side during her wild animal rescues: helping turtles cross the road, building toad abodes in the backyard, and placing fallen baby birds back in their nests. He seemed to be on the same trajectory as Morgan, eager to be a helper and a voice for the voiceless. She knew those qualities were probably still somewhere inside him.

Morgan realized that Elle was staring at her, waiting for her to go on.

"And I can tell he still is. Mack and I haven't had a chance to talk or hang out much in a while. It's good to reconnect with him. And you."

Elle smiled, the relief obvious on her face. "He said the same thing. He really misses you."

Tears tickled the corners of Morgan's eyes and she stared at her menu to keep them from spilling. It was too early to feel so emotional.

The screen door slammed, and everyone turned to watch as Mack walked in. His face was red, and his forehead shiny, but he still looked like the king of the island.

"Caught 'em!" He smiled in triumph. "They were driving away, but I chased them down the street like a lunatic and they finally stopped."

"Aw, baby. Yay!" Elle said, rubbing his back as he sat down.

He locked on to Morgan and studied her face, concern wrinkling his brow. "What's wrong?" He glanced at Elle. "Did you ask her yet?"

"*No*," she scold-whispered back at him. "And everything is fine, we were just talking about the weather."

"Ah, got it." Mack widened his eyes at Elle, then looked down at his menu, whistling softly.

Elle cleared her throat. "Since my fiancé almost blew it, I might as well do it now instead of over drinks at dinner. Morgan, our wedding is going to be nontraditional in a bunch of ways, but we're still doing some of the old-fashioned stuff, like having a group of friends and family with us at the altar. There aren't going to be 'bridesmaids' and 'groomsmen,' just 'honored attendants,' and we're picking them jointly." She paused and her lower lip quivered. "Morgan, we would love to have you standing beside us on our special day."

The weepiness Morgan had been holding back finally broke loose and she sniffled to keep her nose from running. "Seriously?" She glanced back and forth between Mack and Elle as the tears flowed silently down her cheeks.

"Yeah, of course," Mack said softly. He reached out and put his hand on top of Morgan's.

Her heart about cracked in two. It felt like the distance between them was closing at warp speed, and she probably had Elle to thank for it. It was a fresh start for the two of them, and one that she couldn't have envisioned was even possible before he'd arrived on Nantucket. Mack was still the same Mack he'd evolved into, but she could see shades of her sweet little brother now and then, like the sunlight sifting through the trees.

She realized that they were both still staring at her expectantly.

"Well, yes, obviously I will!"

Elle let out an excited whoop as she jumped out of her chair to give Morgan a hug, and within a few seconds they both were teary.

"Mack was so nervous to ask you!" Elle said as she settled back in her seat.

"No, I wasn't," he blustered, trying to step back from the emotions she could see playing across his face. "I knew she'd say yes. How could she not? I'm her baby brother."

Morgan gave him a wry smile but didn't say anything about the fact that they barely kept in touch. But things were going to be different going forward.

"The good news is that you won't have to do any of those ridiculous pre-wedding duties. You can pick your own dress, I just want it to be champagne-colored. There are no bachelor or bachelorette parties, and you can sit with your date during the reception," Elle said.

The corners of Morgan's mouth pulled down. "I'm not sure I'll have one."

"Oh, come on! What about your surfer boy?" Mack asked.

"It's just a summer thing. Nothing serious," she answered, motioning the waitress over.

I've barely even thought about leaving, let alone what's going to happen with Nathan once I go.

"We'll be the judges of that when we meet him tonight," Elle said with authority. "Mack told me he was never going to get married the first time we went out, and now look at him."

Happiness warmed Morgan's chest at the thought of the four of them enjoying the evening together. She felt like a few of the loose ends in her life were finally stitching together into something beautiful and comforting and exactly what she needed.

chapter thirty

Huh. You don't strike me as the Dungeons and Dragons type," Nathan said to Mack in the world's most obvious understatement.

"It was a *long* time ago." Morgan laughed and reached for her champagne glass, already feeling the bubbles. "Mack was into all of that stuff way before Reddit said it was cool to like it. D&D, comic books, superhero movies . . . he was a real trendsetter."

They were seated at a prime outdoor table at the Crew Walk, an intimate grouping of low, slouchy navy couches beneath a canopy that was the perfect spot to see and be seen. Mack had already Instagrammed them, which Morgan realized was his ultimate seal of approval.

The introductions had gone smoothly, with Mack and Nathan sizing each other up and leaning into a chest bump–bro handshake combo that every man seemed to instinctively know. After Nathan turned away from her, Elle had given her an exaggerated thumbs-up and mouthed *Wow!* They'd settled into a fast and easy camaraderie as they worked their way through pre-dinner drinks.

"Morgan is being way too nice, I was a total geek until college," Mack said a little too sharply. He and Morgan exchanged a glance, but he looked away quickly. Mack grabbed the champagne bottle out of the chilling bucket and held it up to the fading light. "I think we need more Avizoise, this bottle's basically kicked. Where's my favorite waitress?" He craned his neck to look around.

Morgan recognized his quick change of topic. Mack never liked talking about who he'd been as a kid. Whenever a throwback challenge popped up on social media, Morgan noticed that he used the same photo, the one from their family trip to Niagara Falls where his body was hidden underneath a yellow rain slicker.

The champagne he'd selected was far from the most expensive on the wine list even though it was over two hundred dollars a bottle, but it was enough to get a gasp out of Morgan when he'd picked it. The meal was shaping up to the equivalent of a month's rent back home, but she knew Mack had something to prove, and for a change she didn't feel the need to make a snarky comment.

"Morgan told me you surf," Mack said to Nathan after he'd ordered from the gorgeous young waitress. "Wish we had more time here, I'd make you take me to your secret spot. I wouldn't call myself a *pro*, but I've done my time on the waves."

Morgan had to hide a smirk. There was nothing Mack couldn't do, according to Mack.

"No way!" Nathan replied. "That sucks you won't have time, this weekend is supposed to be amazing. When do you two head out?"

"Sunday afternoon. We've got our moped ride to 'Sconset tomorrow, then we've got Morgan's dog fund-raiser thing Saturday night. You going to that too?"

"Yeah, I'm basically tagging along all day tomorrow. Hope you don't mind me party-crashing," Nathan said sheepishly.

"No, we'd love to have you come," Elle said. "You can be our tour guide since Morgan hasn't been to 'Sconset yet."

"Hey," Morgan said with mock hurt in her voice. "I think I did a fine job showing you around today."

"Yeah, but your little shopping trip into town set me back a couple hundred. Guess I just can't say no to my girl." He snaked his arm behind Elle, and she leaned against him.

Nathan and Morgan were seated next to each other on the couch, but he was keeping a polite distance from her, probably in deference to Mack. She wished she was pressed up against him, tucked under his arm and wrapped in his delicious suntan lotion scent. But the night was young and if they kept up their pace, it would involve a crapton of drinking, which meant Morgan would eventually end up hanging from Nathan like a backpack.

"What was Morgan like when she was younger?" Nathan asked, leaning back so the setting sun put a spotlight on him. "I want all the details."

"Basically the same," Mack said, then grabbed an oyster and let it slide into his mouth. He gave it a single chew. "Driven. High achieving. Homecoming court. Everybody loved her. Obviously."

Morgan blushed. She'd expected him to throw in something sarcastic about the headgear she had to wear with her braces or her love of boy bands. He usually never missed an opportunity to make fun of her. The changes in Mack kept surprising her.

Nathan let his eyes travel up her body slowly as if he'd forgotten her brother was sitting across from him.

"You were on homecoming court too?" Nathan asked. "Same."

"No way," Elle exclaimed. "Me too! We've got a royal family here."

Mack shifted and cleared his throat. Morgan knew that it was time to switch topics.

"Does everyone know what they're getting?" she asked. "I'm thinking about the pan-seared chicken."

"Not happening," Mack protested. "We're on a goddamned island. Get the lobster! It's my treat tonight."

Morgan started to protest, but Nathan beat her to it. "I can't let you do that, mate. We have to go half at least."

"Then you're gonna have to fight me, bro. This is my thanks for the wonderful hostessing my sister is doing this weekend. It's been way too long, Morgie." Mack raised his glass to her. "I've missed hanging with you."

"Aww," Elle murmured, glancing between them, making Morgan wonder if she knew more about the state of the sibling relationship than she let on.

"Yes it has, Mackie," Morgan said, touching her glass to his, then downing a gulp to keep from getting emotional.

The waitress came over to take their dinner order, and a tipsy feeling that had nothing to do with the alcohol spread through Morgan as she scanned the group. It was perfect. Mack and Nathan both seemed eager to make a good impression on each other, but it felt like there was a genuine connection happening between them as well. Elle already felt like the sister she'd never had. Morgan could only imagine how close they'd become as the years passed and babies came into the picture.

She wondered if the feelings were real or just a trick of the Grey Lady. Everything seemed easier on Nantucket. Tensions eased, relationships mellowed, and nothing mattered other than where to hang out and what to eat. Would she be able to keep some of the magic once she got home?

Home.

The word sent a chill through her. She had less than a week left and she wasn't ready to go back to everything she'd left behind.

Nathan leaned close to her. "What's wrong?" His lips brushed her ear as he whispered, and it sent a tingle along the back of her neck. He pulled away to study her face. "You look worried."

She shook her head slowly. "Not worried," she lied. "Just melancholy. I'm sad my time here is almost over."

He was draped across the couch and finally leaning in close to her while Mack and Elle acted ridiculously cute with each other on the couch across from them.

"But . . . *our* time isn't over," he said softly, his eyes locked on hers. "Or, it doesn't have to be. You're only an hour away from me at home. That's stupid close."

It was the first time either of them had mentioned the future.

"It *is* stupid close."

Nathan ran his finger down Morgan's cheek. They leaned toward each other.

"There's that PDA again." A hoarse voice sounded off from the dock beyond the restaurant.

They jerked apart and saw Brooks waving at them. He looked tidy and sober, but was probably off to change both statuses.

"Hey, Brooks. Where you heading tonight?" Nathan called to him, trying not to be obnoxious about the fact that he was yelling across the crowded restaurant.

"American Seasons for dinner then anywhere and everywhere, baby. We should meet up. Bring your friends. I'll text you." He flashed a peace sign and waddled away.

"Okay, who was that and how do I meet him?" Mack asked, the awe evident on his face. "That dude's got a story, I can tell."

It's like he has a sixth sense for people with money.

"Remember that huge yacht I pointed out today? It's his," Morgan said, pointing toward the docks beyond the restaurant. "His name is Brooks."

Mack turned to Nathan with wide eyes. "How do you know him? Do you think he'd be interested in investing in some prime New York City real estate?"

Nathan chuckled. "I know him through work, but I'm not sure about his portfolio."

"Yeah, he's one of Peachy's many fans," Morgan added. "Or maybe he's *your* fan? He always wants to hang out with you."

Nathan ducked his head. "Nah. Brooks loves everyone."

"Well, if that's the case let's make sure to track him down tonight," Mack said. "I've got some properties that would blow his mind. I'll give you my number so if we miss him you can arrange an intro later."

"Hon," Elle interrupted with a frown. "Please don't work this weekend. No real estate talk. I'm begging you. Let's just have fun."

Morgan recognized the expression on Mack's face as he considered his answer. It was the one that weaponized his charm to plead his case, which usually worked on both of their parents and never Morgan.

"But babe, I . . ."

She widened her eyes at him and tipped her head.

"Okay, okay. No business, I promise."

A laugh bubbled out of Morgan at the unexpected victory. "Holy shit, Elle. You're a certified Mack whisperer. I've never seen that happen before."

She half expected Mack to say something obnoxious, but he laughed along with her, leaving Morgan to be amazed that her brother might have turned into someone she actually liked.

"Ice cream!" Elle yelled as they stumbled down Straight Wharf after finishing dinner. "I want ice cream."

Morgan glanced at Nathan and wound up tripping on an uneven brick in the sidewalk. "Juith Bar?"

"You're drunk, Morgan Pearce." He laughed as he reached out to steady her. "But, yes, the Juice Bar. This way, guys."

"I'm not drunk, I'm *happy*," she shot back at him, tucking herself beneath his arm. "This is fun."

It was a lie because Morgan was both. The bottomless champagne and the fact that everyone got along perfectly made the evening better than she could've hoped. The guys were texting each other memes and sharing private jokes that had them cackling.

Nathan led the group down the sidewalks, past the T-shirt shops that were still open despite the late hour and the crowded restaurants.

"Hold up." Mack stopped in his tracks when he got to the Rose and Crown pub and pointed. "Is that the *line*?"

There were other ice cream shops on the island, but there was something about the variety of flavors and homemade waffle cones that made the spot hard to beat. It was rare not to see people wrapped around the corner waiting for their fix.

"Nooo," Elle moaned, zipping up the Nantucket-red hoodie Mack bought for her at Murray's Toggery. "It's going to take forever."

"You'd be surprised," Nathan said. "They know how to move in there. C'mon, let's get in line. It'll be fifteen minutes, tops."

"*I'm* paying this time," Mack slurred, pointing at his chest.

Morgan realized that he was still smarting over the bill from dinner. Nathan had swiped the bill before Mack could touch it and handed his card to the waitress, and the good-natured scuffle that followed started to feel like the real thing, thanks to all the alcohol. Morgan had gotten a peek at it as Nathan reviewed it and had to stifle a gasp. He'd signed it and then tucked the receipt in his breast pocket, barely giving it a second glance.

They leaned against the gray-shingled building as they waited, watching all walks of life go by. Nathan greeted people he knew, fielding high fives and compliments on Peachy.

"You're like the mayor of this place," Mack said. His cheeks were pink from the day's sunshine.

"Not really, it's just because of my cart's location. I see a lot of the same faces all day. It's a social job."

Morgan slid her hand into Nathan's and he smiled down at her. He'd stopped drinking after his third beer and was still maintaining a polite distance from Morgan despite the fact that she kept grabbing his ass and trying to get him to give her piggyback rides.

"Morgan!"

She looked around and spotted Tess and Cyrus across the street waving at her with Palmer on a leash next to them. She was happy to see them until she realized exactly what it meant.

Tess and Nathan were going to talk for the first time since the great high school heartbreak. She wished she wasn't tipsy.

"Come say hi, you guys!" she shouted back to them. "Meet my brother and his fiancée."

"And me," Nathan said in a quiet voice.

"And you," she reassured him, grasping his arm. "But you already know Cyrus from Bartlett's Farm. And you know Tess too."

"Oh yeah, I have met him." Nathan squinted as they got closer. "But I don't know the girl he's with."

"From *high school*," Morgan whispered.

"But she didn't go to my school," he whispered out of the corner of his mouth as Palmer dragged them over. "I have no clue who she is."

"Hi, hi, hi," Tess said, waving at the group when they reached them. "I'm Tess and this is Cyrus. And Palmer, of course."

The dog couldn't decide if he should try to lick up a puddle of ice cream or greet everyone.

"This is my brother, Mack, and his fiancée, Elle," Morgan said, pointing to them.

Morgan watched Tess take Mack in, then glance at Morgan. "You two look like twins."

No one had said it since they were kids. They grinned at each other like dorks.

"And you both know Nathan," Morgan continued.

"Yeah, forgive me, but how do we know each other again?" he asked Tess, his brow furrowed.

"I went to Jefferson," she replied, her face an expressionless mask.

"Oh, okay, right. We probably yelled at each other at football games." He laughed. "Go Tigers."

"Exactly," she agreed. She fake-glowered at him and raised a fist. "Go Eagles."

Nathan laughed, and Tess caught Morgan's eye to give her a nod that signaled that everything was fine. There would be no reality TV reveal. She breathed a sigh of relief.

Palmer snuffled Morgan's body looking for treats. "I'm broke tonight, mister," she exclaimed, showing him her empty palms. "Not a morsel on me. Sorry, bud."

"His surgery is coming up," Cyrus said, leaning over to thump the dog on his shoulder. He looked up at Mack. "Did you know that your sister basically saved our dog? She diagnosed his hip dysplasia on sight alone."

"Is that a fact?" Mack slurred and punched Morgan's shoulder affectionately, causing her to stumble a step. "Well, that's how she rolls. It's what she does best!"

Mack stopped talking abruptly and went white. She'd told them that she was undercover and he seemed to realize that he was about to step in it.

"Hey, what's the best flavor at this place?" he asked, looking around the group. "I need advice."

It was a clunky segue, but the conversation shifted to a debate about which ice cream was the best. Mack fell back in line beside Morgan as Cyrus and Tess argued about the merits of Crantucket ice cream.

"Sorry about that," he said in a low voice. "I almost blew it. I just like hyping you up."

"It's okay," she whispered back. "Nathan knows."

Mack looked at her with a drunken smile, and Morgan

couldn't tell if he was actually listing side to side or if her vision was swimming. "You like him, don't you?"

She nodded and felt something shimmery course through her. Pure happiness, aided by alcohol, was a heady mix. "I like him a lot," she whispered.

Mack crossed his arms and nodded, glancing between her and Nathan like he was sizing him up.

"Well, I do too. I approve, Morgie."

She didn't need his blessing, but it sure felt great to get it.

chapter thirty-one

I wanna live here," Elle shouted with her arms stretched over her head, gazing out over the dunes to the ocean below. She looked like a model from a tourism ad in a woven fedora and white sundress. "I *love* Nantucket."

It was another perfect day, with the bright sun high in a cloudless sky and the sound of the ocean rolling in the distance. They were midway through the 'Sconset Bluff Walk, a trail that was open to the public, yet was so close to the majestic homes along it that walking it felt like trespassing on private property. The path meandered along the edge of the high bluff, with ocean views running nearly the entire length of it on one side, and quintessential Nantucket homes on the other, most of which were close enough that they could wave hello to the folks sitting on their back porches. The lawns were lush, the climbing roses abundant, and the flags at the tops of poles snapping at attention in the wind.

"You won't let me talk real estate, so I'm not going to mention home prices," Mack said, following closely behind Elle on one of the narrow parts of the trail. "But if you want to live here, I'll make it my mission, babe."

"You guys are gross," Morgan said affectionately. She glanced over her shoulder at Nathan bringing up the rear and smiled. She turned back to Mack just as he stopped to pick up a wrapper someone left behind and stuffed it into his pocket.

"Why would people litter?" he asked, looking out at the water. "Next thing you know it'll blow out there and choke some poor turtle."

Every so often, Morgan caught the sweet scent of honeysuckle on the breeze. A spaniel mix ran out to greet them, followed by a white-haired woman who caught him by the collar and brought the dog back to her porch. Morgan thought about how the walk would've gone if she'd brought Hudson. Given the narrow path and the homes so close by, it would've felt like clocking in for work.

"Mack can't talk about houses around here, but I can," Nathan said. "I heard that the one over there sold for four million last year."

They all turned to gawk at the gray-shingled home with an enviable porch and massive blue hydrangeas bookending it. A trio of rabbits sat munching along the hedgerow, adding to the fairy-tale vibe.

"You want it, babe? Give me a little time and it's yours," Mack laughed.

"Hey, check this out," Elle said, skipping ahead to a section of the path that cut through a wall of a greenery. "How pretty."

Mack whipped his phone out and snapped a photo of her. He paused at the opening. "Morgs, can you take a quick picture of us in front of this?"

She nodded and jogged to them. Nathan joined her as Mack and Elle tried out a few poses.

"Hey, guys, watch out. That's poison ivy," Nathan said, pointing at the shiny plant near their feet.

"Shit!" Mack exclaimed, jumping away. "I'm hyperallergic. I caught a really bad case when I was at camp and now I'm petrified of it. I had it *everywhere*. Like, even on my ass."

"Aw, babe," Elle said, pouting, rubbing his back. "I didn't know that about you."

It wasn't a surprise Mack hadn't mentioned it. Morgan knew he didn't like thinking about that period of his life.

"That's funny, a kid I went to camp with got it really bad too," Nathan said, smiling at the memory. "No one wanted to get near the poor guy. We moved his whole bunk outside and made him sleep there until the counselors caught us!" He shook his head. "Kids are so stupid."

Morgan's heart thudded as she turned toward Mack. He was staring at Nathan with narrowed eyes, his hands curled in fists. She recognized the expression on his face and felt her body tense instinctively.

"Where did you go to camp?" Mack asked in a low voice.

"Camp Crescent Moon, in the Catskills."

Morgan glanced between Mack and Nathan like a spectator at a tennis match as her stomach dipped, making her feel seasick. Mack's posture shifted, first closing in on himself in a shoulder-hunching slouch, then slowly straightening and reclaiming his space, vertebra by vertebra. He seemed coiled with fury as he locked on to Nathan.

"Wait a minute, did you go there too?" Nathan asked, giving Mack a confused look, then glancing at Morgan.

He nodded silently.

"Hold up, no way. Oh my God, it's *you*!" Nathan exclaimed as he laughed and clapped his hands in recognition. "You're Butt Crack Mack, otherwise known as Pork Roll! What a small world. Holy shit, you've *really* changed since then."

Mack didn't answer, and the only sound punctuating the uncomfortable silence was the ocean pounding away at the bottom of the bluff.

"I seriously can't believe the coincidence." Nathan looked at Morgan with a giant smile on his face. "Were you there too?"

"No, I went to horse camp," she replied in a low voice. Morgan wished she could derail the conversation, but there was no way Mack was moving on from the subject. The dangerous shift in the air seemed obvious to everyone but Nathan.

Elle clung to Mack's arm, watching his face with a worried expression.

"We had so much fun that year," Nathan continued. "Wasn't it a blast? Remember when we played capture the flag with Camp Beaver Basin and when we lost, we pushed half of them in the lake? We were such little a-holes."

No one said anything for a moment, until Mack finally spoke up.

"Yeah. You were . . . Nate."

It was the end of the Nathan she thought she knew and the introduction of the Nate she knew too well.

After the realization of who he was, Mack and Elle had taken off on their moped without so much as a goodbye. Morgan wished she hadn't ridden to 'Sconset on the back of Nathan's moped, because she couldn't bear the thought of pressing her body against his now.

Nathan followed Morgan down a public staircase from the bluff to the beach below, finding a spot away from the blankets and sandcastles to try to figure out what to do next. They sat down in the sand close to the seagrass. Nathan reached out to take her hand and she let it sit limply in his before pulling it away.

"You have no idea how badly you hurt him," Morgan said softly to him, staring out at the water.

Nathan was silent as he waited for her to continue.

She finally turned to him with tears in her eyes.

"I hated you *so* much."

He recoiled like she'd hit him with a brick, but didn't respond.

"What you did changed *everything* for him. Because back then, before camp, Mack was . . ." She shook her head. "Mack was a normal twelve-year-old kid. Funny. Cute. A little chubby with baby fat. But it was fine, he had a friend group at school." A smile flickered across her face at the memory. "He was so damn excited for camp that summer. But when he got there, someone gave him the nickname 'Pork Roll.' And now I know that was *you*." She glared at him. "My parents told him to ignore it when he called home crying. But then it got worse when he caught poison ivy. And you obviously know the rest."

She picked up a handful of sand and let it drain through her fingers, waiting for the "it was just a joke" defense, but Nathan remained silent, his face ashen.

"Do you know that I cursed your name for *years*? 'Hate' and 'Nate' go really well together," she said with a harsh laugh. "Mack told me the whole camp joined in but that you were the ringleader. You're the one who came up with the names."

"Morgan . . . I'm so sorry."

She ignored him. "You would think that back then, before cell phones, what happens at camp stays at camp, right? That it's far enough away from home that it wouldn't impact real life. Well, a few kids from our school were there, so when they went back in the fall, the nicknames did too. The bullying continued, and Mack went from the kid just doing his thing to everybody's target. I've gotta say, your nicknames had staying power. Points for that."

"Can I explain—"

"No, hold on. It doesn't end there." Morgan paused to gather her thoughts as her sadness shifted to anger. "I did what I thought was right, trying to be a good big sister and standing up for him. But that made it *worse*. People teased him and said he was a pu—" She stopped herself from using the word. "That he was weak because a girl was trying to fight his battles for him. And it made him hate me. No matter what I did, I was wrong. We went from being best friends to . . . nothing."

Nathan stared out at the water, still silent.

"Obviously, he turned things around," she continued. "After high school he started working out and evolved into the Mack you see now. But his entire life feels like one big 'fuck you' to the way he was treated as a kid. It's like he's still got something to prove to the world."

Nathan let out a long, shaky breath, head hanging.

"I have to apologize to him. I need to talk to him."

"No, you need to talk to *me* first, and I'll decide if that should happen," Morgan shot back at him, still her brother's protector.

Nathan nodded, his mouth in a tight line.

"I was an asshole," he said, his voice was coarse with emotion. "Even back then, on some level I knew I was the worst. But it didn't stop me."

"Why, though?" Morgan's voice cracked with emotion. "What drives someone to be so . . . *cruel* to other people?"

Nathan finally turned to look at her. "I was an angry kid, but I know now that it was just a cover for how sad I was." He let out a hard exhale. "It took a lot of therapy to figure that out. My parents never had a great marriage, and things got even worse right before they divorced. I tried to be perfect, so that I didn't make things harder for them. And I think on some level I thought I could be the glue that kept them together. When they finally split, I crash-landed. I was mad at the world and anyone that wound up in my crosshairs."

"So why did you say you had fun at camp just now, if you realized that you'd been horrible to everyone? You acted like Mack was in on it, like it was just kids being goofy."

Nathan rubbed his hand over his face. "That's one of the worst parts. I managed to block stuff out or remember it as something other than it was. In my memories, the poison ivy stuff was just a bunch of kids having fun, being stupid together. Clearly, I'm wrong."

"Yeah, kids just *love* being ostracized," she scowled.

"There's nothing else for me to say but I'm so sorry."

The sound of children laughing drifted over to them.

"That's not me anymore, Morgan," he continued. "You know that."

She was silent as their time together flipbooked through her mind, each happy memory tinged with the knowledge of what she'd discovered. Nathan *was* different, but would it be enough for Mack? She didn't think it was possible for him to forgive the person who'd basically ruined his young life.

Morgan worried that the cruelty was still crouching somewhere inside Nathan, just waiting for the right trigger. Or was he the kind of person who managed to tame it and save it for certain people, the way her clients did at the clinic? Was he one of those people who yelled at the receptionist if they were running a few minutes behind schedule? Or snapped at a waiter when he got his order wrong?

"I don't think you should come to the gala," she said, still refusing to look at him. "I'm going to be busy for most of the night, which means you'd be alone with Mack and Elle. That's obviously not a good idea."

"I get it," he said, his voice quiet and sad. "Do you think he'd talk to me, though? Before he leaves?"

Morgan shrugged. "No clue; now it's up to him. Doubtful, but I'll ask."

"I've got his number. I could text him."

"Please don't," she replied.

She stared out at the waves he'd helped her master a few weeks before. It felt impossible that sunny, smiling Nathan was the same person as Hateful Nate. He'd changed, yes, but Morgan wasn't sure that she'd be able to look at him the same way again knowing what he'd put her family through. And Mack might not be able to forgive Nathan, which would make a future with him impossible if she wanted to rebuild her relationship with her brother.

Would it come down to a choice between them?

Even as she sat a few feet away from him, raw and angry, a

tiny part of her wanted to creep over to Nathan and take him in her arms. His entire body telegraphed the pain he was in, and she'd always been drawn to help beings in distress. As much as she hated him for kicking off the torment that changed her brother forever, she had to remind herself that he'd been just a boy at that point as well, navigating his own pain.

But he had also admitted that Nathan continued to be Hateful Nate until well beyond childhood. Did she even know him, or was Nantucket Nathan just another side of his personality?

chapter thirty-two

Morgan woke up the next morning in a sweaty panic, star-tling Hudson when she jerked upright. She fell back against the bed, heart racing while he dug at the covers so he could move underneath and distract her. He snuggled against her, tucking his paws against his body so he could rest his head on her shoulder. She stroked his head while she tried to piece together the dream that had left her sweaty and anxious, but all she could remember was the ocean, black and heavy, pulling her under, like the water was tar.

The rest of the day after the big reveal had passed in a blur. Morgan had gone to a quick pre-gala planning meeting, then on to an evening at Cisco Brewers that was supposed to have been a foursome. The night had bordered on frantic with nonstop games of cornhole and Uno while the three of them pretended that the shit hadn't just hit the fan and splattered all over their formerly perfect reunion. It was like Morgan and Mack had reverted to the high school versions of themselves, doing everything in their power to not talk about anything that mattered.

Morgan forced herself to head to the main house to make coffee, and Mack met her in the kitchen with sleepy eyes and messy hair shortly after.

"Hey," he said as he reached down to pet Bernadette and Hudson. "You hungover too?"

She shook her head. "I drove, remember?"

"Right." He poured a cup of coffee.

"Elle still sleeping?"

Mack nodded. "She went all in last night."

"You did too." Morgan paused and picked her next words carefully. "So . . . how are you feeling today?"

"A little groggy, but I'll make it."

He'd misunderstood the question. Morgan studied the Pak-Reynolds-designed faux bois coffee mug to stop herself from asking how he was *feeling* feeling. She'd been burned so many times when they were younger that she knew better than to push him.

"So, what now?" Mack asked, staring into his mug.

It was as good an invitation to talk as any, and she jumped on it.

"I told him not to come to the gala with us tonight. There's no way—"

Mack leaned onto the counter and frowned at her. "Yeah, about that. Elle and I decided to skip it if that's okay. We thought it might be nice to grab dinner alone and keep it chill on our last night. Do you mind?"

"Of course not, no problem. It's going to be lame anyway."

"Hardly," Mack snorted. "If I was in the right frame of mind, I'd be there scoring new clients. But I'm just not feeling it."

"I get it."

The silence stretched out until she couldn't take it. She wasn't going to miss the chance to at least try to talk everything out with him while it was just the two of them.

"You have to know I had no clue who he was."

She held her breath as she waited for him to respond. The old Mack punched back any time someone got too close to his feelings. The new Mack considered the admission in silence.

"Yeah, no kidding," he finally said. "How could you? We were kids. Neither of us look the same. Thank God." He ran his hand through his bedhead.

A shadow passed over Mack's face, and for a second Morgan could see the boy he'd been back then. She felt a piece of her heart chip away.

"It probably doesn't matter to you, and I totally understand, but I need you to know that Nathan's different. He wants to talk to you, Mack. He's not like that anymore. People evolve and I promise you he has. He volunteers with kids, if you can believe it. But nothing erases how he acted back then," she added.

Morgan realized with a start she was talking Nathan up, not just to try to change Mack's viewpoint of him, but also to explain why she'd been sleeping with the enemy.

"Yeah." Mack took a deep breath and exhaled slowly. "People do change. Definitely. I'm happy to hear that he's different. The world needs fewer shitty people." He paused, and the only sound was rhythmic thumping as Hudson scratched himself. "We've all changed since then."

Morgan felt a heaviness lift. Maybe there was a way through the mess?

"But that doesn't mean I can get past it," Mack continued, still looking down at his mug.

The floor went wavy beneath her feet.

"The suffering that I had to go through because of him . . . do you get it, Morgan? I mean, you probably don't because everybody loved you, but it was *relentless* for me. All because of him. Nate Keating lit the fuse that blew my life to hell. I'm sorry, but I don't have it in me to forgive him. Good for him for owning his shit and wanting to make good with me, but I owe him *nothing*." Mack paused and lowered his voice. "And I hope that makes him insane."

Morgan's stomach twisted as she realized that there was no right way to respond.

If she applauded the fact that he was prioritizing his mental health and refusing a reconciliation, it meant that she had no future with Nathan. But she also couldn't try to force his forgiveness because it meant she was putting Nathan's feelings over Mack's. And they'd only just started rebuilding their relationship.

"I know you like him and whatever, but that's how I feel," Mack said with a shrug. "You can do what you want, it's your life. Just know that I want nothing to do with him. Nothing."

Mack padded to the sliding door and walked out to the yard while Hudson glanced between them and tried to decide who to comfort first.

They had thirty minutes before event kickoff, and the catering staff was running around making sure the tables were set and the swag bags were hung on the backs of every chair. Morgan had to admit that the overflowing pink flowers, hanging lanterns, and hurricane lamps had transformed the simple white tents into something swanky enough to justify the $150-per-head ticket price.

After checking in to see if she could help with anything, Morgan tried to fade into the background. The energy in the place was too much for her. All she wanted to do was go back to the pool house and collapse on the couch with her volunteer comfort dog.

Sydney spotted her from across the room and made a bee-line for her.

"I need to tell you something," she said, looking lovely in a pink strapless dress and holding a beautiful bundle of ranunculus. "And you're not going to like it."

Morgan's shoulders slumped. "What now?"

"Hold on, are you okay?" Sydney studied her face. "What's going on with you?"

Morgan shook her head glumly. "Too much to get into. Family stuff."

Sydney reached out and grasped her arm. "I'm sorry to hear that. Your brother and his fiancée are visiting, right? And they're coming tonight?"

"No, they decided to go to dinner."

Morgan was tempted to briefly fill her in on what had gone down, but there was no way she was going to kick down the dam holding everything inside.

"Ah, okay," Sydney nodded, a knowing expression on her face. "Got it. Anyway, on to the *other* bad news: Abby okayed a few VIP guests' dogs at the last minute and she set up a make-shift barking lot."

Morgan closed her eyes. "How many dogs? Do you know?"

She scrunched up her face. "Um, fifteen?"

"Does she have separate areas for big and little dogs?"

Sydney shook her head.

"And how tall is the fence?"

She gestured to knee height. "It's a very . . . *cute* space. Great for photo ops."

"And awful for dog safety," Morgan muttered. "I can't believe she went and did it anyway."

"Well, at least it wasn't a carte blanche invitation to *all* of the attendees' dogs, thanks to you. But that means I'd love for you to clone yourself and be in two places at once." She grinned at Morgan. "Backstage with the dog models and in the barking lot. We need someone like you watching over everything."

She sighed. "I'll do my best."

"You leave this week, right?" Sydney asked.

Morgan nodded. "Wednesday, first thing."

The stress tentacles flicked along her spine, creeping up toward her temples at the mention of her departure.

"Pat is ready for Hudson anytime, so if you need to transition him over to her earlier this week just let me know."

The realization that she needed to get ready to say goodbye to Hudson slammed into her. One of Beacon of Hope's other foster homes had found a forever home for their last foster dog and now had space for him. It was a quiet household without any other pets so it was a good fit for Hudson, plus when Morgan had spoken to the foster mom on the phone, she'd seemed knowledgeable about dog behavior. It was going to be a great fit for him while he waited for his happily-ever-after.

"I seriously can't thank you enough for everything you did for us. I know this"—Sydney gestured around the room—"was a lot. And the way you worked with Hudson. Just amazing. Thank you for being so generous with your time." Sydney gave her a meaningful look and reached out to squeeze her arm again. "I hope you were able to find some peace while you were here."

Morgan reached up to place her hand on top of Sydney's. "I did. And thank you for your support and guidance."

They held on to each other in silence as a moment of acknowledgment passed between them.

"Okay then," Sydney said, plastering a smile on her face even though her eyes were welling. "I'm off to find our dictator, I mean, our *organizer*."

Morgan managed a laugh. "I'm just going to grab a drink, and then I'll go back to the model holding area. Is that allowed? I'll pay for it."

Sydney waved her hand at Morgan. "Please. Drink all you want on us, you deserve it."

Morgan headed for the bar, skirting the edge of the venue, feeling very underdressed. It wasn't that it was a formal event, it was just that she felt . . . drab. Like all the color she'd gained in the past weeks had drained from her, leaving her looking as pale and wan as she'd been the day she arrived.

She ordered a glass of Prosecco and felt eyes boring into her back. She pretended she didn't notice.

"Hey, I know you," the voice said.

Morgan turned around to see the yacht playboy of Nantucket, grinning at her. "Brooks, hello again. You're early, we're still setting up."

"It's Soda Boy's girlfriend! Where's your Soda Boy?" He glanced around the tent. "I wanna raise a glass to him."

She had no desire to get into it with Brooks. "Not here. And it's a busy night for me since I'm a volunteer, so . . ."

"Well, I'll be seeing plenty of him soon enough, right?"

She shot Brooks a confused look and grabbed the glass of Prosecco the bartender held out to her.

"The deal! We signed the deal and I'm investing in Peachy. We've been chatting for a while and we both agree that we're a great fit. Parallel industries, you know?"

He's actually doing it. He's growing already.

Despite everything that had gone on in the past twenty-four hours, she was proud of him.

"What do you mean, 'parallel'?" she asked, hoping it might give her some insight, since she wasn't sure if she'd ever have the chance to talk to Nathan about it.

"Oh, you don't know?" Brooks pointed at himself. "I'm Madge's Cookies. Nathan and I are both in food, so it makes sense. I really believe in what he's doing."

Morgan nearly choked on her drink. Madge's Cookies were in every lunch box across the country.

"Let me tell you, that guy of yours is smart. Nathan was *super* careful vetting potential investors. He was pretty close to losing it all, so we signed the deal in the nick of time."

She frowned. How was she just learning all of this now? "What do you mean?"

"The guy's broke as a joke," Brooks laughed. "He invested every last penny into Peachy and never gave up. I *like* that about him."

The pineapple emergency . . . working the cart every day instead of hiring a kid to do it . . . suddenly Morgan realized that Nathan had been keeping secrets of his own from her. Maybe he'd been ready to make his own confession after she'd told him about her job, only to decide that Morgan couldn't take on more stress? Smiley, sunshiny Nathan had been on the verge of financial ruin the entire time she'd known him and she'd never had a clue.

"When did you sign the deal?" She could barely ask the question because of the lump in her throat.

"Today! That's why I'm surprised you two aren't out celebrating. Once he scales up, he's going to be in a *very* comfortable position, if you know what I mean."

"I need to, uh, I need to head back since more people are arriving," she stuttered, pointing behind him. She couldn't fake it with him for much longer.

"Of course," Brooks replied. "I'm sure we'll be seeing lots of each other in the future." He held up a tumbler of amber liquid. "To Soda Boy!"

Morgan swished her glass through the air, then downed her Prosecco, wishing it was something stronger to help her blot out the mess that her life had become.

chapter thirty-three

The two other volunteers that were supposed to be helping to avoid canine chaos backstage were off gossiping in the corner, so Morgan was on her own. The energetic young golden in the holding area was trying to get all of the other dogs to chase her and every time she jumped into a play bow, the woman in the sheath dress who was her co-model got dragged along a few steps. The beagle mix was yodeling his head off, and the rest of the dogs looked like they wanted to stage a pack coup and take off for the water.

Sydney kept popping in with the countdown and Morgan realized that she was watching the clock with her. She just wanted the night to be over so she could go home and try to figure out how to salvage what was left of Mack and Elle's visit.

The stress tentacles were tightening around the base of her skull, but this time the heaviness felt different.

Nathan.

The loud retch snapped her back to the chaos in the tent. Morgan scanned the room looking for the source. There were two dogs rolling on the grass play-fighting, a few standing around looking like wallflowers at a high school dance, and a puppy holding court in front of her fans. The second she spotted the culprit, the hairs on the back of her neck prickled.

The tan shepherd mix named Duke was hunched over, his neck stretched forward, and the corners of his mouth pulled back in a grimace. Morgan glanced at his handler, a bearded man in suspenders and Nantucket-red pants engrossed in conversation with a woman wearing a black shift and overlarge pearls.

Morgan watched the dog again. He adjusted his stance, shifting his weight from side to side, keeping his head hanging low. He retched again, silently this time. A small trail of drool hung from his mouth. Anyone looking at him would probably think he ate something that didn't agree with him, but Morgan knew better.

Fuck.

She approached the dog slowly and after a few seconds the man noticed her staring.

"Hi there. Isn't he handsome?" he asked Morgan with a smile. "He's already got a few people interested in him. Are you looking?"

Morgan shook her head wordlessly, scanned the dog again, and dropped to her knees next to him. Duke barely acknowledged her. He paced as far as the leash would allow, head down. His belly was distended and when she touched his stomach, it felt taut and hard.

"He's bloating," Morgan said in a sharp voice, looking up at the confused pair. "We need to get him to a vet. *Now.*"

"He's what?" the pearl woman asked.

"Isn't that the thing where the dog eats too fast and something happens to the stomach?" red pants guy asked. "He hasn't eaten in a while, it's probably not that."

"How long has he been acting like this?"

"He was fine a few minutes ago. He was playing with Bailey." The man gestured across the tent.

Abby flitted into the holding area, clipboard in hand with Sydney a few steps behind. "Start thinking about lining up, people," she called out to the group in a bossier-than-normal voice. "We've got fifteen minutes."

Morgan stood up and cupped her hands around her mouth. "Abby!"

She looked around for the source and seemed startled when she realized it was Morgan. Abby looked her up and down as she stomped over to her. "Yes?"

"Duke has bloat, we need to get him to an emergency vet right away."

She pointed to the dog.

Abby pursed her lips together and glared at Morgan. "I'm sure he's fine. He just needs to calm down a little. It's overstimulating back here. Besides, Duke and Miles walk second, they'll be done in a few minutes."

Morgan didn't have the time to argue with Abby. Bloat was a life-threatening condition and every second mattered.

"I'm *one hundred* percent sure it's bloat." She stared Abby down, daring her to argue back. "If he doesn't have surgery to untwist his stomach, he'll die."

Duke paced away from them. The tension of the exchange was drawing stares from the people nearby, and Sydney walked over to join them.

"What's going on?" she asked.

"Nothing," Abby said in a pissy voice. "Duke needs to relax, but our dog walker is convinced that he's sick or something."

Oh no she didn't.

There was no other way to handle it. She was doing this. Morgan took a deep breath, drew herself up to her full height, which gave her a few inches over Abby, and unleashed on her.

"Listen to me," she said in a low voice that sounded like she was negotiating with kidnappers. "I'm not a dog walker, I'm a fucking *veterinarian* and this dog is going to die if we don't get him into surgery. *Now.*"

The expletive hit Abby like a crack across the cheek, and the rest left her wide eyed.

Sydney caught Morgan's eye and nodded in support.

"Where is the emergency vet here? I can take him."

"They have on-call hours, I'll reach out," Sydney said, already dialing.

"Well, if you say so," Abby squeaked out, her voice small. "I mean, if you think he's in danger . . ."

"I just talked to Dr. Neuman. She'll be ready for him," Sydney said, pushing past Abby. "I'm coming with you."

Abby seemed to realize that there was nothing else she could say, and she watched them gingerly lead Duke from the tent. The massive yard outside the festivities was mostly dark beyond the walkway lights to the tent, so none of the revelers could see the three figures quietly making their way to the valet.

Morgan sat in the sand on the narrow beach and watched Mack taking pictures of Elle with the Brant Point Lighthouse in the background, repositioning himself over and over again to avoid getting any of the fishermen in the shot. They were headed for the airport later that afternoon, but Morgan insisted they visit the picturesque spot. Since they weren't going to see the Nantucket landmark from the ferry, at least they'd get to experience it on the beach. She could already envision the filtered pictures on Mack's Instagram feed.

She leaned back on her elbows and stretched her legs out in front of her, letting the sun warm her skin even though nothing she did could relax her. She still felt twitchy around Mack even though he'd reassured her over and over that he wasn't upset with her.

The close call with Duke the night before still weighed on her. The surgery had been a success thanks to the calm confidence of the veterinarian, a woman named Sheila who Morgan had immediately felt a kinship with. Since she wasn't licensed to practice in Massachusetts, the best Morgan was able to do was assist during the procedure like a technician, but even that was enough to remind her how much she loved her job.

If only saving animals was the extent of it.

Her phone vibrated in her pocket and for a second, she thought it might be Nathan, but he'd agreed to wait for Morgan to reach out. It was her mom, texting that she was going to FaceTime them.

"Mack," she yelled. "Mom's calling and wants to see us."

Mack and Elle jogged over to where she was sitting and plopped down beside her in the sand as the phone started ringing.

"There are my babies," Jean squealed when she saw them sitting side by side in the sand. "Look at you two. You *three*," she corrected when Elle leaned in closer. "Your father and I love the pictures you sent us. The one of you at dinner was wonderful."

The photo was of the four of them squeezed on a couch at the restaurant, Mack, Elle, and Morgan laughing and looking at the camera and Nathan staring at Morgan like she'd cast a spell on him. Morgan had forgotten that Mack had sent it to her, and no one spoke for a few uncomfortable seconds.

"Everyone looks so tan and happy," Jean continued, oblivious.

"That would be your son putting filters on us," Morgan finally said, shooting him a look. "I'm still fish-belly pale."

"It's healthier that way," Elle added, fighting with the wind to keep her hair out of her mouth.

"Did you have a wonderful time together?" Jean asked, her eyes shining with excitement, like she was talking to a trio of celebrities.

They'd already agreed not to say anything to her. There was no reason to drag her into the drama when all it would do was give her tension headaches and stomach problems. Morgan let Mack take the lead.

"It was amazing," he replied, beaming his biggest social media–smile at the screen. "Elle and I love Nantucket. And it was great catching up with this one." He crashed his shoulder into Morgan's, really selling the fact that the sibling bond was alive and well.

"Oh, I can't tell you how happy that makes me," Jean replied, her eyes welling. "This is all I've wanted for so long. You and Elle are leaving this afternoon, right, Mackenzie?"

"Yup, in a couple of hours. But we'll definitely be coming back."

"And, Morgan, you leave Wednesday morning?"

"Mm-hmm, first ferry of the day."

They chattered about their favorite parts of the weekend

while Morgan stared out at the horizon. The slow ferry chugged by and she could see people on the deck throwing pennies into the water, magically guaranteeing their return trip. She waved at them and felt a moment of unexpected community when nearly everyone waved back at her.

Her time on the island was nearly over, and she felt like she was leaving with a different kind of anchor around her neck. It wasn't the dread and emptiness she faced every day back home, or the brief bursts of panic that popped up at unexpected times just to keep her on her toes. Thanks to Cynthia, she felt like she had some coping strategies she could use for those issues.

It was the bone-deep sadness of realizing that Nathan wasn't going to be a part of her life.

They hadn't made promises to each other, but up until everything blew up on the bluff walk, she'd had no doubt that they were going to continue what they'd started, minus the magic of their vacation vibe. Now she couldn't see a way forward with him if she wanted to be back in Mack's life. *She* knew that Nathan had changed, but Mack wasn't willing to let him in. And based on what she'd watched her brother go through, she couldn't blame him.

Morgan tuned back into the conversation just as her mom was suggesting a family trip to the island the following summer. She glanced at the ferry fading in the distance.

When she left, she wasn't sure if she was going to throw a penny in the water when she passed the lighthouse or keep it in her pocket.

chapter thirty-four

A nd now for the nap that never ends," Eugene said, leaning back against the chaise lounge by the pool. Bernadette was dozing in the space between his knees, belly up to the sun.

"You earned it," Morgan replied from her spot next to him. "If I were you, I'd stay there for the rest of the summer."

"I plan to. I wish Karl would stop staring at the numbers and relax a little now that it's over."

"Hey, we all celebrate in our own ways."

Morgan glanced at her phone for the millionth time. It wasn't like Nathan was going to reach out to her, so there was no reason to keep checking. And she wasn't sure how she would even feel if he did. The fallout was still felt fresh enough to make her feel bruised.

She'd told him not to contact her.

So why do you want him to do it anyway?

Morgan felt like she needed to put some physical distance between herself and the damn phone to keep from obsessing and second-guessing, so she stripped off her cover-up and headed for the pool. Hudson watched her from his spot in the shade next to her chair.

She wanted a reset, to quiet the mess inside her head for a few seconds. Instead of dipping her toe in to check the water temperature, she stood at the edge of the deep end and steeled herself for whatever would happen when she hit the water. She held her breath, then stepped off into the blackness.

The shock of the cold made her lungs constrict.

Now do you see why you need to check, idiot?

She swam to the surface, gasping.

"We forgot to turn the heater on," Eugene said. "Are you dying?"

"Yes!" she shouted back, treading water. "This is torture."

Hudson stood at the edge of the pool watching Morgan. He barked and paced a few steps. Then without any warning, he launched himself into the water.

It was a first for both of them. Morgan rarely did much real swimming, choosing to wade in the shallow end or float on the inflatable raft instead. The most Hudson ever did was stand on the highest step with the water just covering his feet, watching her like a lifeguard.

But Morgan's messy splashing must have seemed out of character, so Hudson dog-paddled to her and gently placed his mouth around her forearm.

"Hud, what are you doing?" she laughed. "Are you rescuing me? But I'm okay."

He didn't let go as he swam toward the shallow end, gently pulling her along.

"You're saving me," she murmured, paddling her feet to help him along.

He finally let go once they reached the stairs, then climbed out of the pool and shook off.

"That dog is something else," Eugene said in amazement. "Wish I'd recorded it. Bernadette would just watch me drown."

"He really is amazing," Morgan said as she gave him a kiss on top of the head, then ran to get her towel. "Are you guys sure you don't want to adopt him? Please?"

"Honestly, I don't think he'd be happy with us," he replied, pursing his lips at her.

She was about to respond when her phone rang. She ran to it without remembering to keep her cool, her heart in her throat.

Damn it. Sydney.

Morgan tied her towel around her chest and tried not to sound depressed as she answered.

"Are you sitting down?" Sydney asked. "Because I think we found the *perfect* adopters for Hudson!"

She scowled as she stared into the pool's black depths. The last "perfect adopters" Sydney had mentioned never even submitted an application. She knew nothing mattered until anyone interested in him had jumped through all of the necessary hoops *and* gotten her blessing in addition to the rescue's. Sydney seemed to want to rush Hudson's happy ending before Morgan left, as if sending her back to reality knowing that he was in his forever home would make her feel like her first fostering quest was a success. But Morgan didn't want the slightly damaged supermodel going to just anyone.

"Okay, tell me."

"Their names are Faith and Brandon. Young couple, no dog right now, but they have tons of dog experience, she works from home, big fenced backyard."

"Not bad."

"I stalked her Insta and she seems wonderful. An earth-mother-granola kind of person, makes lots of bread. They're flexible about meeting times. If you're too busy packing up, I can have Pat handle it, but I thought you'd want to check them out."

"Of course I do," she answered, biting her lip and watching Hudson watch her. "Let me, uh, figure some scheduling stuff out and call you back."

"Perfect."

She perched the phone on the edge of the lounge chair, trying to keep it away from her wet towel. Eugene had a novel open on his stomach and was pretending like he wasn't eavesdropping.

"All okay?" he asked.

"Yup," she nodded. "Potential adopter for Mr. Baywatch."

"Oh, isn't that interesting?" His emphasis on the word "interesting" left little doubt what he meant. "Mission accomplished, right?"

"Yeah, maybe," she answered. "Hopefully."

Morgan splayed on the lounge chair next to him and started mapping out the screening questions she'd ask the perfect couple. Her phone rang again, and she assumed Sydney was calling back with another tidbit about Hudson's future people. She reached for it and sent it skittering to the cement below.

"Damn it!"

She flipped it over and saw that the call was already connected. "Sorry, dropped my phone. What else did you find out?"

"Hey . . . uh . . ."

Nathan.

Her eyes went wide as hope sparked inside her. She jumped

up from the chair and speed-walked to the pool house with Hudson on her heels.

"Hi," he continued. "I'm sorry for calling."

The relief that flooded her system was completely at odds with the dark thoughts darting in her head. It was like there was a disconnect between logic and her physical response to the sound of his voice. Because logic dictated that she should still feel as angry at him now as she did when she'd found out who he was.

But what she was feeling wasn't anger. It was something nuanced that she couldn't put her finger on.

Morgan settled on the couch with Hudson clocked in at her side and waited for Nathan to say something. She'd left the air-conditioning blasting, so she pulled the blanket off the back of the couch and huddled under it, her wet bathing suit making her feel even chillier.

"I know you told me not to call, but I had to." He took a deep breath. "I was hoping we could meet up before you go, just to talk. I still feel like there's more to say."

Morgan squeezed her eyes shut. She'd played through all of the possible outcomes of her last few days in Nantucket and kept coming to the same conclusion. It took her a few seconds to work up the courage to actually say it.

"That's probably not a good idea."

"Why not?" It came out in a shocked rush.

Saying it out loud clawed away at her.

"The truth is, I want to see you. I miss being with you." A dull pain drummed in her temples as she admitted it. "And that's not good."

"No, it's amazing, Morgan," he said softly, and she swore she could hear him smiling.

"Nathan, I'm still . . . *processing* everything. And a little part of me still sort of hates you. Or, the idea of you. I can't just flip a switch and feel okay about everything. And neither can Mack."

He exhaled. "I was going to ask."

"He doesn't want to talk to you. I tried. But it's his choice. He has to do whatever it takes to stay okay." Talking about Mack kicked up her protective instinct.

A painful silence settled between them.

"I understand," Nathan finally replied. "But I wish he would at least hear me out."

"Well, he left yesterday afternoon, so . . ."

Hudson slapped his paw on Morgan's thigh, demanding attention, so she massaged his silky ears.

"Here's the thing," she began, the words crowding in her mouth until she forced them out. "It would be too easy to see you. Because being with you just feels . . . *right*. And because of that, we'd probably sweep all of that stuff from the past under the rug and focus on the future. Once we both got home we'd keep hanging out, because living an hour apart is nothing, right?"

"Exactly. It's stupid close."

He sounded too hopeful. What had to come next wrung out her heart.

"And maybe, if things go well, we'd still be hanging out during the holidays." She cringed a little at the presumption. "I mean, we could just as easily wind up hating each other once we're off island. But feasibly, we could still be . . . together. And Thanksgiving is only a few months away. But the fact is, it's not like I could invite you to share some turkey and sweet potatoes with the Pearce family. Same with Christmas. Have you even thought about how awkward that would be for *you*? Sitting there fake smiling because Mack won't even glance in your direction? And then next summer, when Mack gets married . . . would I have to go alone?"

"But what if he changed his mind?" Nathan asked in a rush.

"What if he *didn't*?" Morgan shot back, feeling a tickle of anger mixing in with her sadness. Hudson crawled halfway onto her lap and rolled onto his back, exposing his belly. "I've spent half my life exiled from my brother, and now it finally feels like we're figuring our shit out. How do you think he'd react if he found out we were still together?"

"Did he tell you not to see me?" Nathan demanded.

"He would *never* do that. He left it up to me."

The line went quiet.

"So that's it," Nathan said in a flat voice.

The sadness slammed into her and she let her head fall back against the couch and closed her eyes against the pinprick of tears. "Yeah, I think it has to be."

"But what if I talk to Mack?" he asked again. "Give him a chance to do a . . . what do they call it? A victim impact statement? And then I could apologize. *Really* apologize, from my heart. And explain the work I've done on myself."

Memories of Mack crying to their mom when he was little, his face contorted with anguish, came flooding back. Of being in school assemblies and watching him walk to his seat as people muttered *Butt Crack Mack* at him and made elephant noises. Of trying to be there for him only to have him blow up at her.

"I don't think it would matter."

"Can I still text you sometimes, just to check in? See how you're holding up with work and everything?"

The acknowledgment of her mental health was a reminder that he knew her more intimately than anyone.

"And see if you've changed your mind?" he asked in a quiet, pained voice.

"No," she managed to choke out. "It's not healthy to let this drag on. And I can't just be friends with you, so it's best if we don't talk."

"Are you taking the fast ferry?"

The question didn't make sense until she realized that they could potentially bump into each other while he was working. "No. Don't worry, I won't be on Straight Wharf, you won't have to see me."

"But what if I *want* to?" Nathan asked, almost pleading.

She avoided the question. "Look, you're going to be busy anyway. I saw Brooks and he told me he's investing. Congrats." She paused a beat and realized that she couldn't stop herself from asking what had been on her mind since the conversation with Brooks. "He said that things have been . . . challenging for you. Why didn't you tell me?"

Nathan let out a joyless laugh. "And what would that conversation have sounded like? 'Hey, Morgan, can you buy these frappes for us because I'm broke?'"

"Well, I was pretty open and honest with you," she reminded him in a quiet voice.

He let out a long, ragged sigh. "You're dealing with so much, Morgan. I didn't want to stress you out with my troubles. And I had a feeling that the deal was going to go through. I figured once we'd finished celebrating it, then maybe then I could tell you how close I was to losing everything. Because at that point my bank account would just be a funny part of Peachy's origin story, not something that kept me up all night."

"You could've told me. You didn't have to hide it from me."

"I should have told you, but I didn't want to give you a single reason to not want to be with me," he said softly. "And look how things wound up, I went and did it anyway."

An ache spread in her chest as she realized that it was probably the last time they'd talk. She punched down the weepy feelings so she could end the call without losing it.

"I should go."

Hudson flipped over to stare at her with his bottomless brown eyes when she sniffled.

"If that's what you think is right, then okay. But I know this is a mistake."

"Thanks for teaching me how to surf, Nathan," Morgan said, trying to ignore the pain in his voice. "I had an amazing time this summer. Good luck with everything."

Morgan hung up just as Nathan started to say something. She stared at the phone waiting for him to call back or text, and when five minutes passed, she tossed it on the couch next to her with a strangled sigh.

Hudson stood up, examined her from head to toe, and pulled his ears back. Morgan knew what was coming if she didn't straighten herself out.

"I'm fine," she said to him, trying to keep the sadness from registering on her face, but failing. He launched himself against her, covering her face with kisses as the tears started to fall.

She thought she'd be heading home with an arsenal of new

coping strategies and a co-pilot who could take the wheel when she needed support. Nathan had said he'd be there to protect her, and she only had herself to blame for believing it was possible.

Morgan sniffled and Hudson's licking got more insistent. When he stood up to place his front paws on her shoulders for a better angle, Morgan finally had to push him away.

"I'll be okay, just *stop*!"

He crouched at her tone, a wounded expression on his face.

"Oh, Hudson, I'm sorry," she said as her eyes welled again. "I didn't mean it. I'm sorry."

Morgan reached for him and he padded into her arms, snuggling into a ball so he could fit on her lap. She tried not to hug him but failed. He didn't seem to mind, pushing against her and nuzzling his head against her cheek.

Hudson was exceedingly good at his job. Though her heart still felt heavy, within a few minutes her tears slowed.

She leaned away from him, stared into his eyes, and knew exactly what she had to do.

chapter thirty-five

Morgan zipped up her yellow Nantucket hoodie and looked back at the dock from the top deck of the ferry. Eugene and Karl stood at the end of it, waving to her with Bernadette on a leash next to them. Morgan waved back and mustered up a convincing smile. The Pak-Reynoldses had no idea that she was leaving almost as bad off as she'd been when she arrived, but in a different way.

The Grey Lady was wearing her veil of mist for Morgan's early-morning departure, but she'd learned enough about the peculiarities of the island's weather to know it would burn off into another gorgeous day. She tried not to think about what she would've done if she weren't leaving. Bernadette's meds. Breakfast for two out of silver bowls in opposite corners of the kitchen. A quick walk for the sassy senior. A longer training walk for the handsome boy.

And hanging out with Nathan.

Her heart clenched.

Morgan cleared her throat and gave the guys one last wave,

then moved to the other side of the boat so she could watch the lighthouse pass.

"Let's go, mister."

She glanced down at Hudson and looped his leash around her hand, accidentally catching it on her silver Nantucket bracelet. He grinned up at her and wagged, excited to be on the adventure at her side.

The decision to adopt Hudson had come on during a speed round of second-guessing her entire life the day before she left. Was she ready for a dog? Was Hudson *her* dog? Could she find the time to juggle work and his needs? Would she feel lost if he wasn't in her life?

Resounding yeses across the board.

And having him with her made leaving Nantucket a little less depressing, like at least one of the things that had made her summer perfect was going to stay in her life.

Sydney had squealed when Morgan called her with the decision, swearing that she'd predicted the outcome the first time she saw them together. She made Morgan promise to send her updates and be better about posting on social media so she could keep up with them. The last thing Sydney had said as they were hanging up sounded like a puzzle at first: "Remember, Morgan, you can't start a car with a dead battery."

She knew exactly what she meant. It was Sydney's gentle way of encouraging her to continue going to therapy. As tough as some of the sessions with Cynthia had been, Morgan appreciated the clarity they gave her. And she knew there was still so much more for her to unpack.

Morgan and Hudson were practically alone on the deck given it was a Wednesday and barely past seven. Tourists usually arrived or departed on weekends. She leaned against the railing and watched the lighthouse slide into view. There were a few fishermen already out, and she raised her hand to wave at them. They all waved back.

Even though the slow ferry was indeed slow, they were rounding the bend to the open waters faster than she was prepared for. There weren't any other tourists on the deck to make the moment feel noteworthy, which helped keep Hudson from feeling frantic about the new experience. The few men clustered on the far side of the ferry were dozing in their plaid shirts and work boots.

Morgan dug into her jeans pocket, throwing a guilty glance over her shoulder to make sure no one was watching. She pulled out the penny and held it in her palm, trying to figure out if she really wanted to do it.

Yes. She loved Nantucket, despite the way everything had ended. It would always hold a special place in her heart.

Morgan closed her eyes, cranked her arm back, and tossed the penny into the surf.

By the time the ferry slowed as they got closer to Hyannis, her Nantucket notebook had a few new pages of scribbling. After feeling weepy and depressed as the island faded from view behind her, Morgan realized that something had to change, and it was bigger than finding a therapist at home. She couldn't allow herself to lose everything she'd gained while away. Nantucket needed to be the line that separated the terrible before from the improved after.

She was tired of feeling sad. She hated that she had a secret fantasy to run away from her dream career and open a flower shop. Thanks to Cynthia, she now realized that working harder wasn't the way to outrun the bleakness she felt every morning when she woke up. And she didn't want poor Hudson suffering because she couldn't drag herself out of bed on the weekends.

Morgan closed the notebook and squinted into the morning sunshine, nibbling on the end of the pen. She wished the weather weren't so damn perfect. Hudson dropped his chin onto her lap and sighed.

The PA system crackled on, and a voice directed passengers to pack up their belongings and discard trash before disembarking. Morgan sighed and stretched out her back, then scooped her wind-tossed hair into a messy bun.

"You ready for our next adventure?" she asked Hudson, and he wagged in response.

The voice came over the system again. "Ladies and gentlemen, please hold for an important announcement."

Morgan could see land in the distance, which meant that the fantasy was one hundred percent over. The next dose of reality would be fighting traffic for six hours or more.

"Hi everyone, sorry for the disruption. This will only take a minute." A different voice said over the intercom. "Morgan Pearce, I hope you can hear me."

She froze.

What the hell?

Nathan.

It didn't make sense, his voice blasting out over the ferry intercom, and for a second she wondered if she was dreaming.

"Hi, Morgan, it's me," he continued. "I know doing this is risky, so I wanted to make sure you have an out. We'll be in

Hyannis in under five minutes, and if you don't want to see me, you can just get off the ferry and not look back. But I wanted to talk to you in person and tell you that this message was sanctioned by both the Nantucket Steamship Authority . . . and Mack Pearce."

He paused. It took Morgan a few seconds to grasp what he meant.

He talked to Mack?

"I'll be heading to the top rear deck if you'd like to join me there." He paused. "And if you don't, well, I understand."

The intercom clicked off.

Morgan clung to the railing feeling woozy and weak-kneed. Nathan was *here*, on her ferry. She felt herself grinning stupidly as she looked around, trying to figure out where she was in relation to where he was going to be.

She realized that she was already in the meeting spot, the only person on the hard, bright blue chairs. Morgan stood up and Hudson hopped off and shook the sleep away. There was no way Nathan could miss her in the empty space, but she walked to the very back of the ferry, near the flapping American flag, and leaned against the fence.

The seconds ticked by with no sign of Nathan, so Morgan tried to calm her nervous stomach by turning around to look at the trail of whitecaps left behind by the ferry. Within a few seconds she was mesmerized by them.

Foamy, mushy waves.

And then he was beside her, as if she'd wished him there. She gazed at him and felt like she couldn't draw in a full breath.

It was like the moment in *The Wizard of Oz* when everything went Technicolor. In the four days since she'd seen him, it was

as if Nathan had transformed into a brighter and more beautiful version of the man she held in her head. Were his eyes always
that blue or was it the just the way the sun was reflecting? Was
his top lip *really* that plush? The sight of him standing just a few
feet away smiling at her was a dream she hadn't allowed herself
to have made real. Morgan had to hold herself back from leap-
ing into his arms, and she could tell by his tightly crossed arms
that he was forcing himself not to reach for her as well.

Because they both knew the second they touched, there
would be no time for words, and there was so much that still
needed to be said.

Hudson seemed to come out of his trance and finally realize
who Nathan was. He jumped on him like he'd never had a single
lesson as Nathan laughed and petted the ecstatic dog.

"Hi," he finally said, standing up to look into her eyes. The
wind tossed his hair around and he ran his hand through it to
try to tame it. "I'm glad to see you."

"What are you even doing here?" she asked in a rush, even
though his announcement had summarized it perfectly.

"Please don't be upset. I really wanted to do this in person."
He cleared his throat. "I got a call yesterday. From Mack."

Her eyes went wide with shock. It was the last possible reason she'd imagined for him ending up standing in front of her.
When he'd mentioned Mack in the announcement, she assumed
that he'd reached out to her brother against her advice.

"What . . . what did he want? What did he say?" she stam-
mered.

Nathan gazed out at the water, looking like it was a struggle
for him to put it all into words.

"We both said a lot. I apologized a few million times."

Morgan squinted up at him, using her hand to shield her eyes from the sun.

"And then I let him talk," Nathan said, his face grim and his mouth in a tight line. "I wanted him to have a chance to say everything he needed to say to me." He shook his head. "It wasn't easy to hear. I mean, the stuff he went through, because of *me* . . ." Nathan broke off and Morgan thought she saw tears in his eyes. He cleared his throat. "But I needed to hear it. He yelled, he cursed me out, told me that he used to wish I'd die . . . and I understood. All of it. After a while he gave me a chance to talk, and I told him how much I've changed. The work I've done on myself. Then he said that he'd never seen you happier than you were in Nantucket." He turned sheepish. "I guess he thought that I had something to do with that because he told me that you were going to be on this ferry and gave me his blessing to come talk to you."

They both went quiet and stared out at the water, realizing the enormity of the gift Mack had given them. Forgiveness, and a future.

"But what happened?" Morgan asked, still confused by the turn of events. "What prompted him to call?"

"Elle, I think." Nathan said. "She was the push he needed."

Morgan suspected that Elle was also the reason why Mack had ended up in Nantucket in the first place. She made a mental note to give her sister-in-law-to-be an endless hug the next time they were together.

The ferry was nearly into port and had slowed to a putter.

"I want you to know that I planned to respect your boundaries, Morgan," he continued. "I wasn't going to reach out to you since you told me not to. But everything changed when Mack called me. He didn't want to speak for you, but he gave me enough hope to show up on your ferry uninvited and pay off the crew to let me use the intercom." Nathan said, the corner of his mouth kicking up into a grin. He turned to gaze out at the dock speeding toward them and seemed to realize that their time was almost up. "Now it's up to you. I can get off this ferry and buy a return ticket back to Nantucket or . . ."

"Or what?" she asked as hope bubbled up inside her.

"Or . . . I could hang out with you for the next twenty-four hours? You told me you don't have to go back to work for a few days, so I thought I could help you ease back into reality and then head back to ACK to finish up my season. Archer is staying with my buddy so I'm basically wide open." Nathan still seemed fidgety, like he still wasn't sure how she was going to react to him, given that he'd forced the meeting she said she didn't want to have.

But that was before.

Before she understood that the mistakes of the past didn't define the future. That fences could be mended, and bridges rebuilt if they were given the proper care and attention. That forgiveness felt better than grudges.

The way he was looking at her . . . his pained eyes never leaving hers. His face, naked with hope.

"But why just twenty-four hours?" she asked, still watching him carefully.

"I thought you might need time to acclimate alone, before your real life cranks up again." He paused and looked down at his flip-flops. "I've been doing some reading about how to be a good support for you, Morgan. I want to be there for you. If you'll let me."

The overwhelming need to touch him came over her like a fever, leaving her dizzy and hot. Before he could say anything else, she fisted her hands in Nathan's T-shirt and wrenched him closer, pausing for an instant to look into his eyes before going up on her toes and pressing her mouth to his.

She felt the shock of the move register on his lips for an instant, and then felt him relax into the kiss, meeting her move for move. She circled her hands behind his neck as his arms wrapped around her waist, holding her tightly like he was worried she might slip away. There was no need for Morgan to use words since the answer to his question was in her kiss.

I understand. The past is gone. Stay with me.

They lurched apart as the ferry jostled to a stop, and Hudson let out a warning wuff. Morgan pulled away from Nathan reluctantly.

"We're here," she said softly.

"So we are," he answered, staring into her eyes.

The noise of people disembarking carried up to where they were standing. She assumed that at some point a crew member would chase them off the ferry, but for the moment she was content to wait.

"I'll answer your question with my own: would you be interested in helping one tightly wound dog and his equally fragile human relax for a *few* days before going back to the real world?" Morgan asked.

"Yeah," Nathan's worried face finally broke into a smile. "It's actually *all* I want."

As expected, a few minutes later one of the crew appeared on the deck carrying a trash bag, shooting looks at them that made it clear their cinematic moment was over. Nathan took Morgan's hand and the three of them headed off the ferry together.

When she finally put her foot down on land, Morgan expected it to feel momentous, like everything had changed. Instead, it was a quiet victory. She still had work to do to find her equilibrium, but as she gazed at Nathan and Hudson walking beside her, she realized that nothing would ever feel quite as bleak again.

Hudson bumped his nose against her leg, and Nathan looked at her and seemed to read her expression. He leaned down to kiss her gently. "You okay?"

"Yeah, I am," Morgan answered, smiling at him. "Better than okay."

And for the first time in ages, she knew in her heart that it was true.

epilogue

It was a perfect night," Morgan said as she leaned back in the white Adirondack chair set up on the beach and gazed out at the water. She smoothed the front of her long champagne-colored chiffon dress, but it was hopeless: the thing was a wrinkled mess from dancing and sweating.

Nathan turned and looked back over his shoulder at the tents where the crowd was still screaming along with the band. "Doesn't look like it's even close to over. The Pearce crew really knows how to party."

Morgan laughed. "Give the Nowak family some credit. Elle's dad was the one who tore his pants doing the Twist."

Nathan joined Morgan staring out at the stars twinkling over the ocean. "Mack and Elle look really happy." He reached for her hand and she tucked it into the familiar spot.

"They do."

It was their first time back on Nantucket since the summer before, and it felt like they'd never left. In the few days before the wedding, they'd caught up with old friends, visited their favorite spots, and even gotten some surfing in.

The only novel part about seeing Sydney again was that they were doing it in person, since they still talked frequently. And watching Palmer romp full-tilt with Bernadette in the Pak-Reynoldses' backyard nearly brought her to tears. He was as agile and playful as a young dog should be, a testament to the surgeon's skill and Tess's rehab.

"I wish we could stay longer," Nathan said.

"Same, but it works out that I can meet with Shepherd and Kit on the way home. It's the first time the whole team will be together since they hired me."

The quick trip to Boston would cement Morgan's place as A Dog's Dinner's new veterinary liaison. After courting her for months, they'd finally convinced her to come on board remotely and part-time, so she could still juggle her growing relief veterinary practice. Among the notes she'd taken on the ferry home the summer before was the idea that she could transition from the grind of daily practice life to relief work. It was a niche she was perfectly suited for, where she was temporarily hired into practices in need of someone to cover shifts for doctors on maternity leave or sick leave. It gave her complete control over her schedule, leaving her to embrace the parts of her career that she loved and distance herself from the parts that drained her. The changes, plus her ongoing therapy, had transformed her life into something she loved.

"Yeah, I talked to Shep and Kit, actually," Nathan said, still staring at the water. "Told them you wouldn't be there until Tuesday."

Morgan screwed up her face. "Why would you do that?"

"I thought we might as well enjoy this little vacation for as long as possible," he shrugged.

"But the dogs!" she protested. "Rebecca is dropping off Archer and Hud at home tomorrow night."

Their dogs no longer existed as separate entities. They were always mentioned in the same breath: Archer and Hud, the two dogs that had started off their relationship with teeth and blood, but with Morgan's guidance they'd found their way to brotherhood. Her camera roll was filled with photos of the two of them sleeping with their legs braided together.

"Taken care of. I talked to her, too."

Morgan frowned. "I don't get it, why wouldn't you check with me first?"

"Because then it wouldn't be a surprise," he said softly, shifting in his chair to face her.

"What wouldn't?"

"This." Nathan dropped to his knee in front of her.

Morgan's hands flew to her mouth as he pulled a small black box from his pants pocket.

"I figured Nantucket was the perfect spot, since it all started here. I fell in love with you on this sand and in that ocean. Our journey together began on Nantucket, so I figured that the next part of our lives together should start here too." He gazed up at her and drew a shaky breath. "Morgan Pearce, will you marry me?"

She fell out of the chair and onto her knees in front of him, then threw her arms around Nathan, her tears hot against his neck.

She couldn't find words to express her shock. Morgan clutched the box against her palm so the ring wouldn't fall out and get lost in the sand while squeezing Nathan tightly enough to get a grunt out of him. When they finally pulled apart, they both had tears in their eyes.

"Yes!" Morgan sobbed. "Yes forever."

Nathan wiped away a tear on her cheek with his thumb, then leaned in to kiss her.

"You have to promise me something, though," he whispered, leaning his forehead against hers. "This has to be our secret until after all of Mack and Elle's events are over. I don't want to step on their weekend, okay?"

Morgan smiled through her tears at the way Nathan kept looking out for Mack.

"Of course. I won't tell a soul."

They kissed again, savoring the secret pact they'd just made, witnessed only by the moon.

"Put the ring on, would you? I'm stressed about all of this sand," Nathan laughed and sat down.

"Right, the ring!" Morgan exclaimed, realizing that she hadn't even looked at it yet. Nathan took the box from her hand, then slipped the ring on her finger. It was hard to see in the darkness, but all that mattered was that it felt like it belonged there.

"I love it," she sighed, holding her hand up so that it was framed by the stars.

"You can't even see it," Nathan teased. "But I'm glad."

"I can tell that it's perfect," she sighed. "Oh my God, my mom is going to *die* when she finds out. Another wedding!"

"But you can't tell her yet," Nathan pleaded. "Okay? We all know Jean can't keep a secret. We need to keep the ring hidden."

"Right, right," Morgan said, still twisting her hand back and forth and squinting at the ring in the darkness.

"I'm serious, this stays between us until we get back. Can you do that?"

"Of course I can." Morgan nodded at him and raised her chin. "I'm strong."

Nathan pulled her into his lap and wrapped his arms around her. He pressed his lips to the top of her head, making her feel like she was about to burst from happiness.

"I know, you're the strongest person I've ever met."

And after everything she'd been through, she finally believed that she was.

acknowledgments

I love the discovery stage of writing books because I get to talk to people whose input can change the course of the story during a conversation. That happened more than a few times when I interviewed Dr. Sally Foote and Dr. Sheila Newenham, two incredible veterinarians referred to me by pet professional resilience coach (and dear friend) Colleen Pelar. Our conversations were frank, occasionally distressing, and always interesting, and they helped me understand the ups and downs of their profession. Thank you for your candor; your input was invaluable. And Dr. Newenham, extra thanks for fielding way more questions than you signed on for as this book took shape.

I deepened my understanding of veterinary compassion fatigue thanks to Veterinary Social Work Clinician Jeannine Moga, MA, MSW, LCSW. Our discussion about "crispy vets" and how to recognize when someone is silently struggling was a window into just how overwhelming the condition can be. Thank you for the important work that you do.

During a dinner with friends I realized that a fellow guest sitting across the table from me was willing to share more than just appetizers. Mindy Cohen, MSW, LCSW, was generous enough to invite me into her office to discuss the language of therapy, as well as her methods for creating a nurturing and supportive environment, like allowing dogs to come too. Thank you for helping me give Morgan's time in therapy more dimension. (And for letting my dog Millie tag along with me to our meeting!)

I never expected that a chance meeting over island-made soaps and skincare at the Sustainable Nantucket Farmers & Artisans Market would lead me to another wonderful book resource: the Supple Sirens themselves: Shantaw Bloise-Murphy and Bianca Brown! Thank you for giving me a local's perspective on Nantucket life and answering my weird questions about stuff like whether the proper term is *on* Nantucket or *in* Nantucket. (I cheated and used both.)

Eternal gratitude to the team that's with me every step of the way as an idea goes from "what if" to "the end." Forever thanks to my superhero agent, Kevan Lyon—I still pinch myself every time I remember that I'm a "Lyoness"! I'm also lucky enough to have an editor who replies to my late-night, stressed-out emails *way* quicker than she should. Kate Seaver, thanks for helping me discover the real story within my story. And when it comes to creativity, talent, and drive (and patience!), no one beats the dream team of Bridget O'Toole, Dache' Rogers, and Mary Geren. Huge thanks to you and the rest of the unbeatable Berkley team!

As always, giant thanks to my people, from my parents, who have given our family the gift of Nantucket, summer after summer, to my mother-in-law and father-in-law for always buying way more of my books than necessary, and to my friends near and far. The biggest thanks go to my uncredited co-author, my husband, Tom. You listen to every unhinged plot rant and help me find a way through the confusion.

Finally, thanks to *you*, the readers. I can't begin to tell you how amazing it feels to stumble on a beautiful Insta post that you created featuring one of my books (and usually a dog too—thanks for that!) or the rush of getting a message telling me that you loved what I wrote. I'm humbled and honored by your continued support!

dog friendly

VICTORIA SCHADE

questions for discussion

1. Do you think Morgan was in denial about her mental state at the beginning of the book? Why or why not? What subtle signs did you pick up on that signified her need for support?

2. Had you heard of veterinary compassion fatigue prior to reading *Dog Friendly*? Did reading the book give you new insights into what veterinarians face?

3. One of Morgan's secrets was that she'd never fostered before. Have you ever tried fostering a dog or cat? What was your experience like?

4. How did Hudson play a role in Morgan's recovery? Do you think her time on Nantucket would've been different if he wasn't with her?

5. Initially Morgan agreed to surf with Nathan just to get closer to him, even though she had to conquer some fears to do so. In what ways did surfing with Nathan impact Morgan?

6. Morgan kept her profession a secret from Nathan, even as their relationship developed. Do you think she should've been more open about it earlier?

7. Bullying during childhood can have a lifelong negative impact. Do you think Mack's reaction to his childhood bully was justified? Have you or someone you loved ever been bullied? How do you feel about the person now?

8. Morgan and Mack had a complicated relationship, but despite their differences and emotional distance, they both still felt a pull to each other. Have you ever been estranged from a family member? Were you able to find a way to have a relationship?

Victoria Schade is a dog trainer and speaker who serves as a dog resource for the media and has worked both in front of and behind the camera on Animal Planet, as a cohost on the program *Faithful Friends*, and as a trainer and wrangler on the channel's popular Puppy Bowl specials. She lives in Pennsylvania with her husband, her dogs Millie and Olive, and the occasional foster pup.

Ready to find
your next great read?

Let us help.

Visit prh.com/nextread